DRAKON'S PREY

BLOOD OF THE DRAKON

DRAKON'S PREY

BLOOD OF THE DRAKON

N.J. WALTERS

This book is a work of fiction. Names, characters, places, and incidents are the product of the author's imagination or are used fictitiously. Any resemblance to actual events, locales, or persons, living or dead, is coincidental.

Entangled Publishing, LLC
2614 South Timberline Road
Suite 109
Fort Collins, CO 80525
Visit our website at www.entangledpublishing.com.

Select Otherworld is an imprint of Entangled Publishing, LLC.

Edited by Heidi Shoham
Cover design by Kelly Martin
Cover art from Shutterstock and BigStock

Manufactured in the United States of America

First Edition April 2017

Thank you to my readers who have embraced my drakons and asked for more.

Prologue

"Your sister has left town."

Karina Azarov looked up from her computer and waited. Silence was a weapon, and she wielded it with the skill of a master. She was the youngest ever leader of the Knights of the Dragon, a position she'd held for the past decade. If everything went according to plan, she'd hold the position indefinitely.

The man in the doorway stared back at her, and one corner of his mouth quirked upward. No, he wouldn't play the game, wouldn't spit out any information without her asking. Matthew Riggs, her latest lover, was anything but normal.

She sat back in her chair and crooked her finger. He stepped into her office and closed the door behind him. He was tall and well-built. He had the body of a lethal killer and a mind that would rival Machiavelli. He would have fit in well with the Borgia family. He was ambitious.

She planned to use his aspirations to further her own.

He stopped on the other side of the desk. He didn't shift impatiently or cross his arms defensively. No, he looked more amused than anything.

"Well?" She didn't have time to waste on more games.

"Your baby sister decided to take a trip to the West Coast. Washington State, to be exact." He raised one eyebrow in query. "You know anything about that?"

"You don't question me. Ever." Her voice was icy, each word exact. Matthew might be her lover, but she was the one in charge. Always.

"Maybe it's a coincidence," Matthew offered.

She scowled. He didn't believe that any more than she did. "I want two men out there watching her until I find out what's going on." Technically, Matthew worked for Herman Temple, another member of the Knights, but she knew he had plans of his own. And right now, they aligned with hers. "Have her apartment searched." How had her quiet little sister found out about Washington?

He inclined his head slightly. "As you wish." There was none of the deference she was used to from others in his tone. Maybe that was why she found him such a stimulating lover. He was tireless in bed and ruthless out of it. For now, she found him amusing. If he overstepped his boundaries...well, there were other ambitious men out there.

Matthew turned and walked back to the door. Before he opened it, he glanced over his shoulder. "I'll be back later."

"I'm sure you will." She kept her expression contained until he was gone. Only then did she allow herself a small shiver of delight. Yes, Matthew was a talented lover. And he was very useful, for the time being.

She drew her phone out of her pocket and contacted her head of security, a man she trusted implicitly. "I need two men at the cabin we discovered in Washington State. Seems my little sister has decided to pay a visit." She hung up, knowing it would be handled quickly and efficiently.

Karina rose from her chair and walked over to the shelf

that contained her parents' picture. Valeriya had been in her office several days ago. Karina had left her waiting in the hallway, but her little sister had entered when she'd gone upstairs to get her purse. It had set off an internal alarm, but Karina knew there hadn't been anything for her sister to find. She was nothing if not careful.

Still, something had made her sister take a trip west. It wasn't unusual for Valeriya to travel. She did so often. For inspiration, she claimed. But it was suspicious that she would head to the place where the dragon had been.

Most people had no idea such creatures existed. Katrina planned to keep it that way. If she controlled a dragon, or several, she'd be the most powerful woman in the world. Dragons not only had great wealth, but when ingested, their blood healed all illness, actually prolonging life. Dragons were the key to immortality, and there were many people who would pay dearly for such a thing.

She shivered again, her lust for power much greater than her attraction to Matthew.

Karina peered around the room. Had she missed something? Valeriya wanted nothing to do with the family business, had shied away from it all her life. Now she wrote silly children's books, including a series about a loveable dragon.

Karina curled her lip. As if any of those creatures could ever be brave and heroic. They were cold-blooded, dangerous beasts, only looking out for themselves.

Karina strode back to her desk and peered down. There wasn't much there—her Montblanc pen, a pad of paper. The wastebasket was empty. Her desk drawers contained nothing but pens, pencils, and writing supplies. She was very cautious.

Her gaze was drawn back to the small pad of paper. She'd written the GPS coordinates of the cabin on that pad. She'd removed the paper and had taken it with her.

She picked up the innocuous little white pad and ran her fingertips over the top sheet. The slight impression of writing was there.

Karina tugged open one of the desk drawers and drew out a pencil. She ran the lead lightly over the paper. It was very faint, almost unreadable, but the numbers were there. Had her little sister been smart enough to do such a thing? And what was she doing in Washington?

There was nothing there but an airstrip and an old cabin. Her people had already checked. It was a safe house Darius Varkas had used while running from her. She'd lost him, but she'd find him again. It was only a matter of time.

For now, she'd keep an eye on her sister. She viewed this as a betrayal. Valeriya had always professed her disinterest, her distaste, for the family business, for the Knights of the Dragon. Well, her baby sister had just put herself in the middle of this war, and as far as Karina was concerned, she'd chosen a side. And it wasn't the right one.

"Weak." She practically spat the word as she ripped the sheet of paper off the pad, folded it, and tucked it into her pocket. She wouldn't allow her sister, or anyone else for that matter, to derail her plans.

Chapter One

Valeriya Azarov leaned against a towering pine tree and took a deep breath, inhaling the cool, fresh air. She'd left her rental vehicle parked some ways back, figuring it was safer to scout the area on foot rather than just drive right up.

Truthfully, she didn't really have much of a plan at all. She'd impetuously left her home in New York and flown all the way to the West Coast on a whim. No, not a whim. Her sister was looking for someone, a Darius Varkas. Valeriya might not want anything to do with her family's dubious legacy, but she knew more about it than Karina suspected. Valeriya's paternal grandparents had shared all they knew about the Knights of the Dragon, figuring the more she knew, the better prepared she'd be to defend herself.

Valeriya shivered and tugged her coat more closely around her. Even with her heavy jacket, sweater, and long-sleeved top beneath it, she was cold. It was late October in the mountains.

She pushed away from the tree and started walking again. She'd used the GPS coordinates she'd discovered in her sister's office to plot her course. Karina had no idea she'd found them. It had been sheer instinct that had led her to run the tip of a lead pencil over the empty pad of paper and take an etching. She really hadn't expected to find anything, and had been surprised when a set of numbers had shown up.

"You didn't think this through," she muttered. No, as usual, she'd jumped in headfirst without a plan of action. As soon as she'd discovered what the numbers were, she'd hopped on the first plane and headed to the Cascade Mountains.

"At least you had sense enough to pay cash for the plane ticket." No need to alert her sister to what she was doing. Karina was suspicious enough as it was, always wanting to know what Valeriya was up to and who she was spending time with.

As far as she knew, she hadn't been followed, and she'd spent her first day settling in to be sure. That didn't mean things wouldn't change. In spite of her precautions, Valeriya imagined her sister would know soon enough where she was. Karina always did.

She glanced down the narrow dirt road heading toward of her destination.

What had she hoped to accomplish? Certainly, the mysterious Darius Varkas wouldn't be here. Her sister would have already had the area checked out.

No, Valeriya had to know what was going on. Karina had been excited when they'd had dinner the other evening. Not many would have been able to tell, but Valeriya wasn't most people. She'd grown up with Karina. There'd been a barely suppressed anticipation surrounding her sister. That mood usually didn't bode well for others. Karina was ruthless and would stop at nothing to get whatever she wanted.

Her sister had been indoctrinated by her parents when she was young. Valeriya still found it hard to believe that dragons were real, but her grandparents had assured her they were.

As a young girl, she'd always felt sorry for the dragons. They couldn't help what they were. Why should they be hunted?

Oh, she knew that technically they called themselves drakons and were half human and half dragon, but as a child, she'd always thought of them as dragons. It was a hard habit to break.

Something moved off to her right, and Valeriya froze. There were bears and all sorts of other wild animals in these woods. She was a city girl. The wilds of Central Park were more her speed.

A large creature dashed across the road in front of her. Valeriya screamed and then slapped her hand over her mouth. A deer. It was only a deer. Her heart pounding, she leaned forward and sucked air into her lungs.

"Oh God. What am I doing?"

She took another deep breath. She knew why she was here, even if it was most likely a wild goose chase. She'd come on the off-chance Darius Varkas might return. She had to warn him that her sister and the other members of the Knights of the Dragon were after him, believed him to be one of the creatures they coveted. Even if he was no longer at the cabin, she hoped to find some clue to her sister's plans.

She'd played it safe her entire life, keeping her nose out of her family's business. It had been cowardly. She could no longer sit back and take no action, not if she wanted to be able to look at herself in the mirror every morning.

She knew her sister was ruthless, had most likely harmed people over the years, but a piece of her couldn't help hoping that maybe Karina would walk away from the Knights. She knew there was goodness and kindness buried somewhere under the greedy ambition that had shaped her life.

Valeriya remembered Karina playing games with her when they were very small children. Her older sister hadn't hesitated to take over raising her when their parents were killed in a car accident.

She rubbed her hand over her face and sighed. Karina was the only family she had left in the world. For that reason alone, she wouldn't abandon all hope. Not yet.

But in the meantime, she had to do whatever she could to thwart her sister's plans. What Karina and the others were doing was wrong.

She should leave. She'd overslept this morning and hadn't started exploring until after lunch. It would be dark in a couple of hours or less. It would take her about fifteen minutes to get back to her rental car and another hour or so to get to her motel.

But she'd come too far to turn back. She wanted to at least explore a bit. Keeping her eyes and ears open for more animals, she plodded along. She'd give it another ten minutes. She'd followed the coordinates on the GPS and knew this was definitely the right direction.

Several times, she stopped and took pictures. Coming out here for work was her cover story, in case anyone asked. Not that anyone would. She didn't have any close friends. Having a sister who ran a covert, powerful international group meant Valeriya couldn't afford to trust anyone. It had taken her two years to discover that her best friend when she was a teen had been the young daughter of a fellow Knight. The girl's job had been to report back to Karina. In exchange, she'd gotten a full scholarship to the college of her choice.

Valeriya didn't fault the girl. After all, college was expensive, and who knows what might have happened to her father if she'd refused Karina's offer. But it had left Valeriya leery of any overture of friendship.

Since then, she'd kept to herself. She rarely dated, either, for the same reason. It was a lonely life, but she had a home and a career she loved. She wasn't about to complain when many people had it much worse.

Valeriya crouched down and snapped a shot of a cute circle of toadstools. She could use this in her next children's book. The ideas were percolating, and she couldn't wait to start sketching.

Her agent was encouraging her to branch out from her dragon books and try something different.

Maybe she'd do a story about fairies. It was easy to imagine a group of mischievous fairies living in these woods. They'd be the guardians of the forest, possibly scaring off those who'd harm the animals and teaching children they needed to be caretakers of the wild and natural places.

The more she thought about it, the more she liked the idea.

Her mind whirling, she was shocked when the road suddenly ended. Before her, nestled in the woods, was a rustic cabin. The wind gusted, and dry leaves skittered across her path. The windows were all intact, so the place wasn't derelict. A large porch spanned the front of the cabin, but there were no chairs there.

It was quaint but not welcoming.

Every childhood fairytale she'd ever read came roaring back to her. There was always a cottage in the woods, and it was usually very dangerous.

A shiver ran down her spine. Valeriya turned around slowly, but there was no one there. She couldn't shake the sensation, though, that she was being watched.

The clouds rolled over the sun, darkening the small clearing. The day, which had been crisp and sunny, seemed colder and more ominous. "The curse of an active imagination," she muttered.

She'd come all this way. The least she could do was go and knock on the door and see if anyone was at home. What she'd say if there was anyone there, she had no idea.

• • •

Tarrant studied the woman tentatively walking toward the front steps of his home. He'd been watching her for quite some time. He'd known she was there the second she stepped onto the road. He had strategically placed cameras that were damn near impossible to detect. Even the men the Knights had sent to snoop around had missed them. They'd looked, but all they'd found was a dusty, abandoned cabin and a small airstrip nearby. Luckily, he'd moved his truck the day before to a hidden garage about two miles away. The building hadn't been breached.

"Who are you?"

As if she heard him, she looked directly at one of the cameras. It was startling, even though he knew she couldn't possibly realize it was there.

She was around five-seven or so. It was hard to tell her shape, as she was bundled in several layers of clothing, but he'd bet she was slender in build. She had long legs encased in faded blue jeans and a pair of sturdy leather boots. For all that, she was no experienced hiker. She'd almost jumped out of her boots when the deer had crossed her path.

He was far too cynical to believe it was sheer coincidence she was here so soon after the Knights of the Dragon had made an appearance. His upper lip curled. He hated knights of all kinds, but he hated that particular group with a passion that simmered deep inside him.

They'd killed Father Simon, a man who'd been his good friend and confidant for decades, the only person—outside of his brothers—that Tarrant trusted. Now he was gone. And all because he'd helped Tarrant's brother destroy a dangerous book that had belonged to the Knights.

Like his brothers, Tarrant had thought the Knights had been destroyed years ago. But like the mythical Hydra, when one head was chopped off, two more were waiting. Now they were back and stronger than ever.

This time, he was determined to hunt them down until there wasn't anyone left who knew about the Knights of the Dragon. They'd left the humans alone for centuries, not wanting to risk killing innocents, but Tarrant was no longer convinced there was such a thing.

And someone had to pay for the death of Father Simon.

Which brought him back to the woman tentatively walking up the front steps of the cabin. He had her picture running through every known database. That was one of the perks of being the best hacker on the planet. He'd find out who she was sooner or later. In the meantime, it would be interesting to see what she'd do.

When he saw her lips moving, he activated the speakers, curious to know who she was talking to. Was she wired?

"You can do this. There's probably no one here. Just knock."

Tarrant leaned back in his chair and stared at the screen. She was talking to herself. Her voice was low and husky and sent a whisper of awareness trickling through him.

She licked her lips and raised her hand. "You shouldn't have read so many fairytales as a child. It's only a cabin."

He grinned before he could stop himself. "You have no idea, little girl." What would she do if she knew what was waiting for her in a hidden bunker deep below the cabin?

She rapped sharply on the door. "Hello? Is anyone home?" She shifted her weight from one foot to the other and glanced up at the darkening sky.

She took a deep breath, put her hand on the doorknob, and turned. It wasn't locked. The hinges on the thick panel gave an ominous squeak.

"Great," she whispered. "Just great." In a louder voice, she called out again. "Anyone home?"

He switched camera views and watched her walk into the

space. She peered around the interior as though she expected someone to jump out and surprise her at any moment. The living room and kitchen area were open. There were two closed doors off to her left. Not surprisingly, she headed there next.

She knocked on the bathroom door and then the bedroom, before opening both. She visibly relaxed when she discovered she was alone. She didn't bother to unbutton her coat or remove the small knapsack from her back as she began to explore.

She went straight for the stone fireplace. "This is gorgeous." She pulled out her phone and snapped several pictures. Phone still in hand, she crept into the kitchen and studied the woodstove. Several pictures later, she wandered into the living area again and ran her hand over the back of the ancient sofa.

Tarrant's entire body tightened. What would it feel like to have her hand on his body? He growled and shook off the sexual tension.

He glanced at one of his many computers. The search was still running. He was checking the DMV one state at a time. He'd match her picture eventually.

She sighed, seeming defeated, and slumped down into the chair. She coughed when a light plume of dust wafted around her. "Nothing. I don't know what else I expected."

His beast stirred to life inside him, as curious about the woman as he was. That was dangerous. He didn't trust her, not for one second.

One of his sensors went off, and he pushed his chair over to another computer. "Son of a bitch." Two men, dressed all in black and carrying assault rifles, were sneaking through the woods. Were they with her, or was she in danger?

He wheeled back to the screen with the woman on it. As if she sensed danger, her head came up. Two seconds later, she bounded from the chair and out the front door, closing it softly behind her.

She crept into the forest and hunkered down beneath a fallen tree to wait.

Now that was interesting.

One of the men moved in close to the cabin and snuck a glance in the window. He went methodically around the small building, checking each window in turn. "She's not in there." Tarrant's well-planted cameras had no trouble picking up the whisper.

"Where the hell is she? The boss will kill us if anything happens to her."

"Maybe we passed her, and she's on her way back to her car."

"Let's hope so."

"We'll head back and watch her rental. If she's not there, or doesn't show within the hour, we'll come back here."

"Roger that."

As Tarrant watched, the two men began a fast, but silent, trek through the woods. One passed within five feet of the woman, but she was well hidden and stayed completely silent.

He expected her to move as soon as the men were gone, but she stayed for another twenty minutes before finally leaving her hiding spot. This was obviously not the first time she'd hidden from someone.

His dragon side wasn't happy, and neither was Tarrant. Whoever the woman was, she didn't deserve to be hunted, and certainly not by the Knights.

The computer dinged, signaling the end of his search. He kept one eye on the woman as he wheeled over to the computer. "Valeriya Azarov. Resident of New York City."

A feeling of dread filled the pit of his stomach. He'd been using his technical skills to run a trace of all the people who had visited Herman Temple, the man tracking his brother Darius. He'd also made a note of anyone the man had visited.

And he'd had a short meeting with one Karina Azarov.

Tarrant wasn't a man who believed in coincidence. Whoever this unknown woman was, she was associated with the Knights of the Dragon.

He threw back his head and roared.

• • •

Herman Temple carefully set his phone on his desk when what he really wanted to do was smash it against the wall. Things were falling apart, and he'd worked too long and hard to allow that to happen.

He glanced out the window and noted his reflection. His white hair was still distinguished, but his posture wasn't as straight as it had been, and his reflexes were slower. In short, he was aging, and he didn't like it. Not one bit.

A knock came on the door. "Enter," he called. He allowed none of his anger and the underlying fear show. When the door opened, he wasn't surprised to see Matthew Riggs there. After all, Riggs was his head of security, even if he was currently sleeping with and feeding information to the current leader of the Knights of the Dragon.

"Sir." Riggs inclined his head slightly, but there was no true deference there. Riggs thought he was so clever, but Herman had been playing these games since before Riggs's grandfather had been born. Dragon blood had kept him alive a long time. But now his source was gone, and his time was running out.

Herman sat back in his chair, his pose totally relaxed, giving the impression he was a man without a care in the world. "Yes?"

"Valeriya Azarov is in Washington State."

Now, that was a surprise. "Why is she there?" He'd always felt that Karina's sister was a weakness to both her and the group. Not that he could talk. His son had ended up being a liability and a disappointment to him.

"Undetermined," Riggs continued. "Karina has sent men to watch her."

"Karina, is it?" Herman enjoyed when Riggs frowned and looked uncomfortable. "No matter. Fuck her if you want, just remember she has no loyalty to anyone but herself." Neither did he, but that was neither here nor there.

Herman pressed his fingers together, forming a steeple, and contemplated his next move. "I want to know why Karina's sister is in Washington. What does she know about the Knights' business?" He pinned Riggs with a steely gaze. "She's not a member of the Knights and cannot be allowed to interfere."

"Yes, sir."

Herman watched his former head of security leave. Riggs still had the title. He couldn't let him know he was being replaced. Not yet. He was much too valuable, especially with his connection to Karina.

Karina must have slipped up somehow. Valeriya must have found out about Washington. And how much else did she know?

Herman picked up his phone and made a call. "Henderson, come into my office." He hung up knowing the other man would hurry. He was ambitious and would eagerly step into Riggs's role. He'd also have no problem disposing of his predecessor when the time came.

The intercom buzzed. Two seconds later, the door opened and Luther Henderson walked in. He was physically big and tough, but he was also incredibly intelligent. Most of all, he was loyal and would not be distracted by a pretty face. Herman had had his eyes on Henderson for a while now. He had no family, no friends, and no romantic connections. In short, he was perfect.

"I have a job for you."

Chapter Two

Valeriya held herself very still as the man passed within feet of where she was hunkered down beneath a fallen tree. She didn't hold her breath, but took very shallow ones. Even after she'd sensed he'd gone, she waited. She was too smart to move too soon.

Once again, her intuition had warned her. All her life, she'd been able to sense danger coming her way in time to avoid it. It was a trait she'd shared with her paternal grandmother. As a child, Valeriya hadn't really understood what the feelings meant, only that something bad happened when she ignored them. Her grandmother had spent countless hours with her, explaining how their gift worked.

It was an early warning system, one that had allowed her to sidestep the minefield of her childhood, making her always aware whenever trouble was imminent. She didn't quite understand how it worked. Only that it did. An icy sensation would skate down her spine, followed by a certainty that danger was nearby.

As she'd grown older, and with her grandmother's

encouragement, she'd tested the talent, sharpening her skills. Her grandmother had also counseled her to keep quiet about her gift, to not even share the knowledge of it with her parents and sister. Not that Valeriya would have. Just thinking about doing such a thing had made her feel ill, as though her intuition was warning her against such an action.

As a child, it had left her feeling like an outsider in her immediate family. As an adult, she was glad she had kept her silence.

Now her gift not only alerted her when there was danger nearby, she was also able to determine from which direction it was coming and from whom. It had served her well as a woman living alone in New York City, but she'd honed it to a razor's edge while growing up in a household that was the hub for the dangerous Knights of the Dragon.

She relied totally on her instinct and intuition, trusting it implicitly. It had never steered her wrong.

Her shirt was stuck to her skin beneath her sweater and coat. She might have sweat buckets and her heart might still be beating a tad too fast, but she'd held fast and was safe, for the time being.

She slowly eased out from under the fallen tree. It took a bit of work as some of the branches tangled in her coat and backpack. There hadn't been time for her to remove it.

What were those men doing here? They weren't high-ranking members of the Knights like her sister, but foot soldiers, assassins. Was the cabin under surveillance? Or had her sister sent them here for her?

God, she was stupid. Her sister might not be the only person keeping an eye on this place. She knew they all spied on one another. There were no secrets from the Knights of the Dragon.

Maybe they were just doing a sweep of the place and keeping an eye out for Darius Varkas or anyone else who showed up here. That was just as likely.

She shivered as the cold wind bit into her skin. Valeriya stood with her arms wrapped around herself, wondering what she should do next. The men were gone, but they might be watching the road. Maybe they'd found her car, even though she'd pulled it off the road. And if they had, it would be easy for them to trace her back to the motel where she was staying.

Something vibrated beneath her feet. She held her hands out at her side to steady herself as the ground seemed to buckle slightly. Was it an earthquake? It passed but left her feeling more unsettled than ever.

Valeriya cautiously made her way to the porch, dropped down onto one of the steps, and leaned against the railing. "What am I going to do?" Several scenarios ran through her head, including driving straight to the airport, flying home, and pretending she'd never left. If her sister wasn't aware she'd left New York, she might never have to find out.

Another option was getting all the cash she could out of her bank account and running. Her instincts were screaming that her life was about to get a lot more dangerous. But running would only work for a short time. The Knights had contacts everywhere and would eventually find her. She wasn't exactly equipped to live off the grid.

Her sister had impressed upon her the last time they'd spoken that she wanted Valeriya to join the Knights in their quest to find and capture all the dragons in the world. If she discovered Valeriya had come here, Karina would view it as a betrayal.

A shiver skated down her spine. She honestly wasn't sure how far her sister would go if she refused to fall in line. And it wasn't only Karina she had to worry about, but the other Knights.

Valeriya hoped that if her sister discovered where she was, she wouldn't act rashly. Valeriya didn't think she would.

Not out of any sense of family loyalty, but because it would make Karina appear weak to the other Knights.

She'd acted without thinking through the consequences. Her sister had stayed out of her life for so long that she'd allowed herself to believe she was well and truly away from the Knights and their nasty business. Obviously, that was wishful thinking on her part.

She'd paid cash for her trip, but that precaution probably made little difference. She'd still had to book the plane ticket under her own name. Her skills didn't run to acquiring a fake ID. Her sister, or one of the Knights, was probably monitoring her activities. And there was no way Karina would believe the trip here was for research for Valeriya's books.

So be it. She couldn't willfully sit on the sidelines any longer. And if there was one thing she knew about the Knights of the Dragon, it was that if you weren't with them, you were against them.

She straightened her shoulders. "If the Knights know I'm here, I might as well check out of the motel and stay for a while. If anyone shows up, I can warn them they're in danger." And if the men came back, she'd hide once again, assuming they weren't waiting for her back at her motel.

If her sister had sent them, she might have ordered them to simply watch and see what she did. That was the more likely scenario. Karina always said that information was power.

Not for the first time, she wondered how her sister could follow the life path she'd chosen. They'd inherited money and several lucrative businesses when their parents died. And Karina was a sharp businessperson, more than able to handle all the responsibilities that came with both. They could have been a real family, been true sisters, if not for the Knights. But her sister had always chosen them above Valeriya.

She glanced up at the darkening sky and sighed. If she hurried, she could reach her car before dark. Still, she was reluctant to leave. She couldn't put her finger on why, but this place drew her. Deep inside, her intuition was demanding she stay, as if there was something very important to be discovered here.

"I'll be back," she whispered to the wind. "I'll be back tomorrow." She had no idea if this Darius Varkas would return here, but if he came, she was determined to protect him. Being a writer and illustrator, and self-employed, she could stay as long as necessary. In the meantime, she'd work on new sketches and ideas for her next book.

It wasn't much of a plan, but it was all she had.

Valeriya pushed herself off the porch and took the first step toward the road. It was surprisingly more difficult than she'd anticipated. "I'll be back," she repeated. She broke into a run and kept it up until she got a stitch in her side and her lungs burned. She slowed down, but only until the pain subsided enough for her to run again.

She almost cried with relief when she saw her car and there was no one waiting. She was happy she didn't have to confront the unknown men. Maybe they hadn't been looking for her at all.

Her hands shook when she pulled her key fob from her pocket and pressed the button for the lock. It gave a beep, and she yanked the door open and slid in. She was still wearing her backpack. She twisted around until she was able to remove it.

It was fully dark now, but the stars were coming out. Valeriya took a deep breath, started the car, and headed back toward the motel. In her mind, she was already compiling a list of the supplies she'd need if she planned on staying at the cabin for a while.

• • •

Tarrant watched Valeriya run away. The primitive urge to

chase her sang in his blood. He wanted to catch her and bring her back.

Mine.

He ignored the whisperings of the beast that lurked within him. The only reason he was able to let her go was because she'd whispered she'd be back. For some reason, he believed her. And even if he didn't, he could find her. There was nowhere in the world she could hide from him.

He'd lived for thousands of years and had his finger in almost every aspect of business. His communication empire was vast, far larger than that of any single country in the world. He controlled the airwaves and had since the very beginning, when telecommunication had been nothing more than the idea of madmen.

He'd made billions, but it was the power that was more important to him than the money.

Restless now that she was out of sight, Tarrant turned back to his computer and began to search for information. Before he slept, he'd know everything there was to know about Valeriya Azarov and her sister.

His fingers flew with increasing speed over the keyboard, bringing up information on multiple screens. Not surprisingly, Karina Azarov was involved in both technology and pharmaceutical businesses. The Knights were heavy into pharmaceuticals, trying to find ways not only to control drakons, but also to be able to reproduce drakon blood in a lab. His lips curled. Good luck with that.

He was more interested in Valeriya. She looked as exotic as her name, with her long, black hair and her clear green eyes. He ignored the way his body responded to thoughts of her. Yes, he was aroused, but that was to be expected. He hadn't been away from his lair in months.

He stared at the screen and blinked. Surely this couldn't be right. Valeriya Azarov was a children's author. She wrote books about…dragons. Tarrant didn't know whether to curse or laugh. Out of curiosity, he downloaded her books. He'd check them out later.

In the meantime, he dug deeper. Finding the information he needed was child's play for him. Karina was older by eight years. She'd taken over raising her younger sister after their parents died when Valeriya had been fifteen.

Karina had stepped up to head the family businesses and had travelled the world. Valeriya had spent much of her time with her grandparents, her father's parents. He doubled-checked the information. Yes, she now lived in those same grandparents' apartment. They'd willed it to her when they passed.

"So you don't live with your sister." He ignored the sense of relief. "Doesn't mean anything." She was most likely still involved with the Knights.

His stomach growled, a reminder it had been hours since he'd eaten. He didn't bother checking the clock to see how long he'd been down here. Time had little meaning to him. He'd lived for thousands of years and would live for thousands more. The one thing he had plenty of was time.

He stood and twisted his head from side to side, cracking his neck. He stretched his arms overhead to work out the kinks in his shoulder muscles as he walked toward the elevator. He stepped inside when it opened. "Up." The controls were voice activated and keyed to four specific people—him and his three brothers. When he reached the top, the door opened and he stepped out. It shut behind him with an ominous thud. No one could get into his computer lab unless he let them in. It was one of the most secure facilities on the planet.

Tarrant strode down the hallway, bypassing the bedrooms and heading straight to the kitchen. He wasn't in the mood to cook, so he dug in the freezer, pulled out two large pizzas, and shoved them in the oven. He grabbed a beer from the fridge, wandered into the living room, and sprawled on one of the two large sectional sofas. Since his brothers were on his mind, he decided to check in with them.

He retrieved his phone from his pocket and dialed. His brother answered on the first ring. "Everything okay?"

That was Darius—blunt and direct. "Good"—he paused and checked the time—"evening to you, too."

"Cut the crap, Tarrant. Are you okay?"

He knew his brother was worried about him, but there was no need. "I'm fine. I did have more visitors, though. This is becoming a very popular spot." He had to hold the phone away from his ear as Darius swore. "I hope Sarah isn't around to hear you talking like that," he teased.

Sarah Anderson was a librarian, a human who'd put her own life on the line to warn Darius about the Knights. Herman Temple had hired her to find a book of vast power, one that could have been used to hunt and trap his brother. She'd found the book, but when she'd realized Temple's intent, she'd taken it and run, her actions leading her straight to Darius. His older brother was head over heels about the woman. Darius's dragon half had decided Sarah was his mate, and his human half agreed. There was nothing Darius wouldn't do to protect her.

"Sarah is down on the beach with Ezra. They decided a bonfire would be nice."

Tarrant couldn't help but smile at the image of two fierce drakons catering to the whim of one delicate human female. "And why aren't you with them?"

His brother mumbled something.

"What was that?" Tarrant asked, even though he'd understood his brother perfectly.

"I got sent to the house for the marshmallows. There. Are you happy now?"

"Very." He'd take his amusements where he could get

them.

"You had visitors. Knights?"

"Yes." He pushed off the sofa and headed back to the kitchen, taking his beer with him. "Two armed men, but that's not the most curious part."

"Then what is?" Darius's impatience came over the line loud and clear.

"A woman showed up first."

"A woman? Who is she? And don't tell me you don't know yet." Darius knew him so well.

"Valeriya Azarov." Saying her name had his cock twitching. He ignored his small brain and listen to his larger one. "Children's book author from New York."

There was silence. "Are you serious?"

"Completely." Then he threw in the tidbit that would most interest Darius. "Her sister is Karina Azarov, who had a meeting with Herman Temple."

Darius swore again. "Then she's with the Knights."

Tarrant shook off the fury that welled up every time he thought about his friend's death. "Undetermined. The men seemed to be looking for her, and she did her best to avoid them." For a woman who didn't seem at home in the woods, Valeriya had been hyperalert and very good at concealing herself. How had she known they were there? Because she *had* known. It was a mystery, and one he would solve.

"You be careful."

Tarrant opened the oven and pulled out one of the pizzas. It was hot, but he was a drakon—a little heat didn't bother him. He tossed it down on an oversize cutting board, selected a knife, and cut the pizza into quarters. He turned off the oven so the second pizza would stay warm but not burn. "I'm always careful. You're the one out running around and getting into trouble."

Darius and Sarah had survived a deadly encounter with

the Knights. Thankfully, they were both okay and were safe on a privately-owned island off the coast of Maine. "And how is Ezra?" Their brother was even more reclusive than Tarrant, and that was saying something. They might have had the same sire, but they'd all had different mothers. Their personalities were totally unique.

"You know Ezra. He doesn't have a lot to say, but he likes Sarah. He's already talking about teaching her to scuba dive next spring."

That was impressive. Ezra didn't like sharing his private island with anyone. "What is she, a drakon whisperer?"

Darius laughed. "Maybe. All I know is she's mine." There was an underlying warning that Tarrant heeded. As much as he enjoyed teasing his brother, it wasn't smart to poke the sleeping dragon.

"She's all yours," he agreed.

Darius sighed. "Shit, I'm being an ass, aren't I?"

Tarrant laughed. "Since you're my older brother, I must agree with you."

"You would. Listen, don't take any unnecessary risks. The Knights are far more organized and well equipped than we thought."

"Don't worry. I have no plans for becoming a blood donor so some Knight can prolong his life." That was the primary reason drakons were so sought after by the Knights. Their blood could heal any wounds, cure any disease, and prolong life. And with the onset of DNA research, he knew the Knights would be experimenting on drakons in ways he didn't want to think about.

"Call if you need me, and I'll come."

Tarrant rubbed his hand over his face. He could always count on his brothers. "I know you will. Give Sarah my love."

"No, I will not. I'll tell her you said hello."

Tarrant was still laughing when the line went dead. He

tossed his phone aside and practically inhaled the first pizza. Then he went to the oven and retrieved the second one. That was half gone when he picked up his phone again. He knew Darius and Ezra were fine. That left Nicodemus.

He dialed the number and it rang three times before it was answered. "Tarrant, my man, what's on your mind?"

Tarrant shook his head. He could hear the noise in the background—people shouting, bells ringing, and music. "Where are you?" He didn't know how Nic could stand to be around so many people all the time. It would drive Tarrant crazy.

"Vegas, baby. And I'm on a hot streak."

They all had hobbies, things they collected. That was the dragon part of their nature, their need to gather and hoard treasure. For him it was information and gadgets. For Nic, it was artwork of all kinds. He could outfit several world-class museums and not even make a dent in his collection. They all worked and invested to finance their collections, but Nic also gambled.

"You take too many chances." Nic put himself too much in the public eye.

"Don't worry. I'll lose enough so the casino doesn't get too angry." He spoke to someone nearby. "I'll just be a second." Then he came back on the line. "Do you need me for anything?"

Nic might come across as devil-may-care, but he was a drakon and would come if Tarrant needed him. "No, just checking in. Be careful."

"Will do."

The line went dead, and Tarrant tucked his phone away and finished off the pizza. Now that he'd talked with his brothers and eaten, there was nothing else to occupy him but thoughts of Valeriya.

"Shit." He cleaned up what little mess he'd made in the

kitchen and then retired to his bedroom. He could watch any number of sporting events on television, but he wasn't in the mood. He didn't need much sleep, either. He could go days without rest. In fact, he couldn't exactly remember the last time he'd slept well. Not since the death of Father Simon.

The lights came on in his room as soon as he entered. There were sensors in the floor that registered his weight and automatically turned the lights on. It was the same in every room. They could be manually controlled as well. He went straight into the bathroom and stared at himself in the mirror.

Dark circles rimmed his eyes. He might be a drakon, but even he needed rest sooner or later. His face was all planes and angles. He looked as though he'd lost weight. He hadn't been eating regularly enough. He needed a heck of a lot more calories than a human did.

He removed his phone, put it on the vanity, and stripped off his clothes, tossing them into the laundry hamper. He'd deal with that tomorrow. The shower stall was large enough to accommodate him. Tarrant turned the water on and stepped beneath the spray. It cascaded over his body like a caress.

An image of Valeriya popped into his head. He wondered where she was now, what she was doing. His dick came to full attention, and he sighed, knowing he had to do something about this little problem or he'd never sleep.

Giving in to the inevitable, he soaped his chest and arms, and then he went lower. He grasped his cock in his hand and slid his fist up and down. His groan reverberated, making the tempered-glass wall shudder.

He remembered how she'd slid her hand over the back of the sofa, and imagined it was her smaller, softer hand on his shaft. He didn't even know what she looked like out of the heavy bundle of clothing, but that didn't matter. Something about her drew him.

His dragon rumbled inside him. Oh, yeah, the beast liked

her, too. Tarrant had lived for a very long time. He'd seen the most beautiful women throughout the ages, and had even slept with some of them. But none of them held a candle to Valeriya.

His stroke quickened and his balls drew up tight. He roared when he came, shooting his release over his stomach. It was purely a physical exercise, like feeding his hunger for food. There was no joy when he was done, no satisfaction, only emptiness.

He swore and cleaned himself up. Silence surrounded him when he turned off the taps. He was used to being alone, preferred it. But tonight, he didn't want to be alone. Tonight, he wanted her with him.

Growling, he dried off and tossed the damp towel over the rod. He couldn't allow himself to become distracted by a pretty face, no matter how much he wanted her. For all he knew, she could be working for the Knights. In times gone by, they'd tie a virgin to a stake to try to lure a drakon. That hadn't exactly worked out well for the Knights. Drakons weren't the stupid beasts most humans thought them to be.

Their dragon sires had been more basic in their needs, but their sons combined the instincts and strengths of a dragon along with the intellect and cunning of their human mothers. A deadly combination.

Valeriya wasn't exactly an offering from the Knights to tempt him to show himself. She had come alone. Or mostly alone. She may have hidden from the armed men searching for her, but that might have been nothing more than a ploy. Maybe they suspected Darius was still around or that he might come back.

The thought of her being sent to seduce his brother made smoke billow from his nostrils. He got his dragon under control before he set fire to his home. He strode into the bedroom and threw himself down on his enormous bed. He closed his eyes, but that lasted all of five seconds.

He sat up and reached for the tablet on the bedside table. He pulled up the first of the three books he'd downloaded. Valeriya had not only written them, she'd illustrated them as well.

He scrolled to the first page and started to read. It was a story of acceptance and friendship, and the hero was the dragon. That surprised him. He'd expected some tale where the dragon was vanquished. When he was done with the first book about the friendly little dragon named Damian, he started the second. The illustrations really were beautiful and multilayered, something both the children and the person reading them the story would enjoy. Valeriya Azarov was not only beautiful, she was very talented.

Chapter Three

Valeriya was exhausted by the time she made it back to the motel. The nearby store had already closed its doors for the evening. She'd have to shop for supplies in the morning. There had been no sign of the two armed men on her drive, but they were nearby. She sensed them.

With her grandparents gone, there was no one else in the world who knew about her talent. If her sister ever discovered what Valeriya could do, she had no doubt Karina would find some way to exploit it. Her sister would stop at nothing to get what she wanted. If that meant she had to pressure, maybe even hurt, family in the process, she would.

Valeriya had lived her entire life waiting for her sister to decide she was a liability. That was one of the reasons she'd always lived her life the way she wanted. She didn't expect to have a long one.

They might be sisters, but they'd become more like strangers with each passing year. Karina was immersed in the world of the Knights, while Valeriya had stayed as far away from them as possible. Maybe that had been a mistake.

Maybe if she'd made an effort with her sister when they were both younger, Karina wouldn't be cold, so driven.

Valeriya climbed out of the car and listened. There was nothing but quiet. Then a vehicle rumbled in the distance, and an owl gave a lonely hoot. A shiver raced down her spine. She grabbed her knapsack and headed to her room.

She knew the second she stepped inside that someone had been there. The back of her neck tingled, a sure warning sign. There was nothing overtly out of place, but she caught the faintest hint of soap. And it wasn't hers.

Mostly likely it was one of the men who'd trailed her to the cabin. Either that or they had friends.

Hands shaking, she shut the door and slid the bolt home. Not that it would keep them out if they decided they wanted in. There was a single chair sitting next to a small table. Valeriya dumped her pack on the bed and dragged the chair over and slid it under the handle. If anyone broke in, it would at least slow them down some.

She slumped down on the end of the bed and buried her face in her hands. She was tired of always having to look over her shoulder, of being followed. Her older sister had been controlling her life since their parents died. Valeriya was sick of it.

She wished she'd never heard of the Knights of the Dragon, wished her family had chosen another path. She rubbed her hands over her face and pushed off the bed. "Shower."

Ignoring the rumble of her stomach, she went into the tiny bathroom and turned on the shower. While the water was heating, she collected a pair of green flannel sleep pants and a long-sleeved white thermal top to change into when she was done.

Steam billowed from the shower/tub combo. She quickly stripped and stepped into the tub. The spray pummeled her relentlessly. She knew the water was hot, but she couldn't seem to get warm.

Her reaction was a combination of fear and hunger. She knew that, but it didn't ease her trembling or chase away the chill.

When she was showered and dressed, she padded barefoot back into her room. The thin carpet on the floor did little to chase away the chill, so she donned a pair of fuzzy white socks. For good measure, she grabbed a hoodie from her bag and tugged it on as well.

She wanted something hot, so she filled the small kettle. While she was waiting for it to boil, she dug her laptop out of her knapsack. She discovered two granola bars at the bottom of the bag and ripped one of them open. They weren't much, but they'd take care of the worst of her hunger.

Valeriya took a big bite and settled on the bed with the laptop perched on her thighs. "It's time to do some looking." She knew her sister probably had someone on staff who could hack into her computer, but Valeriya no longer cared. If Karina knew she was here, she knew it had to do with the Knights' business.

She typed a name into the search engine. "Darius Varkas." She'd avoided doing this up until now, half afraid she'd find the man's obituary. She had no idea why her sister was so interested in him, only that he was likely in grave danger.

He might even be a drakon.

Valeriya had never seen one and didn't want to. The only way she'd ever see a drakon was if the Knights had captured one and her sister decided to show her. And Valeriya couldn't bear the thought of seeing such a thing. It was an abomination, what the Knights did. She knew many of them drank drakon blood to prolong their lives and cure them of illnesses. She'd even heard whisperings it gave some humans extra powers.

The kettle whistled, startling her. Valeriya set aside her computer and made a cup of tea. She ate the last of the granola bar and tossed the wrapper. "Stop procrastinating," she ordered. She climbed back on the bed and set her mug of tea on the bedside table.

Taking a deep breath, she pulled the laptop back onto her thighs. There were quite a few entries for Darius Varkas. He was a businessman, his headquarters in New York. Not surprising, then, that Karina came to the city. It certainly hadn't been to visit Valeriya.

She snagged her mug and took a sip of the hot tea, keeping her hands cupped around the mug to allow the heat to seep into her skin. Mr. Varkas was in mining. Earth drakon. She immediately shook off the thought. Lots of people were involved in mining. It didn't mean they were drakons. Of course, they might be, or they might come in contact with one.

Valeriya knew she was grasping at straws but continued to search a bit more. There was nothing of a personal nature in the articles she found about him. And no pictures, either, at least none she could find.

She erased her browsing history and leaned back against the pillows. "What now?" She sipped her tea and thought about the cabin. There was something there. She was sure of it. Maybe she'd missed something, some clue that would help her discover more about why this place was so important to her sister.

Since the men she'd seen earlier hadn't descended on her motel room to do more than snoop, she assumed they'd been ordered to simply watch. That order could change in a heartbeat if Karina, or whoever had sent them, decided she was too big a liability.

It might be smarter to run, but Valeriya decided to head back to the cabin. The door had been unlocked. She'd move in and stay for a few days, maybe longer. She'd work on ideas for her new book and also keep an eye out in case Mr. Varkas returned, assuming he'd been there in the first place.

All she had to go on was her instinct, some coordinates scratched on a pad of paper, and snippets of an overheard phone conversation between her sister and someone else.

She closed her eyes and sighed. "You're no James Bond." She wasn't cut out for skulking around. She didn't have the right skills or mindset.

Her stomach rumbled again, so she reached for the second granola bar. She could almost hear her sister warning her not to eat it, to watch her weight. She ripped open the wrapper and took a big bite. Unlike her sister, who was willowy and tall, Valeriya was sturdier, curvier. No amount of dieting and exercise had changed it, so she'd eventually accepted and embraced her body for what it was. She wasn't fat, but she'd never be skinny.

"Stop it," she muttered. Disgusted with herself, she tossed the empty wrapper. She wasn't a child any longer, searching for approval from her parents and sister. A disappointment—that's what she was to them. She knew it but no longer cared. As far as she was concerned, they were a much bigger disappointment to her.

They'd killed people under the guise of being righteous. And she was worse because she'd done nothing to stop them.

It didn't help that she knew there was nothing she could do. They had followers in high places in both government and law enforcement. Besides, if she opened her mouth and told the police or FBI her family headed up a secret group that hunted drakons—dragon-like creatures—she'd be institutionalized.

She shivered at the thought as she tossed a fresh teabag into her mug and added hot water. No, she could do nothing without destroying herself. And in the end, it would do no good. The Knights would continue on, even if her sister or other high-ranking members were imprisoned or dead.

The best thing, the only thing she could do, was warn Mr.

Varkas if he or anyone who knew him returned to the cabin.

Valeriya did the one thing she could to take her mind off her sister and the Knights. She dug out her sketchbook and pencils. She did much of her work on her laptop and tablet these days, but nothing beat sketching with paper and pencils. That's where her ideas really came alive.

She took her fresh cup of tea back to the bed. This time, she crawled under the covers. She glanced at her knapsack. There were probably messages on her phone, but she doubted any of them were important. They rarely were. The pictures she'd taken earlier today were on there, but she could work from memory for now.

She opened the new sketchbook and selected a pencil. She meant to draw a fairy, really she did. But as she drew the woods, she felt his presence—a dragon. She smiled, liking the idea of a secret dragon lurking in her woods.

Valeriya lost herself in the work, stopping only long enough to use the bathroom. She resumed as soon as she crawled back into bed. She did sketch after sketch, creating a world of fairies and dragons. She'd thought to start a new series, but maybe she could do a crossover with her popular books featuring Damian the dragon. Maybe Damian wandered into the fairy woods.

Her head was full of ideas when her eyes finally closed and the pencil slipped from her fingers. She woke hours later with a crick in her neck and sunshine beaming in on her.

She groaned and squinted. "What the heck?" She put her hand down to push herself upright and something crinkled under her palm. Her sketchbook. Valeriya sighed and rubbed her free hand over her face. She'd fallen asleep while working…again. Wasn't the first time and wouldn't be the last.

Her neck was stiff, so she rolled it from side to side. Once she was satisfied she hadn't done any permanent damage, she slid her legs over the side of the bed.

Anticipation raced through her. She had a lot to do this morning. She needed to check out of the motel, get some supplies, and head back to the cabin. Maybe it was dangerous, but she didn't care. The Knights were watching her. For all she knew, Darius Varkas might be watching her, too. He was either a drakon or a powerful, rich businessman. Either way, staying in a secluded cabin without the owner's permission was foolhardy.

Valeriya snorted. "Why start being sensible now?" She may have burned her last bridge with her sister by coming here. Time would tell. The only path was the one forward.

"If nothing else, I'll get a book out of it." She knew she'd done some of her best sketches last night. She'd even written snippets of dialogue and story to go along with them. At this rate, she'd have the bare bones of the book done within a week. It would only be a matter of refining her drawings and storyline after that.

Valeriya stood and stretched. She'd get dressed and hit the coffee shop for some breakfast before purchasing supplies. Plan in place, she began to gather her things.

• • •

Tarrant woke in a foul mood. He knew his brothers would argue that was no different than any other day of the week. That he always woke in a foul mood. But this was worse than normal. He'd spent the night dreaming of her.

He swore as he padded naked out to the kitchen and started a pot of coffee. Once the brew was underway, he went back to his room and hauled on a pair of jeans and a long-sleeved cotton shirt. By the time he got back to the kitchen, there was enough coffee brewed for him to fill his large mug.

He sighed as he took the first hit of the day. Coffee was one of the greatest inventions of mankind. Forget flight and space travel. They would never have gotten off the ground without coffee.

The phone rang as he was considering his options for breakfast. It was no surprise it was Darius. He answered and put the call on speaker. "Yeah?

"You have your coffee yet?" his brother asked.

"Fuck you," Tarrant shot back. He opened the refrigerator and pulled out a package of bacon.

"That would be a no, I take it."

"I'm having my first one now. I finally got some sleep last night."

"You haven't slept well since you got word of Father Simon's death, have you?"

Tarrant didn't like the concern in Darius's voice. The last thing his brother needed was to be worrying about him. "I've been busy," he shot back. "Where's Sarah?"

Darius practically purred. "She's still sleeping. I wore her out last night."

Not what Tarrant needed to hear. Not only did he not want to picture his brother and his woman getting it on, he was also jealous. All he'd had were dreams to keep him company. And while the dreams had been hot, waking alone had brought him back to reality in a hurry.

"Not sure you want Sarah to hear you talking like that," Tarrant warned. "Women can be funny about certain things."

Darius chuckled. Sarah really was a drakon whisperer. He'd only been half kidding when he'd called her that last night. Anyone who could make his serious brother actually laugh was a miracle worker.

"Was there a reason for your call? Not that I'm not happy to hear from you." Tarrant put two large grill pans on the stove and loaded strips of bacon onto them. He was starving.

"Just checking to see if any of your guests have shown up again."

"No alarms have gone off, but I haven't checked my computers yet this morning."

"Wait. Has the world come to an end? You haven't checked your computers yet this morning?"

Darius's humor was beginning to annoy him. "You're a real comedian. I'm going to warn Sarah about your new sense of humor."

Darius growled long and low. This time Tarrant smiled. It was fun to tease his brother.

"She loves me just the way I am," Darius asserted.

Tarrant swallowed the last of his coffee and refilled his mug. "Yeah, we can't all be that lucky."

"I'm sorry." Tarrant could picture his brother's frown.

"Don't be. At least one of us should be happy." Tarrant flipped the bacon. "Look, I'm going to have breakfast and then check things out. I'll call if I discover anything." The sizzle and pop of bacon fat was making him hungry. "You be careful, and keep a watch. Remember, you're the one the Knights have targeted."

"I won't forget. Talk to you later."

Tarrant turned off his phone and concentrated on cooking. He scrambled a dozen eggs to go with his plate-load of bacon. By the time he'd finished eating, he was on his forth cup of coffee and starting to feel half human. His pun made him smile. He was half human, half dragon, too. But he was all drakon.

He put his dishes in the dishwasher and headed down to his computer lab. His security rivaled the best in the world. It was his companies that most governments and corporations called on when they needed a system designed.

As always, something inside him settled when he walked into his most private domain. Here, he could access the world's secrets at any given moment. Darius liked shiny rocks and minerals; Tarrant liked information.

He pulled his chair up to the screen and began to sift through all the data that had accumulated while he'd slept. He kept track of it all—business, banking, politics, wars, social trends. It all interested him. He had a voracious appetite for knowledge of all kinds.

Still, his mind wandered back to his dreams.

He swore and closed his eyes, to better capture the memory of Valeriya. He'd fallen asleep reading her children's books. He'd never tell his brothers that. They'd never let him live it down, especially Nic.

He'd actually enjoyed the adventures of the likeable dragon who pretended to be tough to hide his insecurities. But what had really drawn him in was Valeriya's artwork. Her pictures were clever and layered. You could glance at them and enjoy the story, or you could give them a second look and see the hidden bits and pieces, like the owl in the tree or the mouse crouching beside a rock.

There was an innocence about the drawings that tugged at him.

He snorted. There'd certainly been nothing innocent about his dreams last night. They'd been X-rated all the way. He'd had her naked in his bed. He might not know what she looked like beneath her clothes, but in his dreams she was curvy and voluptuous, just the way he liked a woman.

Tarrant didn't understand the current trend of women wanting to starve themselves. Maybe it was because he'd lived through many different eras, but he liked a woman who looked like a woman. Strength was also attractive. Strong women, curvy women, but not skinny ones. To him, that mean hard times and poverty.

He'd also lived long enough to know every culture and every age had its own interpretation of beauty and it would eventually change once again. Such was the way of the world.

His Valeriya had full breasts that fit his palms to perfection.

She had curved hips that cradled him as he buried his cock deep and thrust.

He groaned and opened his eyes. He was aroused again, and it wasn't the least bit comfortable. And what the hell was his thinking? She wasn't his Valeriya. She didn't even know he existed. And it was going to stay that way.

His dragon grumbled and growled inside him, but Tarrant ignored his beast. His job was to keep the Knights from finding out about him, not invite one of them into his life.

He ignored the ache in his chest and concentrated on work. Information never failed him, never let him down. He depended on himself and his brothers. That was the best way to survive.

He'd just finished reading the last of the reports when an outer perimeter alarm went off. His heart leaped, and anticipation flooded through him. Was she back?

He clicked on the cameras and watched as a car drove down the rutted dirt road to his cabin. He focused one camera in on the driver. A slow smile slid across his face.

"You came back."

Just as she'd promised yesterday, Valeriya was back. But for how long? And where were the Knights?

Tarrant checked all his alarms and put his private lair in lockdown mode.

He watched as the car slowed to a crawl. She'd have made faster time walking. Finally, she pulled up in front of the cabin and climbed out of the car. She turned in a complete circle and peered up at the bright blue sky.

Chapter Four

"I'm back," Valeriya whispered. She knew there was no one around to hear her, but she couldn't help feeling as though she was being watched. But she didn't feel threatened, not in the least. It was more of an awareness than a sense of danger.

The cabin really did belong in one of her books. It was rustic, but the porch running across the front softened it slightly. She could picture it with some comfy chairs and a table to hold an iced tea on a hot afternoon or a hot chocolate on a cool one.

A bitterly cold wind whipped through the trees, making her shiver in spite of her warm clothing. She popped the trunk of the car and pulled out several of the bags of supplies she'd purchased. She carried them up the stairs but paused in front of the door. It was one thing to stop and look around the place. It was quite another to move in. What if the owner showed up?

That's what she wanted, wasn't it? The owner would have to know Darius Varkas, wouldn't he? Maybe Varkas owned the place, maybe a friend did. She wasn't sure how to search property records to find out.

"Stop dithering." She turned the handle of the door and stepped inside. Nothing happened—the world didn't end, and no one called out, accusing her of breaking and entering.

Valeriya carried the bags straight into the kitchen and set them down on the tiny counter space. She was being generous calling it a kitchen. It had mismatched cupboards and a refrigerator that didn't just look retro, but was.

Because she wasn't sure how reliable the refrigerator was, she'd bought all canned and boxed food. Not the tastiest choice in the world, but certainly the smartest. And since it would probably only be for a short time, she could live with canned meat, veggies, and fruit instead of fresh, and crackers instead of bread. She'd gone heavy on the soup, as that was fairly nutritious and quick to prepare.

She studied the stove and groaned. It wasn't gas or electric. It was a woodstove. "I'll be lucky if I don't burn the place down," she muttered. No, she would be positive about this situation, even if it killed her. She was smart. She'd figure things out.

She went back to the car and dragged in her suitcase, knapsack, more bags, and one final box of supplies. It took her several trips, but she finally finished.

She carried her suitcase into the bedroom. It was a small space that contained a bed and a chest of drawers. Not exactly the most welcoming place. There wasn't even any bedding on the bare mattress. Thankfully, she'd been able to purchase a sleeping bag from the local store. She went out to the living room, grabbed the sleeping bag, and carried it back to the bedroom.

"Not exactly the Ritz, but it will do quite nicely." It was like camping out. Or as close to camping as she wanted to get. She liked having a roof over her head and a mattress to sleep on at night.

The bathroom had running water. She wasn't quite sure how that worked, but she wasn't about to question it.

Valeriya went back to the kitchen and unpacked her supplies. The cupboards were surprisingly clean, so she loaded her canned and boxed food inside. She ran water and rinsed the old metal kettle several times before filling it.

It was time to face the stove.

She set the kettle on the cast-iron top and looked around for some wood. There was a box with a couple of logs, but no more. "That won't last long. There has to be wood around somewhere." After all, they had a woodstove and a fireplace.

She let out her breath in a huff. "You can do this." She needed the constant reminder and the pep talk. There was a back door off the kitchen. This door was also unlocked, so she opened it and stepped out onto the small back stoop. There was no shed, at least not one she could see.

Undaunted, she went down the two stairs and began to search for the woodpile.

• • •

Tarrant was fascinated by the way Valeriya talked to herself. The pile of things she'd brought with her made him relax. It was obvious she was planning to stay for a while. He ignored his sense of relief and followed her movements as she walked around the cabin.

He'd seen her staring at the woodstove and knew she was intimidated by it. That didn't stop her, though. He only hoped she didn't burn down the cabin or hurt herself.

"Around to the other side," he muttered.

She paused and then walked around the side of the cabin and off to the left.

He growled with frustration as she took the long way around. Her cry of delight when she spied the neatly stacked pile of wood in the rustic lean-to made him smile. Most women didn't get that excited when they received diamonds.

Valeriya hurried over and began to load chunks of wood into her arms. She overdid it and stumbled several times on her way back to the house. The first time it happened, Tarrant lurched forward, as though he could reach through the screen and catch her.

She carried the wood into the house and dumped it into the box beside the stove. Then she went back for another load.

"Damn woman didn't learn anything the first time around." He watched with mounting anger as she overloaded herself again and again. She made a total of five trips to the woodpile before she was satisfied she had enough wood for the stove and the fireplace. He was just glad she hadn't hurt herself…yet.

The way she was staring at the woodstove was making him nervous. Still, she didn't just throw some wood inside and light a match. She studied it, checking the flue and the oven. She practiced removing the metal covered tops with the handle and returning them to the top of the stove.

She tore bark from the wood to use as kindling and stuffed it around several chunks of the wood. Finally, she seemed satisfied and reached for the box of matches on a shelf next to the stove. He held his breath as she lit the match and set the flame to the edges of the bark. It flared and she pulled her hand back.

Tarrant watched, as fascinated as she by the flames. They lowered and almost flickered out, but the wood finally caught. "Woo hoo!" she shouted, and did a little victory dance, wiggling her hips and jumping around the kitchen.

He couldn't look away from her hips. He just wished she wasn't wearing the damn coat.

When Valeriya settled back down, she set the metal cover back into place and pulled the kettle on top of it. Then she rubbed her hands together and turned to stare at the fireplace.

• • •

Valeriya was feeling victorious. She had a fire going in the woodstove and the kettle boiling. There was something very primal and satisfying about making fire. The most she'd ever done before was light a candle.

Now that the stove was going, it was time to face the fireplace. This was her main source of heat, and it was cold outside. She'd freeze tonight if she didn't figure out how to keep a fire going.

She should have looked it up online before she'd left town, maybe watched a video or two. The locals had warned her she'd get spotty to non-existent internet service so high in the mountains.

She'd figure it out. She went into the living room, crouched down beside the fireplace, and looked up the chimney. She couldn't see if it was blocked, but there was a metal lever. It was stiff, but she got it to move and opened the flue partway.

Next came the firewood. She set several large logs in the grate and used more bark as kindling. Using the matches from the kitchen, she lit the bark. Flames flared and then receded. "Come on," she coaxed. She leaned forward and gently blew on the embers. She'd seen that in a movie once, and it did seem to help.

She prayed and lit another match.

It took much longer than the woodstove had, but finally she had a cheery fire going. She sat back on her heels and stared at the flames. She was exhausted. Gathering supplies had been nerve-wracking. She knew there were men in town keeping a watch for her. What she wasn't sure of was whether or not they'd seen her leave town. She hadn't sensed anyone around her or seen a car following. And she'd been looking for them, not only visually but also with her gift.

All the way on the drive up, she'd half expected a vehicle to overtake her. What would happen after that, she really didn't know. It had almost been a shock when she'd arrived here without them making contact.

She could only hope they were still watching her motel room. That since they'd already checked out the cabin, they wouldn't bother with it again. At least not for a day or two, until they realized she wasn't still in town.

She wasn't foolish enough to believe they wouldn't come back, probably sooner rather than later. Chances of Mr. Varkas showing up were low, especially if he caught wind of the men skulking around. The smart thing for her to do would be to leave, but she just couldn't make herself do that. Not yet.

There was some reason she needed to stay. She didn't question the sense of knowing deep inside. She only hoped she wasn't making a huge mistake, one that might cost her dearly.

Unpacking, carrying armloads of wood, and starting two fires had worn her out. The combination of stress and physical activity had depleted her reserves. She hadn't eaten since breakfast. That was hours ago, and it had only been some toast and tea at the local diner.

"Time to eat." Talking out loud made her feel not quite so isolated. Besides, there was no one around to hear her, so it didn't matter. Living alone, she was used to talking to herself. She also did it while she worked on her books, reciting the story out loud to decide if it was working. Since she wrote books for children, and they were likely to read aloud, it made sense for her to do it, too.

Steam was finally billowing from the spout of the kettle. Valeriya hurried to the kitchen and shifted it over to the other side of the stovetop. The small cast-iron stove was radiating heat, and it made her realize just how chilled she was.

She opened several cupboards and found the dishes. The mugs were old, but there were no chips or cracks in them. She rinsed one and then dug out her selection of teabags. She chose a berry blend. As she poured hot water into the mug, her hand was shaking from a combination of cold, fear, and hunger.

She'd bought a dozen containers of soup. All she had to do was add water to the container, let it sit for a minute, and then stir. She decided on chicken noodle. She was in dire need of comfort food.

While the soup was doing its thing, she carried her tea into the living room and set it on the scarred coffee table. Then she went to the bedroom and collected her sleeping bag. The way things were looking, she'd be better off spending the night out here in front of the fireplace. The sofa was an ugly shade of green, but it was better than the floor.

It took her a few minutes to settle on the surprisingly comfortable sofa with her sleeping bag wrapped around her. She had the soup cradled in her hands and her tea within reach.

The flames crackled merrily in the fireplace, and the chill was starting to come off the air. She had food, shelter, and warmth. Now all she had to do was wait and see if anyone showed up.

• • •

Tarrant sat back in his chair, sipped his coffee, and watched Valeriya eat soup from a plastic container. Some tendrils had escaped her ponytail and lay haphazardly around her neck and shoulders. Her skin seemed even paler than before. She looked tired.

She was curled up on the sofa, covered by a navy-blue sleeping bag that looked new. He was glad she had it, as there were no blankets on the bed. He found he didn't like the idea of her being cold.

She was proving to be more resourceful than he'd imagined. And that worried him. Was she truly what she seemed, or was she working with the Knights?

Either way, he'd watch her. As the old adage went, keep your friends close but your enemies closer. And he was much closer than she realized. His bunker was just below the cabin, only a short climb up the hidden staircase. Friend or enemy, it was certainly no hardship to watch her.

When she finished the soup, she finally removed her coat. He leaned forward. "Come on." He wanted to see what she looked like beneath that bulky garment. He groaned in frustration as she kept the sleeping bag around her. "Why couldn't she have come during the summer months?" He'd love to see her in a halter top and pair of shorts.

There was more than enough heat down in his lair, and Tarrant was starting to sweat. Imagining her in a tight pair of shorts raised his body temperature by a few degrees. It had also made his dick jump to life.

His phone rang, distracting him from his physical discomfort. He sighed and answered. "I told you I'd call if I learned anything." Honestly, Darius was worse than an old lady.

"Darius told me not to call, but I was worried."

A smile touched his lips, and Tarrant felt the warmth of her concern wrap around him. "Hey, Sarah." She really was a drakon whisperer. Even he hadn't been able to stay suspicious of her for long, and God knows, he was a mistrustful bastard. "How are things on the other coast?"

She laughed. "I'm loving Ezra's island. I mean, who owns an island?"

"We all do." He had several in various locations around the world.

"Get out. Darius didn't tell me that."

Knowing he was going to aggravate his brother, Tarrant gave Sarah more information. "Ask him about the one he has in the Caribbean."

Sarah gasped. "You mean we could be somewhere tropical and warm? Somewhere away from the Knights?"

Shit, he hadn't meant to stir up quite that much trouble. Before Tarrant could explain, Sarah was talking again.

"Of course, we couldn't leave the country. Not with you, Ezra, and Nic here and the Knights searching for a drakon."

His brother had found a one in a million, maybe even a one in a billion woman. Even Nic, who loved to gamble, would never have bet on any of them finding someone like Sarah.

"Now tell me about the woman who came to the cabin?"

Tarrant didn't want to talk to anyone about Valeriya. She was his. Possessiveness welled up inside him, and he had to force it back. "I'm keeping an eye on her."

"She came back?" She started to speak but then had to stop and placate Darius. "I told you I was calling him," she informed his brother in the background.

Tarrant couldn't help but grin. Darius had his hands full with Sarah. She was independent and strong. His glance went back to the computer screen. Valeriya was still curled up on the sofa. She was also proving to be independent and strong.

"I have you on speaker," Sarah told him. "Your brother is worried about you."

"Nothing to be concerned about. Valeriya came back. She seems to be alone, but I expect the Knights are out there somewhere."

"Be careful." Darius was a man of few words, and blunt to a fault, but Tarrant never doubted for one second that he would lay down his life for any of his brothers.

"That's my middle name," he quipped.

Darius snorted and Sarah shushed him. "Just don't take

any risks," Sarah told him. "The Knights don't know about you," she reminded him.

"I'll call you when and if I know more." He ended the call, tired of talking. He wanted to watch Valeriya.

Her eyelids slowly closed and she dozed off in front of the fire. He wanted to wrap his large body around hers and warm her, comfort her, protect her.

"Shit." He raked his fingers through his short hair and kept one eye on her as he went to work. His business empire didn't run itself. Thankfully, he needed little sleep and could skim documents in a fraction of the time it took most humans. He could read and process huge amounts of information very quickly. It was a talent, one that had allowed him to build the empire he had. He spent several hours taking care of the most pressing work and firing emails off to top staff.

In the meantime, he was also running in-depth searches on all the known Knights and their associates, compiling dossiers on them all. It was tedious work, but then again, he thrived on this kind of job. Information was his life's blood.

When an outer perimeter alarm dinged, he wasn't surprised. He'd been expecting company.

He brought up the cameras and nodded when he noted the men from yesterday moving silently through the woods. They were both wearing nondescript dark clothing and had their faces covered, but he could tell it was the same two by their builds and the way they moved.

From everything he'd observed, they weren't with Valeriya. Either that or they were pretending not to be. He turned on the audio and was surprised to hear them talking.

"This is such a shit assignment," the man in the lead complained.

"You don't know that," the other pointed out.

His partner stopped and faced him. "We're glorified babysitters."

Tarrant willed them to say more, but they went silent. They were heavily armed and dressed all in black. Camouflage would have been a better option for the woods, but they still blended well with the forest.

They crept up to the cabin. Tarrant grew more tense the closer they came. It wasn't himself he was worried about, but Valeriya. She was unarmed and vulnerable.

The leader of the two sidled up close to the cabin and peeked in the window. He moved away quickly and went back to his partner. "She's sleeping like a baby."

The other man snorted. "I wouldn't mind having her in my bed. She's got some serious curves."

"She's got good tits, but she's a little too heavy for my liking."

Tarrant's entire body shook. Scales began to form on his arms. "No." If he shifted down here, he risked destroying some, if not all, of his computers and other specialized equipment. There simply wasn't enough room for his dragon. The beast wasn't happy. It wanted to destroy both men, to stomp them into the ground and then set them on fire for talking about Valeriya like that.

"I'll protect her," Tarrant promised. His voice was low and guttural as he struggled with the other half of his nature. The dragon was more primal and wanted to protect what he considered his. And he'd decided that Valeriya belonged to him.

He glanced at the screen. "They're not going inside." If they did, he'd kill them. That helped his dragon settle back down.

Valeriya's eyes suddenly popped open and she sat upright. Her gaze went directly to the window that the Knight had peered through only seconds before. Just as she had the day before, she seemed to be aware that there was some threat nearby. It was the kind of instinct he usually associated with animals, not humans.

She shoved the sleeping bag off her legs and slowly moved toward the window. He noted that she stayed off to the side and cautiously peered out.

There was nothing to see. The men were too well hidden.

Valeriya rubbed her hands up and down her arms. If he didn't know better, he'd say she knew they were out there. Interesting, since the men didn't seem to think she was aware of them.

When she tugged the drapes shut, Tarrant got a sinking feeling in his gut. She did know they were out there. Was this a trap? Or was Valeriya playing some deeper game?

Was she hoping to find or capture his brother? If she wanted to advance in the ranks of the Knights, that was the sure way to do it. Maybe she thought the book Darius and Sarah had stolen was still around. Tarrant didn't think the Knights were aware it had been destroyed. They might suspect it, but they couldn't know for sure unless Father Simon had told them. And Tarrant knew that hadn't happened.

There was only one way to discover what Valeriya was really up to.

Tarrant settled down to watch, waiting as the minutes ticked away and night slowly arrived.

Chapter Five

To say she was feeling a little unsettled was an understatement. Valeriya knew there was someone outside in the woods. She could sense them watching her. But it was more than that. Something in the air had changed. The cabin, which had felt welcoming and warm, now seemed sinister and dangerous.

"It's just your imagination," she assured herself. "Just because it's dark outside." And it was pitch black. There were no streetlights, no ambient light from other houses or businesses. She was totally alone except for the men skulking in the woods. She hoped they were freezing their butts off out there.

At least they seemed content to simply keep an eye on her. Good thing, since there were no locks on the doors and she doubted pushing a chair in front of them would stop the men for long if they decided they wanted inside.

She added another log to the fire and went back to the sofa. She'd been working all afternoon, refining her ideas for her new book. They were flowing, as were the sketches. She probably had enough for several books. The real work would come when she started polishing both the story and the art. When you were dealing with children, both had to have an immediate impact or you'd lose the reader.

She tugged the sleeping bag over her legs and thought about making some supper but couldn't work up any enthusiasm. She munched on a cracker from a box she'd brought over earlier.

"I want a pizza. With gooey cheese and lots of roasted veggies." Her stomach growled in agreement. If she were home, she could nip around the corner to Gino's and get exactly what she wanted. There was no nipping around the corner to anything out here. Civilization was more than an hour away by car. And even that wasn't real civilization. More like an outpost.

What was she doing here? She'd put her life in danger on the slim chance she could help save a man from whatever fate the Knights and her sister had planned for him.

All her life, she'd felt helpless when it came to the Knights, but no longer. Now she was actively doing something. It might not be much, but it was all she could do.

Valeriya knew her sister wasn't going to allow her to stay on the sidelines much longer. She'd had sensed it the last time they were together. And she trusted her senses. They never led her astray.

And right now, they were screaming that she was in danger from some unseen foe. Was it the Knights or someone else? She wished her grandparents were still alive. They were the only people who'd ever truly loved and accepted her. Her grandmother had used her intuition to avoid getting tangled in the web of the Knights, and she'd taught Valeriya to do the same. It had worked for years, but it seemed as though her luck was about to run out. She was getting in deeper with each passing second.

She rubbed her fingers over her forehead. God, she

wasn't cut out for a life of danger. She was an ordinary woman who wanted an ordinary life. She had a job she loved, but her family history meant she'd never been able to make connections. The one thing she'd always wanted was a family of her own, and it was the one thing she'd never have.

"Stop with the pity party." She was disgusted with herself. She had no right to complain about her life. It had been one of comfort and privilege, bought with the blood of others.

If it came to it, better to be dead than to live a lie any longer. And if she could help one person, one drakon, along the way, she'd count her life well lived.

There was still a chance whoever was watching her would leave her alone. She'd stay a couple of days. If Darius Varkas didn't show up, she'd go home knowing she'd done all she could do. It had been a long shot to think she'd find him here. She had a life waiting for her back in New York. It might not be much by some people's standards, but it was hers, and she'd fight to hold on to it.

The evening had closed in early, and Valeriya decided to call it a day. She set her sketchbook on the coffee table, in case she got any more ideas later. She went to the bedroom long enough to collect her sleep pants and top and carry them to the bathroom. She took a quick shower, not sure how long the hot water would last, donned her night clothes, and added a pair of thick socks. In spite of the stove and the fireplace going all afternoon, there was still a chill in the cabin, especially in the bedroom.

She packed away her clothes and grabbed her hoodie. Layers were the way to go. She grabbed her hairbrush and took it to the living room. She was really starting to feel the chill.

The fire was crackling away in the grate, but it was a little low. She added another log. She should probably do the same with the stove, but it seemed wasteful since she wasn't planning on making tea until the morning. She had no idea how long the wood supply she had would last, and didn't want to waste any. Chopping trees wasn't really in her skill set.

She went to the window and peeked around the edge of the curtain she'd drawn earlier. All she could see was darkness, but she knew they were out there.

The windows groaned as a blast of wind struck them. She lowered the curtain, went back to the sofa, and curled up under her sleeping bag. She should probably crawl into it, but liked it better spread out as a blanket. The sofa was facing the fireplace so heat shouldn't be a problem during the night.

She picked up her brush and ran it through her damp hair. The repetitive action soothed her nerves, but she couldn't keep it up all night. She finally set the brush aside and braided her hair.

She shivered, and not because of the cold. Something was going to happen, and it wasn't going to be good. But there was nothing she could do about it. She could only deal with whatever occurred. She was on her own out here in the wilderness. There was no one to help her but herself.

Valeriya was lonely. In the city, it was easy to ignore the pangs of loneliness among so many people. Out here with just the wind and the unknown men waiting in the woods, she felt just how alone she truly was.

No one would know if she disappeared or was killed. Her agent and publisher would care, but that was mostly because of their business relationship, not because they were friends. She wasn't sure if Karina would be upset if something happened. How sad was that?

She sighed and pulled her covering tighter around her. She'd always dreamed of a hero coming to rescue her. As a child, it had been a dragon—a big, fierce creature who would protect her from her family. As an adult, she'd realized she had to save herself. So, she'd left home and struck out on her own. She'd built a life, and most days she didn't even think about her sister or the Knights.

But at moments like this, she felt more like a child than an independent woman. And while she no longer wanted or needed a man to save her, a friend wouldn't go amiss.

She closed her eyes and pulled up the image of her childhood imaginary friend. Not surprising, it had been a drakon—a child who could be both human and dragon. She'd always thought that was the coolest thing ever. Still did, which is why she wrote about it. But the dragon in her book was just that—a dragon. The world wasn't ready to know about drakons, even in children's fiction.

She hadn't thought about her imaginary friend in years. He'd have grown up like she had. He'd be a man now. The image of a tall, dark-haired man popped into her mind. Suddenly, she wasn't cold at all.

• • •

Tarrant watched the screen for hours, stopping only long enough to get something to eat. Even then, he'd taken his laptop with him so he could keep an eye on both Valeriya and the men watching her.

The men were currently camped just out of sight of the cabin. One of them was sleeping while the other kept watch. They had to be cold, but they hadn't built a fire.

Valeriya, on the other hand, had a small blaze going in the old stone fireplace. She was curled up on the sofa, looking both innocent and beautiful. She'd rooted around for a bit but had eventually settled. That had been hours ago. She'd been asleep for quite some time and her fire was getting lower as it devoured the wood. Dawn was close.

It was time to make his move.

He pushed away from his desk and went to the titanium

door that guarded his domain. He opened it, stepped inside the elevator, and the door silently slid shut behind him. "Up." The voice-activated elevator began to move upward.

Maybe what he was doing was stupid. No, scratch that. It was extremely stupid, but he was tired of waiting for the Knights to make a move. It was time for him to make one of his own.

Valeriya was a pawn in the game between the Knights and the drakons, whether she realized it or not. She either had information or value. Maybe both. She might be exactly what she seemed to be, or she might be working with the Knights. Either way, he'd find out.

He stepped out of the elevator and made sure his computer lab was secure. No way would he give her access to it. Even if she could get past all his safeguards, which she couldn't, he'd never trust a woman with his secrets. Not when his brothers' lives were at stake.

He stalked down the hallway and into the living area, stopping in front of the hidden staircase. His heart was racing, not with fear but with anticipation. He would soon have her locked away in his home with his other treasures.

"She's not a treasure," he reminded himself as he opened the door and started up the staircase. "She's a hostage. A pawn. A useful tool in the war." His beast wasn't happy with his assessment, but the fact Tarrant was going to collect her calmed the creature.

He paused outside the entrance to the cabin and listened. There was no sound. He pressed a hidden lever and the wall slid silently away. Tarrant stepped into the kitchen. As a safety precaution, he closed the door behind him. The kitchen cupboard slid back into place. No one looking at it would ever imagine it hid a staircase.

Tarrant walked lightly on the floor. He knew where every creaky board was. It took him only a few steps to reach her.

He stopped on the back side of the sofa and peered down at Valeriya. The image on the computer screens hadn't done her justice.

Her full lips were slightly parted as she breathed deeply. Her skin was pale and smooth. Her hair was black, but even with it braided he could see the sheen reflecting the firelight.

She had to be cold, because she had the covering tucked up to her chin. Even as he thought it, she shivered. He remained motionless. He was hoping she was a deep sleeper and wouldn't wake while he moved her. Otherwise, he'd be forced to subdue her.

If she called for help and the men from outside came to her defense, things could get ugly.

She rooted around some but settled back to sleep. Tarrant waited several minutes before moving around to the front of the sofa. He reached down and gathered her in his arms, sleeping bag and all. She was light, especially with his extraordinary strength, but he felt invisible fetters begin to wrap around him.

He almost put her back and left.

Then she sighed, her breath warm on his neck, and snuggled closer.

Tarrant was lost, and he knew it. He carried his precious cargo back to the kitchen and activated the switch to open the door. He had to go almost sideways down the stairs, but he soon had her in his home. He carried her down the hallway and paused outside his bedroom before silently swearing and taking her to the guest room.

The baseboard lights, activated by his presence, came on low. He set her in the center of the bed and reluctantly released her. She snuffled around and frowned as the cool bedcovers touched her skin. "Drakon," she whispered before settling down once again.

Tarrant froze, and the fine hair on his nape rose. Did she

know he was here? Did she know who and what he was? Was this nothing more than a setup?

But Valeriya was breathing deeply and her body was limp. Unless she was the best actress in the world, she was sleeping.

He forced himself to leave her. He still had work to do.

The door didn't have a lock, but she wasn't going anywhere. There was no way she could leave without getting by him, and that wasn't going to happen. He hurried back out to the living room and up the hidden staircase to the cabin. He didn't bother with the food in the cupboards. It was all canned and boxed and would be fine.

He went to the bedroom and gathered her clothing, tossing what was laying around into the case before closing it. Her knapsack was in the living room. He paused long enough to grab her laptop, tablet, and sketchbook.

The fire was low enough that it would burn itself out by morning, so he left it alone. In under two minutes, he was back in the secret staircase. He breathed a sigh of relief when the door to his home shut behind him. Only he and his brothers had access. Valeriya Azarov wasn't going anywhere.

Something inside him settled. He carried her suitcase down the hallway and set the bag in his room. He'd go through it later. He had to get rid of her computer first. He took her knapsack back to the kitchen and drew out her phone, computer, and tablet. He had no qualms about digging in her bag for what he wanted. Her privacy didn't matter. Only his safety and that of his brothers did.

He checked her phone to see if she'd been in contact with anyone before he removed the battery and SIM card. She hadn't sent or received any calls. That was unusual and slightly disturbing. Did she have no one in her life? Or was she just cautious? Regardless, there was no way for anyone to use her phone to pinpoint her location, or for her to use it to contact anyone.

Then he did the same with her computer and tablet, searching them before turning off the GPS and removing the batteries. He was tempted to simply destroy all the devices, but he didn't doubt all the story ideas, pictures, and drawings on them were important to her.

Why he cared wasn't a matter he was willing to delve into too deeply.

For all intents and purposes, Valeriya had dropped off the map. She and her belongings were gone. The car was still outside, but he'd left the key on the table just inside the door. If they checked on her at all, the men outside would believe she'd given them the slip.

Tarrant already knew what agency she'd used to rent the car. He called and arranged for them to pick it up, paying the owed fee with a prepaid credit card he'd set up in her name. He was nothing if not thorough. And he was king of the online world. This was child's play for him.

If the men still thought Valeriya was inside, they'd learn differently when the people from the car rental agency came to pick up the vehicle. Tarrant wondered what they'd do then. It would be interesting to watch. Would they leave or would they send more men into the woods searching for her?

Either way, he'd made his first move in this latest war the Knights had started when they'd come after his brother and killed his friend.

Satisfied with what he'd done, he tucked his phone away and picked up her knapsack. He paused when he caught sight of her sketchbook. She'd worked nonstop all afternoon, and he was curious. Somehow this seemed much more intimate than checking her phone and computer. But that didn't stop him from opening it.

The first few sketches were of trees, flowers, and several kinds of mushrooms. He recognized them as local, growing in the surrounding woods.

She had a delightful fairy creature seated cross-legged on a particularly large toadstool. The fairy was playing a harp, of all things. A reluctant smile tugged at his lips. Valeriya had the fairy in several other poses. In the margins, she had jotted what he realized were stories ideas and pieces of dialogue.

He flipped another page, and his heart almost stopped. Staring back at him was a large dragon. This was different from the one that starred in her children's series. That dragon was friendly and more childlike. This one was fierce and dangerous. Deadly. It was drawn in black and white, and it looked surprisingly like him.

He was halfway to the bedroom before he caught himself. He wanted to demand to know where she'd seen the creature. Since real dragons didn't exist, this had to be a drakon in his dragon form.

Had she seen one that the Knights had captured? Had she been a part of it?

His gut burned, and a fury like he'd never known welled up inside him. He began to shake. Inside him, his dragon roared—not in anger at Valeriya, but in anger at him for daring to think she could be a part of such an abomination.

The Knights were the true monsters, wrapped up in their self-righteous drivel about protecting mankind from evil. What they really wanted was drakon blood to prolong their pitiful lives and give them power.

Too many drakons had died. For too long, they'd stayed in the shadows, not engaging the humans. Always, they had been attacked. It was time to bring the war to the Knights.

And if Valeriya had had a part in any of their atrocities... He couldn't even finish his thought. The idea of hurting her burned like acid in his bloodstream. It was sobering to realize he couldn't hurt her no matter what she'd done.

He'd known she was dangerous to him, but until this moment, he'd truly had no idea just how much. He'd be better off killing her now, before he grew more attached to her, before his dragon demanded he keep her.

A whisper of sound alerted him to the fact he was no longer alone. He glanced down at her sketchbook, all but crushed in his hands, and then slowly looked up at Valeriya, who was standing at the entrance of the hallway.

Chapter Six

Valeriya had been scared many times in her life, but if she combined them all, they still fell short of what she was experiencing right now. The man watching her was gorgeous. He was huge, well over six and a half feet tall, for sure. He had short, jet-black hair, and his facial features were strong, all planes and angles. Her fingers itched to draw him. His eyes were glacial blue. An aura of danger seemed to permeate the air around him.

He was also furious.

It didn't take her intuition, her ability, to tell her that. All she had to do was look at him. She had no idea who he was or how she'd gotten here—wherever here was. Had he drugged her? She didn't feel groggy, but that didn't mean anything. She had no idea how much time had passed. It had to have been a substantial amount, since she was no longer in the cabin.

Waking in a strange room in a strange bed had scared the crap out of her. She had no idea where she was or what, if anything, had been done to her. The only thing that had allowed her to stay calm was the fact she was still fully dressed, with her sleeping bag covering her.

What she found even more frightening was the fact that her gift had failed her. Her intuition always alerted her to danger. Always. Her grandfather had always teased her and her grandmother that they were psychic. They'd both preferred to use the word gifted. It was weird enough to be able to do what she did without the label making her feel even more strange.

And she was procrastinating, thinking of something that really didn't matter because she didn't want to confront the reality facing her.

While she'd been sleeping, at her most vulnerable, someone had taken her.

How was that even possible? At the slightest threat, she should have woken.

Did that mean this man, whoever he was, wasn't a threat? Not likely. All she had to do was look at him to know he was dangerous.

The room where she'd woken up had been stark, but it was no prison cell. And the door hadn't been locked. Of course, now that she was facing the stranger who was her captor, it was no wonder. There was no way she was getting past him. There was a door on the far wall, but it was closed and there was a security panel beside it. No, she hadn't been placed in a cell, but that's what this entire place was—one large prison.

She almost wished she'd stayed in bed with the sleeping bag pulled over her head, rather than leaving the dubious safety of the bedroom to search for answers. But there was no going back now.

"Are you with the Knights?" Better to go on the offensive and act more confident than she actually felt. The fact he didn't blink meant he was aware of who and what the Knights were. Her hopes plummeted and her stomach knotted.

"Now that's an interesting question, isn't it?" His voice

was deep and sent a flash of heat rocketing through her.

She forced herself to look away from him and focused on her belongings strewn all over the large granite countertop. She didn't know who this man was, but his kitchen was like something out of a magazine, with white shaker-style cupboards, gleaming hardwood floors, and stainless steel appliances. Her artist's eye captured it all in a heartbeat.

Then she noticed her phone and computer sitting on the large kitchen island. "You went through my things?" she accused.

He crossed his arms over his massive chest. It was difficult not to notice the way his biceps bulged and the fabric of his T-shirt tightened. "Of course I did."

"Of course you did." Valeriya felt like she'd fallen down a rabbit hole, but this wasn't Wonderland. "And why was that?"

One corner of his mouth turned upward. It wasn't a smile—more of a smirk. "You can't be that stupid."

She bristled at the implication. "If you didn't want me contacting anyone, why didn't you just leave my phone and laptop behind when you took me?" She knew her calm demeanor was a false one and that she was in shock. Good thing. She didn't think he'd appreciate her screaming and throwing things.

She curled her fingers toward her palms.

He stirred and unfolded his arms. He didn't move toward her exactly, but that didn't stop her from feeling threatened. Her legs trembled, but she held her ground.

"I didn't want to leave a trace of you behind. It was better to take everything, disable the GPS, and remove the batteries."

Valeriya had trouble swallowing past the huge lump in her throat. That wasn't good. If he didn't want to leave any trace of her behind, that meant one of her sister's enemies had found her. Karina would have had her taken home. Wouldn't she? Valeriya was no longer sure about anything. But she was under no illusions about the Knights of the Dragon. They were all power hungry and ruthless. Whoever sent him, it could only mean one thing. "You're going to kill me."

His gaze narrowed and he took a step toward her. "And why would you think that?"

She laughed, and there was a slight hysterical tinge to it. Her entire body was numb. She knew her fingernails were digging into her palms, but she couldn't feel any pain. She'd always known she wouldn't have a long life, but until this moment, she'd always had hope.

"You kidnapped me and made sure there was no trace of me left behind. What else could it mean? Tell me this first—did my sister send you, or do you work for another member of the Knights?"

• • •

Tarrant was confused. Not a state of mind he was used to dealing with. His body reacted to Valeriya's closeness. Every muscle was taut, and there was no disguising his arousal. Thankfully, the kitchen island was hiding that rather large fact from his guest. Otherwise, she might have run screaming.

As it was, she was terrified. He could smell her fear and see the fast fluttering of the pulse in her neck. In spite of that, she faced him. She was braver than most men, given the situation.

Maybe she thought she could talk her way out of here if her sister had sent him? Or maybe not, given the fact she thought he was going to kill her. Why would she think her sister would send someone to kill her?

He couldn't stop looking at her. She was no longer wearing a coat or wrapped in a sleeping bag. For the first time, he could get a better idea of what she looked like. His assessment of her had been correct. Valeriya was a curvy woman with ample breasts and hips.

His cock punched against the front of his jeans. He ignored the unruly appendage and continued to study her. Her skin was like porcelain, her lips full and rosy. The color of her eyes seemed richer, deeper than it had through the lens of the security cameras.

"Well?" she demanded.

Tarrant shrugged. "I have no plans to kill you." When she visibly relaxed, he added, "Yet."

His dragon wasn't happy with him, but he wasn't about to take anything at face value. "You hungry?"

Valeriya looked at him like he was out of his mind. And he very well might be. Taking her had been a huge risk, but one he couldn't regret.

"You tell me you have no plans to kill me. At least not yet. And then you want to know if I'm hungry?"

He nodded.

She rubbed her hands over her face. "You're either the most cold-blooded man I've ever met, or you're crazy. Either way, I'm screwed."

"Why are you here?" he demanded, trying to catch her off guard.

"Since I don't know where here is, I can't tell you. You tell me. You're the one who brought me here."

Tarrant felt like kicking himself for his slip. "I meant, why were you at the cabin? It's in the middle of nowhere and not easy to find unless you know where to look."

She tucked her hands into the pockets of the hoodie she was wearing and shrugged. "I was doing research for my book. I'm a children's author." She removed one hand from her pocket and motioned to the sketchbook on the counter. "You've already seen my drawings."

That was the truth as far as it went, but not the whole truth. "How did you find the cabin?" Tarrant started to walk toward her. When he rounded the island, her eyes widened. She took several steps back until she hit the wall behind her.

Valeriya shook her head. "I won't tell you. I won't tell you anything. I won't be party to hurting an innocent person."

He stopped in front of her and looked down into her frightened but defiant green eyes. "No one is innocent." That was a lesson he'd learned a long time ago.

"You can't believe that." She seemed shocked, which ironically made her seem more innocent in his eyes.

"And you can't be that naive." He was angry at the Knights for what they'd done. And he was angry because Valeriya was starting to seem as though she was exactly what she presented herself to be—a children's writer who had the misfortune of being born into a family that was a part of the Knights of the Dragon.

"I'm not naive. I just know not everyone is driven by the desire for power and money."

Tarrant caught her chin between his thumb and forefinger. She didn't try to pull away, realizing it was futile. No, instead she tilted her chin higher and glared at him.

Damned if he didn't like her. He didn't trust her, but he did admire her courage. "You've lived a charmed life if you believe that."

Her entire demeanor changed and became tinged with sadness. "No. It's because I *haven't* lived a charmed life that I believe it."

Taken aback, Tarrant softened his grip and lightly ran the back of his knuckles over her cheek. Her skin was soft, and he caught the slightest hint of lavender, either her soap or lotion.

"What am I going to do with you?" He hadn't meant to ask the question out loud. It was rhetorical anyway. He knew he was going to keep her. He couldn't release her now, even if he wanted to. Which he didn't.

"You can let me go. I won't tell anyone," she promised.

Tarrant almost believed her, but it was too late—for both of them.

He sighed and stepped away before he did something really stupid, like kiss her. His dragon roared to life inside him, liking that idea immensely. Shit, he was going to be stupid.

Before he could gain a foothold of sanity and stop himself, he leaned down and grazed his lips over hers. She sucked in a deep breath and held herself perfectly still. She tasted sweet with a hint of mint. He dragged his tongue over her bottom lip, and she sucked in a breath.

He slipped his tongue inside and groaned as he sank into her heat. He'd kissed hundreds of women over the course of his lifetime, but never had one affected him this deeply.

It took him a second to realize she had her hands on his chest and was pushing him away, or at least trying to. His blood ran cold, and he pulled back. Never had he kissed an unwilling woman.

Her lips were moist, her cheeks flushed. And her pupils were dilated. She might deny it, but she wasn't totally unwilling.

"What are you doing?" she demanded.

"Damned if I know," he answered honestly. He abruptly turned and stalked back over to the counter. He needed something to do so he'd feed her. Maybe some food would help loosen her tongue.

• • •

Valeriya brought her fingers to her lips and touched them. Just as quickly, she pulled her hand away. Thankfully, her captor hadn't noticed. He was busy pulling pans out of the cupboard. Her lips still tingled and her entire body was suffused with heat.

She still couldn't believe he'd kissed her. Was it a tactic

to get her to talk? That dispersed most of the heat in a hurry. Did he think her so lonely, so needy that a kiss or two would make her spill her secrets? Not that she really had many, but he didn't know that.

She could still feel the pressure of his lips against hers, the gentle slide of his tongue into her mouth. It was the best kiss she'd ever experienced. She wasn't sure what that said about her and her choice of men in the past.

"What's your name?" she suddenly demanded. She'd kissed him and didn't even know his name.

He opened the refrigerator door and pulled out several packages.

"Hey." She knew it was crazy to demand anything from this man, but she was past all caution. "I asked you a question."

"And if I answer it, you'll never be able to leave here." The way he said it, with little inflection, stopped her in her tracks.

It was a variation of "If I tell you, I'll have to kill you." It was used in the movies all the time, but Valeriya didn't think this man was joking. "We both know I'm never getting out of here anyway, so why don't you tell me who you are?" Maybe if she befriended him, she could get him to release her.

And then where would she go? The Knights were everywhere.

She swayed as her knees went weak. All she'd wanted to do was warn Darius Varkas about the Knights and go back home to her life. Now she feared she was truly going to die.

"What the hell?" Her captor was around the counter and caught her before she hit the floor. He scooped her up as though she weighed nothing and set her on one of the stools on the far side of the island. "Are you all right?" He hovered beside her but was no longer touching her.

It was as though he was afraid to touch her. She wasn't sure if that was for her benefit or for his. She should be trying to figure out a way to escape, fighting the growing attraction she had for her captor. She wasn't a guest here, but an unwilling visitor.

Unfortunately, it didn't quite feel that way. It suddenly occurred to her that her intuition was silent. Yes, he was a very dangerous man, no doubt about it, but she didn't feel as though he was a danger to her.

Her gift had chosen a really bad time to go haywire.

"What does it matter, if you're going to kill me?" She'd rather get it over with than to drag it out indefinitely. And she really didn't want to be tortured.

He swore, long and fluently, and in a language she didn't understand. Did that mean he wasn't American, or did he simply know other languages?

"Tarrant. My name is Tarrant. And I told you I wasn't going to kill you."

She rested her elbows on the counter to steady herself. "For now. You said you weren't going to kill me right now."

He swore again. "No one is killing anyone. I'm going to make you something to eat. You didn't eat much yesterday."

"You were watching me." She wasn't overly surprised, but it was still a shock. "Are you working with the men who were outside the cabin?" She narrowed her gaze and studied him.

"Hell no." Tarrant seemed insulted by her question.

She shrugged. "What else am I supposed to think?" Then another thought occurred to her. "You're not really Darius Varkas, are you?" She'd never been able to find an actual picture of him, other than a very grainy black and white one that was taken at a distance. But he was a big man, like Tarrant.

He grabbed her upper arms and dragged her right off the seat until her toes were dangling in midair. His strength was astounding. "What do you know about Darius Varkas?"

Valeriya was too scared to speak. She'd known her captor was tough, that he was strong, but this was the first time she truly believed he was a killer. It was in his eyes. He'd swat her like a bug if he had to and have no regrets.

"Well?" He shook her again.

She opened her mouth and tried to talk. Instead, she did something she truly detested. She burst into tears. The fright of the moment was too much. She'd always been a sensitive soul, and this entire situation was really too much.

"Fuck." Tarrant swore. Next thing she knew, she was back in his arms and he was carrying her over to one of the large sofas. He sat and patted her awkwardly on the back. "Stop crying. I told you I wasn't going to kill you."

Valeriya was still crying even as she laughed at his disgruntled expression.

He sighed and shoved her head against his shoulder. He was trying to comfort her in his own clumsy fashion. She found it endearing in a weird way. For all his threats, he was being very kind to her.

"I knew you were going to be trouble the first time I laid eyes on you."

She sensed he was talking more to himself than to her. She got control of her wayward emotions and sniffed back her tears. She also fought the urge to apologize for crying all over him. He'd kidnapped her and might still kill her. He didn't deserve an apology.

"Feeling better?"

"No," she answered honestly. She didn't think she'd ever feel better again. Although, being held in his strong arms felt good, which couldn't be healthy, given the situation. She truly was a mess.

He pushed back a strand of her hair that had escaped her braid. "Please tell me what you know about Darius Varkas?"

Valeriya sighed. What did it truly matter if she told him or not? If he was with the Knights, he likely already knew about the man.

"All I know is my sister is looking for him. I think he's been at the cabin where I was staying."

Tarrant frowned. "That's why you went there?"

She nodded. "I wanted to know why this cabin was so important." She paused and plunged onward, even knowing he'd think her hopelessly naive or stupid. Not that he might not already have that opinion, but she didn't want to reinforce it. "Plus, if Mr. Varkas came back, I wanted to warn him he's a person of interest with the Knights."

"A person of interest," he repeated. "That's one way of looking at it."

It occurred to her that she was still sitting on Tarrant's lap, and he wasn't unaffected by her proximity. She shot off his lap and glared at him. "You're…" She broke off, not quite knowing how to point out his rather obvious erection.

"I'm aroused," he stated. "But nothing will happen that you don't want to."

That wasn't exactly reassuring, since she was proving to have little control and common sense around this man. She'd already let him kiss her. And she'd enjoyed it way too much.

"So you know the Knights are after Darius Varkas?" He seemed more menacing now that she wasn't sitting on his lap.

Since he'd decided to ignore his arousal, she would, too. "I only heard part of a phone conversation, but, yes, that's was my deduction."

"But that doesn't explain the cabin."

Valeriya looked around the large room. Anywhere but at the large man beside her. "There are no windows," she blurted. It was obviously a living room, but there was no natural source of light. Must be a basement of some sort.

"No, there aren't any windows. The cabin?" he prompted.

Valeriya sighed. "I found the coordinates on a pad of paper on my sister's desk."

"You can't expect me to believe she was that careless."

whenever she was near.

When she paced by him again, he wrapped his arm around her and stopped her in her tracks. She stared up at him. He could see the low, simmering fear in her eyes, but she met his gaze steadily.

He sighed and used the pad of his thumb to wipe the remains of her tears from her cheek. "You can tell me more while I cook us something to eat." He didn't say it was breakfast, because he didn't want her to know what time of day it was or how much time had passed since he'd taken her. She wasn't wearing a watch, and with her electronic equipment gone, there was no way for her to check.

She hesitated but then blinked several times and nodded. "Okay."

"Okay?" He wasn't sure he'd heard her correctly.

She nodded again, this time more definitively. "Yes. I don't know who you are, beyond your first name, but from your reaction, I don't think you're with the Knights."

Tarrant snorted and guided her back to the stool she'd been sitting on. "You got that right."

She settled on the stool, rested her elbows on the counter, and propped her chin on her hands. Her eyes were red, her cheeks were still pale, and several strands of hair fell around her face, but she looked adorable sitting there in her hoodie, a pair of green flannel pants, and socks.

Tarrant went around to the other side of the counter before he scooped her up and took her to bed—his bed.

"So your sister is a member of the Knights of the Dragon?" If she was in an agreeable mood, it was best to get her talking. He needed to know whatever she did.

Valeriya nodded. "Yeah, you could say that. Do you have any water? I'm parched."

Impatience ate at him, but he held his peace. He got a bottle of water from the refrigerator and placed it in front of her. She unscrewed the cap and took a long swallow.

He turned back to the fridge and pulled out eggs and bacon. They were quick and easy. He grabbed a couple of steaks, too. He was ravenous again.

Thankfully, he'd just resupplied. He usually shopped in bulk and had freezers filled with meat in a utility room, as well as shelves of canned goods. Sometimes he had groceries delivered to the cabin. He always left the money on the front step and waited until the delivery van was gone before he collected his food. He wouldn't be able to rely on that method for the foreseeable future. Not until this situation resolved itself. But they wouldn't starve.

"Your sister," he reminded her when she set the bottle down in front of her.

She rolled the plastic bottle between her hands. "Our parents groomed Karina from the time she was born to be a member of the Knights."

"But not you?" Tarrant found that hard to believe. He kept his doubts to himself and began cracking eggs into a bowl. There were eight left in the carton, so he did them all.

Valeriya shook her head and hooked a stray lock of hair behind her ear. "No. I was quiet, more sensitive. I know I was a disappointment to them. I spent a lot of time with my grandparents."

He'd already known that from his research. He kept his silence and began frying bacon.

"I liked to draw and paint. Karina learned hand-to-hand combat and how to handle guns." Valeriya shivered. "My parents insisted on some of the same training for me until they discovered I wasn't very good at it." Her smile was sad, and he had to fight the urge to comfort her. "Karina took martial arts, and I was in dance class."

She took another swig of water. "We were as different as night and day. People would come to our home to speak with our father and mother. I was quiet and sometimes people would forget I was in the room."

He couldn't imagine anyone forgetting about Valeriya, but he believed her. He could picture a small, dark-haired girl curled up behind a chair listening to the adults. "And what did they talk about?"

"Dragons." She shivered and wrapped her arms around herself. "I thought it was all a fairytale, a make-believe story. Then I heard them talk about capturing one." She met his gaze. "I didn't think it was real."

He nodded, sensing she needed his agreement. He removed the fried bacon and placed more uncooked strips in the pan. "You were just a child."

"Yes." She gazed into the distance as though seeing a memory. "Just a child." She looked back at him. "But my parents and the others weren't. They knew better, but they didn't care."

"What did they do?" Tarrant knew, but he wanted to hear her story.

"They imprisoned the dragon, and one man spoke of drinking his blood."

"What man?" Tarrant needed all the names he could get.

Valeriya's face scrunched as she thought hard. "Temple. I think his name was Temple."

"Herman Temple?"

She shook her head. "Maybe. I don't know. That's all I can remember. There was a man named Dent and a woman with the last name Picton. They're the only names I can recall."

"What happened then?" Tarrant finished with the bacon and started on the steaks. The meat sizzled when it hit the hot grill pan.

"After the people left, I went to my father and asked him about the dragon." She shuddered. "He was furious at me for listening. He told me that dragons were treacherous creatures that needed to be controlled." Her hand went to her cheek.

Something dangerous welled up inside Tarrant. He knew what her answer would be before he voiced the question, but still he asked. "He hit you, didn't he?"

Valeriya nodded, her gaze on the counter and not on him. "He was very angry. I never asked him about it again, but I asked my grandparents, my father's parents. They told me everything they knew about the Knights, which wasn't a lot. They wanted no part of them, either. My mother was the one who brought my father into the Knights. Her side of the family had been a part of the group since its inception."

Tarrant didn't push her any further. She seemed exhausted. Since the steaks were almost done, he threw the eggs into a large skillet. When they were scrambled, he dumped all the food onto a couple of large platters and set both of them on the island in front of her. "Eat something."

He set out some plates and then made a pot of coffee. When he glanced at her, she was staring at the mounds of food he'd made. He grinned at her shocked expression.

"Is all this for us?"

"I have a big appetite." He couldn't quite keep the heat from his voice. Her cheeks flushed, but Valeriya didn't comment. "Coffee?" he asked.

She shook her head. "Do you have any tea?"

He dug through the cabinet until he found a small unopened box of tea. It was plain, old-fashioned tea. Nothing special. "This okay?"

She nodded as she scooped some eggs onto her plate. "Perfect."

Tarrant filled the kettle and set it to boil. He opened the box and shoved one of the teabags into a mug. He should have known she'd want tea. That's what she'd been drinking most of the day. "Don't you like coffee?"

"It's okay." She picked up a piece of bacon in her fingers

and took a bite. "I prefer tea."

Tarrant was momentarily taken aback. In times past, most people preferred tea, but the modern era was fueled by coffee.

Valeriya grinned, and heat exploded inside him. "Most people find me odd."

He chuckled. "Means there's more coffee for me." When the kettle boiled, he filled the mug with hot water and set it in front of her. Then he piled a thick steak, a dozen pieces of bacon and a mound of eggs onto his plate.

Valeriya was staring at him. "What?" he asked.

"Aren't you worried about your cholesterol?"

It took everything in him not to laugh, but he couldn't stop himself from smiling. "Not particularly."

"It's your body." She managed to eat about one egg and a couple of pieces of bacon, but she didn't touch the steak.

"You not hungry?" He didn't like the idea of her not eating.

"Not really." She sighed and sipped her tea. "Being kidnapped puts a damper on the appetite."

Tarrant ignored her comment. "Tell me about your grandparents."

Her smile was soft and warm. "They were the best. I don't think I'd have made it if it weren't for them. Especially after Mom and Dad were killed and Karina became my guardian. She changed then. Got harder. More focused."

"She's a high-ranking member of the Knights?"

Valeriya's expression grew bleak. "You could say that. Karina Azarov is the head of the Knights of the Dragon."

• • •

He'd kill her now for sure. Valeriya didn't know why she hadn't kept her mouth shut, except that she was tired of all the secrets. If Tarrant was opposing the Knights, he needed all the information and help she could give him. If he wasn't what he seemed and was *with* the Knights, then he already knew about her sister.

Her dreams of going home, of being able to put this all behind her were gone. By taking her, Tarrant had put her squarely in the game with the Knights. It didn't matter who was behind his actions or what was motivating him.

He slowly put down his fork and stared at her. "She's what?"

The little food she'd eaten sat like a lump in the pit of her stomach. "She's the head of the Knights. Just like my mother was before her."

"Your mother?"

She saw the confusion on his face and clarified. "The leader of the Knights is always a woman from my family line."

"Why?"

She shrugged. "That, I don't know. Only Karina knows that." When he looked skeptical, she tried to explain. "Because I didn't take an active role in the Knights, I've always been kept in the dark about most of what goes on. I made no secret of the fact I wanted nothing to do with hurting people."

When Tarrant only raised a questioning eyebrow, she continued. She had to look away from the intensity of his gaze. "My grandparents told me what the Knights do. They also told me how powerful the group is. So, I did what they'd told me to do, and I focused on building my own life. And when my grandparents left me their apartment, I had a home of my own."

That was the short, sad story of her life.

"Yet you write about dragons." Tarrant was on the opposite side of the counter, but he loomed large and fierce. Much like a dragon. She didn't think he'd appreciate the comparison. "Why is that?"

"I know the difference between a dragon and a drakon.

A dragon's base form is the animal, yet it can shift into human form for a short time. It's cold and calculating. A drakon is half human and half dragon. Its base form is that of a human, but it can shift into a dragon for as long as it wishes. It has a human heart."

She sensed his impatience and hurried on with her story. "I couldn't exactly write about drakons, so I wrote about a sad little dragon named Damian." She lifted her tea and took a sip.

"I've read your books."

Valeriya was startled and almost dropped the mug. That was the last thing she'd expected him to say. "You have?" She set the mug carefully down on the stone countertop. "Why?"

"I wanted to know more about you." He brushed it off as though it didn't matter.

"My sister has never read them," she blurted.

"No?"

"She thinks they're stupid and childish." And that had always hurt. As much as she and her sister didn't get along, Karina was the only family she had left in the world.

"They're meant for children, but the themes are universal—acceptance, friendship, honesty," Tarrant pointed out.

Tears pricked her eyes and she blinked them back. "Yes. That's exactly right." This big, powerful man had read her stories about a lost little dragon. On one hand, she was touched he'd read them. On the other, it meant he'd really researched her life. That was scary.

"What's going to happen to me?" She had to know.

Tarrant sighed and walked around the counter until he was standing beside her. He cupped her face in his hands. "I honestly don't know." Then he kissed her.

Unlike the last time, she was ready for him. But the heat and power of the caress still took her off guard. If she'd been standing, her knees would have buckled. The warmth of his hands soaked into her skin. His lips were firm, yet supple.

"Tarrant." She whispered his name this time. Last time, she hadn't even known it. She still didn't know his last name. Not that it truly mattered.

His tongue touched hers, and she leaned inward, wanting more. It was crazy to be drawn to her captor. He might have been kind and held her while she'd cried. He might have cooked her food and made her tea. But she could never forget he'd taken her for reasons of his own. And she had no idea what those reasons were.

She tried to focus on her gift, but it wasn't easy. Not when he was kissing her. There was no sense of danger, only a knowing that she was where she was supposed to be. It didn't make any sense. None of this situation did. Maybe her intuition was faulty, but she honestly didn't think so. It had served her well her entire life.

So maybe, just maybe, it was telling her the truth. Tarrant wasn't a threat to her. Yes, he was big and dangerous and obviously skilled, since he'd managed to take her without her knowing. She should be terrified of him. But she wasn't. If anything, she yearned to get closer to him.

Maybe she was the one who was crazy.

They had to stop. She didn't want to, but she had to. Everything was happening so fast. She needed time to think.

"Tarrant." She pulled away and sucked in a deep breath. This was wrong. It had to be. No matter how right it felt.

Desperation filled her, and she spun away and ran for the only door in the room. She grabbed the handle and pulled. It wouldn't open. She suddenly felt as though the walls were closing in around her. "Let me out." She banged her fists against the door, ignoring the pain that shot up her arms.

Valeriya sensed Tarrant behind her. She whirled around and confronted him. "Open the door," she demanded.

He slowly shook his head. "No."

All her anger coalesced at once. She was angry at the Knights for simply existing, at her sister for choosing them over her, at circumstance for forcing her to take a side in the war between the drakons and the Knights. All she'd wanted was to have her career and a family. Now it appeared as if she would never get to return to her life. And that hadn't been her plan when she'd left.

If she didn't have her books and her apartment, she had nothing.

Then there was Tarrant. He'd taken her from the cabin without her even knowing. She had no idea what his motivation was or what he planned to do with her. The only thing she knew for sure was that he wanted her.

And damn her, but she wanted him, too.

It wasn't fair. But then no one ever said life would be.

She flew at him, beating her fists against his chest, needing to vent her fury. The shock that had kept her calm burned away under the flames of her anger. "I want to go home."

He let her hit him over and over. He didn't flinch, didn't seem to even notice when her fists made contact.

Tears leaked from the corners of her eyes. "I don't want to be a part of this." She'd never asked to be a part of this world, of this war.

"I know." His easy agreement simply angered her even more.

She screamed and tried to turn back to the door, but he simply pulled her into is arms. She didn't want to be comforted by him, didn't want to nestle against the heat of his strong chest. She fought him, but he continued to hug her, to offer silent comfort.

"I want to go home." She sounded pitiful, like a child who was lost. She honestly had no idea where she would even go if she left here. Her grandparents' apartment, which was now her home, was no longer safe, no longer the haven it had been her entire life.

Tarrant scooped her into his arms and carried her down the hall. She had no idea where he was taking her and didn't care. Valeriya felt empty inside. There was no way she could escape this place, no way to escape Tarrant. If he didn't let her go, she'd probably die here.

And if he did let her go, she was probably dead, too. Those men knew she'd been at the cabin, and they'd tell whoever they were working for that she'd disappeared. If they worked for her sister, Karina would not be pleased. At this point, she no longer knew her sister, had no idea what she would do.

Valeriya had held on to a childish hope that Karina would change. That there was enough goodness inside her that she would walk away from the Knights. It had been a fool's dream. She realized that now. Karina could have walked away when she'd taken over the running of their parents' estate. Instead, she'd fought to keep the leadership of the Knights of the Dragon. Valeriya had often wondered what she'd had to do to retain the title when there'd been a small group of men and women who coveted the position.

And if another member of the Knights found her, they'd most likely use their knowledge of what she'd done to hurt her sister before they killed her.

Tarrant carried her into the bedroom where she'd awoken, and laid her on the bed. "Rest. You're safe."

There was no such thing as safety, only the illusion. She rolled over and gave him her back.

Her sleeping bag settled over her. She refused to thank him. She felt him hovering behind her for several seconds before he turned and left. He closed the door behind him, leaving her in darkness but for the baseboard lights.

Peering into the dark, she ignored the tears trickling down her cheek. She was mentally, emotionally, and physically spent. She'd rest. Surely things would look better when she woke.

She laughed, but the sound was anything but pleasant. Her life was a mess and she didn't think there was any way to make it better again.

• • •

Tarrant was not happy. Neither was his dragon half. His arousal had died as soon as he'd seen the panic on Valeriya's face, felt her desperation.

It almost made him wish he could go back in time and leave her in the cabin. But he knew he wouldn't change what he'd done. That would have left her vulnerable. She might not realize it yet, but he'd done her a favour.

He snorted. "Yeah, best to keep that to yourself." He didn't think she'd appreciate his logic.

And speaking of logic, he hadn't checked her luggage yet. Best to do it now while she was resting. He went to his room and lifted the bag onto the bed. As soon as he unzipped it, he caught a hint of her scent. He inhaled deeply, unable to stop himself. His body reacted immediately, every muscle hardening, his cock throbbing.

Swearing, he forced himself to search through her things, checking the bag for any kind of tracking device. There was nothing suspicious, nothing that would tie her to the Knights.

He touched the band of a pair of her underwear before stuffing everything back into the case and zipping it back up. It was bad enough he was invading her privacy. He wouldn't apologize for that. It was necessary. But fondling her underwear was over the line. He dragged his fingers through his hair and huffed out a deep breath.

Not knowing what else to do, he decided to fall back on what he always did in times of stress. He'd work.

He left his bedroom and glanced at the closed door to Valeriya's room. He forced himself to walk to the end of the hall and go through the security protocols to open the door to the elevator. Once he was in his computer lab, he brought up the camera in her room. She was huddled on the bed, her eyes closed.

The urge to go to her, not to make love, but to simply hold her in his arms, was almost overwhelming. He *needed* to care for her. He was in deep trouble. He was acting around Valeriya the same way his brother had around Sarah.

It was as though a part of him yearned for her, knew she was what had been missing in his life. And she wouldn't believe him if he told her.

He turned away from the camera screen and pulled up the news on another. He had research to do and business to attend to.

Chapter Eight

Her head hurt and her eyes were gritty. That's what she got for crying herself to sleep. She was also surprisingly calm, her anger spent.

She had no idea how long she'd slept, but she didn't think it had been too long. It was hard to tell because there were no windows to tell her if it was day or night.

She reached out and turned on the bedside lamp. It gave a soft glow to the room. She rubbed her hands over her face. God, she was a wreck. Her hair was coming down from her braid and she really needed to use the bathroom.

Valeriya stood and padded across the room. She opened the first door. The baseboard lights came on low—it seemed to be a feature of the room—allowing her to tell she'd found the bathroom. She felt around for the light switch. It was easy enough to find and she flicked it on.

The bathroom was gorgeous. There was a full tub and a separate shower. The tiles were earth toned, and big, white fluffy towels sat on a nearby shelf. Unfortunately, she didn't have a change of clothes, and so she settled for splashing water on her face. She dug around the vanity drawers and found a comb and a toothbrush still in its package. She put both to use. When she was done, she felt fresher and her hair had been tamed.

She stared at her reflection in the mirror, barely recognizing the woman staring back at her. There were shadows under her eyes, and she was pale. Not surprising considering everything.

She gripped the edge of the vanity and took a deep breath. Okay, time to review the facts. She'd tried to escape, and she'd attacked Tarrant. And what had he done? He'd hugged her and carried her to bed.

"Don't make him seem better than he is." He'd taken her from the cabin. And other than his name, she really didn't know anything about him or who he was working for.

She left the room, turning out the light behind her. Not knowing where to go, she sat on the side of the bed and rubbed her palms up and down her legs. What could she do? What should she do?

Not much time had passed when there was a light knock on her door. That surprised her. She'd expected him to barge right in.

Tarrant stood in the doorway, blocking out all the light from the hall. "How are you feeling?"

She ignored the shivery sensation that radiated outward from her core to the tips of her fingers and toes. His mere presence was enough to stir her up. "I'm not sure how I should feel." It was best to be totally honest. "I'm being held captive by a virtual stranger."

He made a sound of impatience. "I told you I'm not going to hurt you."

"No," she corrected. "You told me you weren't going to kill me. Yet," she added.

Tarrant stalked across the room and stood in front of her

with his hands on his hips. Seated on the side of the bed, she had a perfect view of his arousal. And considering she was sitting on a bed, that probably wasn't the wisest thing for her to be noticing.

She jumped to her feet.

"I'm not going to kill you. Not now. Not ever."

She felt the truth of his words, but that didn't change everything. "I'm still a prisoner."

The sound that came out of his throat was almost a growl. "You're not a prisoner."

"Then I'm free to go?" She doubted he'd just open the door and allow her to walk away. And honestly, she wasn't truly sure she wanted to leave.

He raked his fingers through his hair. "I can't do that. It's not safe for you out there."

"And you know this how?"

Tarrant began to pace then suddenly stopped. "I need coffee if we're going to talk." He strode from the room and she followed him, curious to hear what he had to say.

She sat on one of the kitchen stools and watched as he filled the coffeepot and set the kettle boiling without her having to ask.

He kept his back turned to her and rested his palms on the countertop. Neither of them spoke until he'd poured himself a cup of coffee and prepared her a cup of tea. He placed the mug in front of her.

"You had men watching you."

Of course, he'd known. She hadn't been acquainted with him long, but Tarrant seemed to be the kind of man who was thorough when it came to such things. He appeared both competent and confident.

"I did." No point in denying it.

He canted his head to one side. "Just how did you know? Because I was watching both you and them, and you knew they were there before you saw them."

Crap, what did she do now?

He reached across the counter and cupped her face in his hands. "Tell me the truth."

"Why? You haven't told me the truth about why you took me." It was stupid to bargain, but she didn't care. She needed some answers.

"I know those men were sent by someone in the Knights of the Dragon. If you're not with them, as you've claimed you're not, then you were in danger."

"But you didn't know I wasn't with them," she countered.

"Not then." Tarrant released her and took a sip of coffee. She missed his touch.

"You hid from them. That was a good indication."

"You really were watching me all along." It gave her the shivers. It was so easy for someone with skills to spy on someone else. She wondered if her sister had been doing the same thing for years without her knowledge.

"Yes." He set his mug down and came around the counter to stand beside her. "How did you know they were there?"

She opened her mouth to lie but found she couldn't do it. "You won't believe me," she said instead.

"Try me."

He was standing too close. She could feel the heat from his body, smell his masculine scent. She fortified herself with a mouthful of tea.

"I have a gift."

"A gift." His tone was neutral, with no way for her to gauge what he was feeling.

"Yes, a gift. My grandmother had it, too. I can sense danger." Best to keep the explanation simple. "It's instinct."

He turned her stool until she was facing him. "It's more than instinct. You knew those men were outside the cabin."

She shrugged, unwilling to elaborate further. "All I know

is that I can tell when someone means to harm me. I always know when there is danger around." She braced for his questions about her talent, not quite sure how she'd respond. She'd already told him more than she'd ever shared with anyone outside of her grandparents.

"And what do your instincts say about me?"

Not what she'd been expecting him to ask. "Umm, I'm not sure what you mean." She didn't want to talk about her feelings for him.

"Yes, you do." He sat on the stool next to hers and cupped her chin in his hand. "Tell me."

She licked her lips and swallowed. This wasn't smart, but she was no longer sure she had any other choice. "You're a dangerous man," she began.

He nodded. "I am."

There was no point in denying what they both knew was true. She was about to push her luck. It was time to find out exactly where she stood with him. "You're no stranger to violence."

He tightened his hand fractionally before relaxing it. "I'm not," he agreed.

This was it. "But for some reason, I don't think you'll hurt me. I shouldn't believe it, since you kidnapped me."

"Rescued you from danger," he countered.

She almost smiled. "Guess it depends on your perspective."

He released her chin and stood. "I am deadly to my enemies." He pinned her with a glare. "Don't become an enemy, and you'll have nothing to fear."

"See." She pointed her finger at him. "I should be scared to death of you, running for my room or trying to knock you out or something so I can escape."

"But you're not."

She shrugged. "I'm still sitting here, aren't I?"

"So you are." He ran his hand over her hair and down the

side of her neck. Heat blossomed in her chest and radiated outward. "What else does your gift tell you?" His low murmur was sexy and made her toes curl.

"You want me." She really didn't need anything extra to tell her that.

"Hmm," he whispered as he leaned down and kissed just behind her ear. "I do."

"I shouldn't want you," she reminded him.

"Why not?" He left a string of kisses down the curve of her neck.

Why not? She couldn't come up with one single reason. "Umm, you're my captor. Yeah, that's the reason."

"Rescuer," he countered.

She knew that wasn't the real reason he'd taken her. Maybe it was a factor, because she couldn't detect any lies when he told her that, but neither was he telling her the entire truth.

He nipped her jaw and then nuzzled his way to her lips. "I want you."

She wanted him, too. It didn't make sense, but it didn't have to.

She pushed all her worries aside to deal with later and focused entirely on their kiss. The heat warmed her from the inside out. Her breasts felt heavy and full, and an ache grew between her legs. Maybe this was nothing more than an interrogation technique. If so, he was very good at it. She'd already spilled all her secrets. She really didn't know that much at all about the Knights.

She had no idea what was going to happen to her, if she'd ever have anything approximating a normal life again. So she might as well grab as much pleasure as she could get. She'd had sex before. Not often, but she wasn't a virgin. But nothing had ever felt as right as having Tarrant kiss her.

He pulled away and stared at her, his blue eyes icing over.

"This won't change anything," he warned.

She knew he was telling her the truth. Even if they had sex, he wouldn't let her go. "I know."

Perhaps she had lost her mind, because all she wanted to do right now was make love with Tarrant. No, it would be having sex. There was no love between them. There couldn't be. There was too much mistrust. Too many secrets.

She still had no idea who exactly Tarrant was or his real reason for taking her. He'd either tell her or he wouldn't. Nothing she could do or say would change that. He was too hard a man to soften with sex.

He kissed her again, but this one was different. It was as though some internal switch had been flipped, as though her agreement had changed everything. If his earlier kisses had been hot, this one was devastating. He ate at her mouth and lips before thrusting his tongue inside and laying siege to her.

All she could do was hold on to his broad shoulders and return the intense kiss. She wanted this man more than she'd ever wanted another. The heat and the power of him was thrilling. It was like being on a roller coaster. She hung on and enjoyed the ride.

She was breathless when he finally pulled back. Her heart was galloping, and she was so warm she was starting to sweat.

"Be sure," he told her. His voice was lower than normal, almost guttural. His face looked like it had been hewn from stone.

There really wasn't any choice for her. Valeriya always went with her instincts. Right now, they were urging her to grab on to Tarrant and never let go. Against all common sense, she was going to do what she always did and listen to her gift, even if it wasn't logical. "I'm sure."

He groaned and scooped her off the stool. He was so incredibly strong, but he was smart, too. She couldn't resist him and she knew why. He reminded her of a knight of old.

Not like the Knights of the Dragon, but a real knight, filled with honor and purpose.

Maybe she was completely wrong about him. It was likely she was. He was probably sleeping with her for his own reasons, and none of them good.

She didn't care. She wanted to taste life.

Tarrant carried her down the hallway and back into the room where she'd been when she'd awakened earlier. She buried the tiny hurt that he wasn't taking her to his bedroom.

He went down on the bed with her and rolled to one side so he wasn't crushing her. Then he was kissing her again, and nothing else mattered. Reality would still be waiting when they were finished. But for now, it was just the two of them—a man and a woman who wanted each other.

It was enough.

Chapter Nine

Tarrant knew this was not a good idea, but damned if he could stop himself. He didn't want to stop. It didn't matter that Valeriya's sister was head of the Knights of the Dragon. And wasn't that a kicker. No, all he wanted was to strip her naked and kiss every inch of her curvy body.

His brothers would kick his ass if they found out he was sleeping with the enemy. Yet Valeriya didn't seem like the enemy. She was an innocent victim in the war. Just as Father Simon had been. He shoved away thoughts of his friend. That way only led to anger and madness.

Valeriya stroked her hands over his shoulders. "Is everything okay?"

Everything was not okay. It would never be okay. Not as long as her sister and the Knights were allowed to live. He wondered how Valeriya would react if she knew he planned to kill Karina and her band of not-so-merry men.

Best not to mention it.

He had Valeriya warm and willing. The last thing he wanted to do was say or do something that would make her change her mind.

Yet the honorable part of him refused to let him go any further. He inwardly cursed himself even as he spoke. "I have to destroy the Knights," he told her.

Her expression was sad but resigned. "I know."

He swore aloud and then kissed her. He hated seeing her so distressed, but there was nothing he could do about it. The Knights had brought the war to him, and he wasn't about to back away and hide. Not this time.

He'd almost taken her to his room, to his bed, but at the last second had brought her back to the guest room. She was getting under his skin enough as it was. Having her as the centerpiece in his room would only make him more possessive.

If his thinking was clear, he'd walk away from her. His dragon roared inside him, not at all happy by that thought. The creature wanted to lock her away, not to hurt her, but to keep her safe.

The time for walking away was past. They were together, and he had to have her.

"Tarrant?" She pulled away and stared into his eyes. "Is something wrong?"

The ambient lighting had come on in the room when they'd entered, but not the overhead one. He'd set it up that way before he'd gone up to the cabin to retrieve her. She would have a harder time distinguishing his features, but he had no such trouble. His preternatural vision allowed him to clearly see her heart-shaped face and straight nose.

"No, nothing is wrong." At this moment, everything was right. He captured the end of her braid and removed the elastic. He tossed it over his shoulder and began to unwind her thick braid. "I want to see your hair." It was black and thick and shiny. He slid his fingers through the thick mass and massaged her scalp.

She moaned. "That feels good."

"It will feel even better," he promised.

He slid his fingertips over the curve of her cheek and along her jaw. She tilted her face toward his touch. "So lovely." He dropped kisses across her forehead and down the slope of her nose as he reached for the zipper of her hoodie.

He unzipped the garment and held his breath, wondering if she would stop him now. Valeriya sat up, and he inwardly moaned. His cock was full and ached to be inside her.

She peeled the hoodie off and tossed it onto the floor. Tarrant growled in approval and she stilled. He watched her throat ripple as she swallowed. "I wish I could see you better."

"Your eyes will adjust," he promised her. If she could see him better, there was no way she'd miss the tattoo that covered the left side of his body from the neck down. If she knew as much about drakons as she claimed, she'd know what he was the moment she saw it. Given his size and the fact he knew about the Knights, she'd have to suspect he was a drakon.

And he didn't want that. He had no idea how she would react. She might run screaming, a distinct possibility, or she might decide to try to use him in some way. Right now, he was nothing more than a man to her, and she wanted him. In spite of everything.

He pushed himself into an upright position and reached for the hem of the long-sleeved top she wore. "May I?"

She nodded.

He slid his fingers under the band and found the smooth skin of her stomach. She was warm and soft. Delicate. He had to remember to be careful with her and go slow. If he hurt her, he'd never forgive himself.

That was a far cry from how he'd felt yesterday when he'd contemplated killing her. But he hadn't known her then. Now that he did, he knew he'd cut off his own hand before he harmed her. Best she never learned that or he was in trouble.

Valeriya Azarov really could lead to his downfall. Tarrant suddenly understood his brother better, and how Darius could have allowed himself to be tamed by a human female.

Her breath caught in her throat, bringing him back to the present. He pushed his hand upward and encountered nothing but bare flesh. She wasn't wearing a bra. He cupped one full mound and gently squeezed.

Valeriya gasped and licked her lips. "That feels wonderful."

His heart raced and the vein in his temple pulsed to the same beat as his erection. He had to see her. He yanked the top up and off her head before she could protest…and he lost the ability to speak.

Her breasts were full and tipped with large nipples in a dark pink color. Her skin was pale and fine. She didn't cover herself or try to hide. Of course, she didn't know he could see as well as he could, and he wasn't about to tell her.

He swooped down and captured one puckered tip between his lips. She yelped and then moaned his name. He wrapped his arm around her shoulders and guided her back down on the bed so she was lying flat on her back. He planted his hands on either side of her body and continued to suck her nipple.

When she threaded her fingers through his hair and held him to her, Tarrant wanted to roar with pleasure. What he did do was kiss a path to her other breast and tease the tender tip. He lost track of time as he nuzzled and licked and sucked the full mounds.

Valeriya began to get restless, moving her legs against the comforter. Tarrant lifted his head and stared down at her. Her eyes were partially closed but shot open as soon as he left her. A fierce glow appeared in them. "Take off your shirt."

It was a command. He was used to being in charge, the one who gave the commands. But he could no more deny her than he could stop the sun from rising and setting daily. He stripped his shirt away and flung it aside.

• • •

Valeriya really wished she could see better. There was some dim light emanating from the baseboards in the room, but it wasn't nearly enough for her to be able to see as well as she'd like. There were no windows in any of the rooms she'd been in, reinforcing her belief she was in a basement or bunker somewhere.

She really had no idea where she was and no longer cared. She was with Tarrant. That was all she needed to know.

He appeared even larger in the shadows. She couldn't really see more than a vague outline. His shoulders were impossibly wide. She reached out and ran her hands down the slope of his arms, marveling at the size and firmness of his muscles.

Knowing if she couldn't see him well, he could see her no better, gave her the courage to keep exploring. Blanketed in the dark, Valeriya became bolder than she ever could have been with the lights on.

She placed both palms on his chest. His skin was warm. She knew it was bronzed from seeing his face, neck, and hands. Whether that was its natural color or if it was a tan, she had no idea. The muscles in his abs rippled as she moved lower. God, the man was ripped.

She really wanted a light on, but she wasn't quite ready to be that exposed.

Tarrant gave another growl. It sounded so real, more animal than human. The fine hair on the back of her neck stood on end.

Before she could begin to second-guess her decision to get naked with him, Tarrant kissed her again. For such a hard man, his lips were supple and softer than the rest of him. He kissed and nipped at her bottom lip before sliding his tongue inside. She didn't really like coffee, but she loved the taste of it when it was mingled with Tarrant's unique flavor. She tangled her tongue with his and then did some exploring of her own.

She wrapped her arms around his neck and tugged him down. His chest pressed against her breasts in the most delicious way. Her nipples were puckered so tight they actually ached. She rubbed them against his smooth chest, groaning as the friction sent rivers of heat running from her breasts to between her legs.

Tarrant ended the kiss, his breath warm on her face. But he didn't stop. He just moved lower, kissing a path along her jawline, down her neck and over her collarbone. She held her breath, but he ignored her breasts this time, leaving a trail of kisses down her stomach. He circled her navel with his tongue.

She knew what was coming next but didn't stop him.

He gripped the waistband of her sleep pants and eased them downward, taking her underwear with it. She could feel the heat creeping up her body and knew she was blushing. It was just as well he couldn't see her all that well, otherwise she'd have been totally embarrassed.

She'd had lovers before, but none of them had been like Tarrant. He was a force of nature—big, bold, and sexy. And right now, he was all hers.

He skimmed his fingers over her ankles and removed her socks. She was naked and exposed.

"Now you." If she was going to be naked, so was he.

Tarrant rolled onto his back and she heard him lower the zipper of his jeans. The shushing noise the material made as he slid it down his thighs seemed overly loud. He turned to pull his pants off and she got a glimpse of the shape and size of his erection.

It was in proportion to the rest of him, which meant it was

large.

Her breathing increased. What had ever given her the idea she could handle a man like Tarrant? He was so far outside her experience.

"Valeriya." He caught her by the shoulders. "Look at me."

She had no choice. She stared into his face, wishing she could see his stunning blue eyes. They were more expressive than he probably believed they were. They could be icy one moment and as warm as a summer sky the next.

"That's it, sweetheart, just breathe." She sucked in some air and concentrated on slowing down her breathing. Now she was embarrassed.

"Again." He rubbed his hand over her hair. It was such a gentle action, so incongruent with such a huge man. He really was special.

"I'm sorry." She hadn't meant to kill the mood.

He cupped one side of her face in his large hand. "I'm not. I have you naked in bed. Now, where were we?" He didn't wait for her reply, but covered her with his body and kissed her.

Valeriya was overwhelmed by his heat and the nearness of his body. His legs were between hers, and his thick shaft was nestled alongside her thigh. His chest was cushioned against her breasts. He had most of his weight resting on his forearms so she wasn't crushed beneath him.

She ran her hands over his arms, shoulders, and around to his back. He was more muscular, stronger than any man she'd ever seen. His cock flexed and pressed harder against her leg.

She savored the kiss. It was surprisingly tender at first, as though he sensed she was nervous. As she relaxed and let herself sink into the mattress, he deepened the caress.

It wasn't long until kissing wasn't enough. Every inch of her body was on fire for him. She wanted more and he was the only one who could give her what she needed.

He broke the kiss and raised his head. His eyes seemed to glow. A trick of the light, for sure. One side of his body seemed darker than the other. She wondered about that until Tarrant started kissing a path down her body. As a distraction, it worked to perfection.

He knelt between her legs and waited.

When she opened them the slightest bit, she caught a glimpse of his white teeth as he smiled. Heat shot through her when he shoved his hands beneath her bottom and lifted. He lowered his head, and Valeriya forgot how to think.

• • •

She smelled so sweet. Tarrant inhaled the scent of her arousal before he dragged the flat of his tongue over the plump folds of her sex. She gasped and bucked her hips. He knew she had some trepidation about what was to come.

If he wanted her more than once—and he did—he had to make sure she received the maximum amount of pleasure. And while he'd like to spend hours exploring her lush body, he knew he was close to coming. Now he needed her to find her pleasure as fast as possible so he could get inside her.

Valeriya had the most wonderful curves. Her waist was supple, her hips rounded. She wasn't exactly small, but he had more than a foot of height on her and over one hundred pounds. That she trusted him enough to allow him to touch her pleased him.

A sly voice in the back of his head whispered that maybe she was tricking him. Maybe she was doing this to get closer to him.

He ignored the voice and traced the slick pink folds of her sex. Her thighs trembled. Whatever her reasons, there was no faking her reaction. She wanted him as much as he wanted her.

He found her clit and concentrated on stimulating the little kernel of nerves. He flicked it with the tip of his tongue, circled it, and then sucked on it. She bucked against his mouth. Incoherent words fell from her lips.

He growled, sending the vibration through her clit. She screamed. She actually screamed as she came. Her entire body went stiff as a board and then seemed to collapse. She was laughing and crying at the same time.

Tarrant wasn't sure if he should be worried or not, but there was no time. He had to have her. He lowered her legs and levered his body over hers once again. He reached between them and guided the broad head of his cock to her opening. She shivered but didn't stop him as he eased forward.

Her body resisted him at first, and she tensed. He dropped his head forward and groaned. "Relax, sweetheart. I'll take it slow." At least he hoped he could. His cock was seconds from exploding. He had to feel her hot, wet heat surrounding him.

"I'm trying." There was a plaintive quality to her voice that he didn't like.

"Everything will be fine," he promised. He kissed her sweet mouth and was relieved when she eagerly welcomed him.

The second he felt her relax, he pressed inward. The head of his shaft breached her opening, stretching her to accept him. She stiffened and then moaned.

Tarrant kept kissing her and stroked her face before cupping one of her breasts. He teased the taut nipple with his thumb. She moaned and undulated her hips, taking him in another inch.

He wasn't going to make it. His balls were trying to crawl into his body. He growled and pushed forward. Valeriya was slick from her orgasm and he managed to gain several more inches.

He buried his face against her shoulder. His lungs were

working hard as he sucked in much-needed air. She stoked his back and shoulders, as if trying to calm him. He could have told her nothing would work. Every touch was pushing him closer to the edge.

Then Valeriya pulled her legs up alongside his hips. The motion pushed him deeper. He was almost there.

He raised his head and peered down at her. Her cheeks were flushed, her lips moist, and her eyes wide and bright. "Finish it," she told him.

He could have denied any other woman. He was a skilled lover, able to control himself and his passion. But this woman made a mockery of his so-called skill. He pushed forward, burying the last of his cock inside.

Her slick walls rippled and stretched to accommodate him. She fit him as snugly as he knew she would, better than he could have ever imagined. Her eyes widened and her lips parted.

"Okay?" He'd pull out if he was hurting her. It might kill him, but he'd do it.

She nodded.

That didn't satisfy him. "Valeriya?"

She shuddered when he said her name. Her inner muscles clutched his dick. He closed his eyes and sucked in a breath, but it was too late. He came, spilling himself inside her. He swore, reared back, and plunged forward several times.

Valeriya shocked him when she cried out. Before he could ask if he was hurting her, he felt the telltale ripples of her pussy. She was coming again.

Tarrant lost it totally. He plunged into her over and over, his big body trembling, her smaller one shaking. He didn't want to stop, never wanted to stop, but eventually not even he could keep going.

He collapsed beside her, finding just enough strength to pull out so he wouldn't crush her. Totally spent, he wrapped one arm around her and dragged her into the curve of his body.

One word echoed in his brain.

Mine.

• • •

Karina carefully set her phone on her desk when what she really wanted to do was smash it into tiny pieces. Her sister was missing. How had two men, both highly trained operatives, lost her sister? The woman was a children's author. She could barely keep up in dance class and hadn't lasted in ballet more than two years. She had no training when it came to evasion tactics.

But the fact remained that the rental company had picked up the vehicle Valeriya had been driving, and her things were no longer in the cabin.

Had her sister had help?

Karina leaned back in her chair and pressed her fingers together. Maybe that was it. But who?

Had Riggs double crossed her and taken Valeriya to Herman Temple? She didn't think so, but there was no denying her lover was ambitious. Maybe Temple had gone after her himself. She didn't doubt he had spies in her ranks. After all, she had them in his.

Her phone rang again. She glanced at the number, not surprised to see it belonged to Riggs. She picked it up and answered. "Yes."

"Your sister is missing."

"How do you know?" she asked. She'd sent two of her own men to watch Valeriya. She realized now she should have sent more. There was a third possibility she hadn't counted on. Maybe Darius Varkas had slipped back and taken her sister.

Riggs made an impatient sound. "You know Temple has

men watching your men. After they pulled out in a hurry, Temple's men checked out the situation and just reported back. He's not sure if she's slipped her leash or if you've taken her in."

She heard the question in Riggs's tone. He wanted to know if she had Valeriya. It was time to make use of her lover.

"I don't know where she is, and I don't like it. She might not know much about the secrets and daily workings of the Knights, but she knows enough. If she falls into the hands of our enemies…" She let the implication speak for itself.

"I'm heading to the mountains."

Karina allowed herself a smile. "I thought you might." She stood and began to pace. "In the meantime, I'll keep an eye on Temple myself. Maybe it's time we had another meeting."

"I'll be in touch," Riggs told her.

"You do that." She ended the call before he did. She quickly pressed another number. It was answered on the third ring. Herman did like to play his silly games.

"What can I do for you, Karina?" Herman was a good-looking man, considering his age, but she'd never been attracted to him. She'd always sensed he'd slit her throat if he thought he could usurp her position with the Knights.

"I think we should meet later today to discuss the latest developments." That was as much as she was willing to say over the phone. "I'll stop by your office." Once again, she ended the call first.

She tossed her phone on the desk and smiled. She could just imagine how furious he was over having to wait around for her all day, having no idea what time she would arrive to meet with him. She was, after all, the leader of the Knights. He'd damn well wait on her.

As for her sister, well, Valeriya wouldn't get far on her own. She pressed the intercom on her desk. It was answered immediately. "Yes, Ms. Azarov."

"I want every resource at our disposal used to find my sister. Track her credit cards, car rental outlets, airports, everything."

"Yes, Ms. Azarov."

She tucked her phone in her pocket and left her office. Whatever it took to find her sister, she'd do it.

Chapter Ten

Valeriya had no idea how much time had passed when she woke. All she knew was that she was naked and alone. She shivered as a chill snaked over her. The covers were tucked tight around her, but without Tarrant beside her radiating body heat, she was cold.

She sat up in bed, keeping the covers tucked around her. The ambient light still glowed from the baseboards, but it was too dark for her to truly see anything beyond shapes. She reached for the bedside lamp. The click seemed overly loud and the light too bright. She blinked several times to allow her vision to adjust.

She'd seen motel rooms with more personality. The space was spartan, with a bed, a chest of drawer, a nightstand, and a chair that sat in the corner. The furnishings and bedclothes was all excellent quality, but it was all in shades of beige and brown. There were no books or paintings or personal items of any kind. And, of course, there was no window.

Her suitcase sat just inside the door of the room. Tarrant must have put it there while she was sleeping. At least she had clean clothes. Her flannel pants, shirt, and hoodie were folded neatly on the chair.

Valeriya sighed and rubbed her hands over her face. What had she done? It was bad enough that she'd slept with the man who'd kidnapped her—any shrink would have a field day with that—but she had feelings for him. Deep ones.

Yeah, definitely big trouble.

She shoved the covers aside and got out of bed. She didn't like walking around naked, not when she didn't know when or if Tarrant was coming back. It was one thing to be naked while they were making love. Quite another to just wander around with no clothing on.

In spite of Tarrant's place being underground, the room was actually fairly warm. Not that it helped with the chill radiating from deep inside her. She feared that might never truly abate. She shivered as the air circulated around her, making her nipples tighten. It reminded her of what she and Tarrant had done. Suddenly, she wasn't nearly as cold.

She grabbed her suitcase and dragged it over to the bed. This was not the time to get aroused. She needed to get dressed and figure out what she was going to do next.

She opened the case to find everything jumbled inside. He'd probably searched her belongings. He hadn't hesitated to check her phone and laptop before disabling them, he certainly wouldn't think twice about going through her clothes.

It was more than a little disconcerting to think about him handling her underclothes. She ignored the flash of heat that crept up her face and pulled out a pair of jeans, a long-sleeved top, and clean underwear.

Valeriya carried her clothes with her as she padded across the floor and opened the bathroom door. Like before, the baseboard lights came on low and she set her clothing on the vanity before turning on the overhead light.

This room might be done in shades of brown, too, but it had a luxurious feel that appealed to her. Valeriya went back to the bedroom and dug around in her suitcase until she located her brush and comb and the bag with her toiletries.

She went back to the bathroom and started the water in the shower running before she laid out her soap, shampoo, and conditioner. She noted there was an expensive brand of all three already in the shower. She grabbed one of the bottles and read the label. It was all natural and smelled like lemons.

She shrugged and tucked her own things back into the small zippered bag. Since the toiletries were already here, she'd treat the situation as though she were in a high-class hotel and use them. She stepped beneath the hot spray and closed her eyes. The water cascaded over her.

She'd really made love with Tarrant. Or had sex with him. Using the term "making love" was almost too intimate, implied too much.

She groaned and rested her hands on the tile. If she was caught up in semantics, she was in bigger trouble than she thought.

• • •

Tarrant was losing his mind. There could be no other reason for watching Valeriya wander around naked in the guest room. He was smart enough not to view the feed from the camera that faced the shower stall. He was aroused enough as it was.

He spun his chair away from the screen and growled.

It had taken every ounce of discipline he'd possessed to leave Valeriya sleeping in bed. He'd wanted to stay with her, with her smaller body tucked against his. It was for that very reason that he'd forced himself to get up and leave her once he'd known she was sleeping.

The searches he'd been running had yielded up some interesting results. There was little about Karina Azarov, other than her name being connected to various businesses. She kept to herself and had competent people in charge of the day-to-day running of her empire.

Some people might assume she was more socialite than businesswoman. Tarrant knew she was cunning, and a killer. It didn't matter if she'd never pulled a trigger herself, although he wouldn't bet good money on that. She was the head of a clandestine organization that would do anything to keep its secrets.

It meant that if Valeriya was what she seemed to be—a woman caught in the middle of this war because of family ties—she was in danger. He didn't doubt for one second that Karina would kill her younger sister if she deemed her a threat.

And if Karina wouldn't, another one of the Knights would.

It was surprising Valeriya had lived this long. Tarrant imagined there were several top-ranking members of the Knights keeping tabs on her, hoping to use her against her sister if they could.

That made sense. In their shoes, he'd have done the same.

His phone rang. He glanced at it and sighed, knowing if he didn't answer it would just ring again.

"Darius is bad enough. I didn't think you were a nursemaid, too, Ezra."

"Fuck off," his brother shot back. In spite of himself, Tarrant smiled.

"Is that any way to greet your favorite brother?" He turned his chair back around and watched the screen. The bathroom door was still closed. His fingers itched to click on the video feed for the shower. He curled his hand into a fist.

Ezra snorted but didn't deny his claim. They were both

loners, eschewing the crowded places of the world. Darius might not like them, but he did dwell in cities for his work. And Nic…well, he was an anomaly none of them understood. He actually sought out people. Tarrant shivered at the horror of being in a place like Vegas with lights and noise and so many damn people.

"What do you want, Ezra? I'm a little busy here." He glanced over at several other screens that were running searches and compiling data for him.

"With the little children's author. Yeah, Darius told me." Ezra paused. "I bet you are real busy."

The tone of his brother's voice made Tarrant bristle. "And just what do you mean by that?"

"She's most likely a plant," his brother bluntly stated. "You need to think with that computer-like brain of yours and not with your dick."

Tarrant took a deep breath and then another and another. He still couldn't speak. What he really wanted to do was rip his brother's head off.

That was a sobering thought. He loved his brother. Had spent his entire life protecting him.

"You're as bad as Darius." Ezra's quiet voice was like a thunderclap in the silence between them.

Tarrant shook his head in denial, even though he knew it was true. He would not allow Valeriya to control him or his actions. She was a means to an end. Nothing more.

"I'm nothing like what our older brother was like with Sarah." Denying his connection to Valeriya felt wrong and actually created a physical ache in his chest.

"You keep telling yourself that." Ezra sighed and Tarrant could picture his brother dragging his fingers through his hair, as he often did when he was exasperated. "Just be careful. The fact you took the woman instead of just watching her tells me you're already gone on her. It's just not like you."

"Valeriya. Her name is Valeriya." She wasn't just some random woman. She was special. Hell, he was four thousand years old and had never felt the urge to grab a woman and run with her before.

As much as it pained him to admit it, Ezra was right. He was acting like Darius had with Sarah. Now that they'd made love, he felt even more possessive than he had before.

"Don't you find it odd that after all these years, both you and Darius are attracted to women at almost the same time. I don't know whether I should be excited or worried."

Tarrant could tell his brother was only half joking. Ezra was also right. "It's too much of a coincidence to be a coincidence."

"What does it mean? Do you think the Knights are controlling this?" Ezra made a growling noise. "No, scratch that. Sarah would die for Darius."

Tarrant wondered if Valeriya would die for him if it came down to a choice between him and the Knights. Did he want her to be that committed to him?

Tarrant's attention was caught by the bathroom door in the bedroom opening. He frowned when he realized she was dressed. He liked her much better naked. Her hair looked damp and was pulled back into a braid. The jeans she wore clung to her hips and the top outlined her breasts nicely.

"If you're done, I've got to go."

"All I'm saying is be careful. If I have to come and rescue your scaly ass from the Knights, I'm not going to be happy. You know how I hate to leave my island." With that parting shot, Ezra hung up on him.

Tarrant focused entirely on Valeriya as she left the bedroom and went down the hallway to the kitchen. "Tarrant," she called his name. She paused alongside the island and looked longingly at the kettle.

After squaring her shoulders, she marched over to the

kettle and added water before setting it on the stove to boil.

"Where is he?" she muttered. He found himself grinning as she wandered around the room, opening cupboard doors and peeking inside. There was nothing for her to find other than dishes, pots and pans, and food.

She left the kitchen area and wandered around the living room. She paused by the security panel with the blinking light. Not surprising, she jabbed at several of the buttons, all the while glancing nervously over her shoulder.

Tarrant stood and went to the elevator in his private computer lab. He stepped inside. "Up." He glanced at the tablet in his hand, watching as she tried another button.

He opened the upper door and stepped out. It shut behind him, sealing his computer equipment safely away from Valeriya and anyone else. Not even his brothers could access it without him. It was programmed so they could leave if they were with him, but not so they could enter on their own.

It was safer for all of them that way.

As he stealthily strode down the hallway, he could hear her muttering. At the last second, he closed down the program on his tablet and locked it. Best not to provide any temptation.

"What are you doing?" He kept his voice mild, but she still jumped and spun around. The look of guilt on her face was priceless.

She straightened her shoulders and glared at him. "This is a door to the outside, isn't it?"

There was no reason to lie to her. "Yes." He set the tablet on the counter before going over to stand beside her. "And it requires my handprint and a code to open it."

He leaned down and sniffed. She smelled like lemons. He knew that wasn't her normal scent, which meant she'd used the grooming products he'd left in the bathroom for her. It pleased him deeply.

"What are you doing?" She took a step back and

frowned. The welcoming, passionate woman from hours ago was gone, leaving a guarded one behind. He was sorry to see the welcome gone from her eyes, but it helped steady him. He needed to be more cautious with Valeriya.

"I'm smelling you," he answered honestly.

She hunched her shoulders slightly. "If you don't like it, it's your own fault. I used the shampoo and soap in the shower."

"I like it. I left it there for you," he added.

"You did? I mean, it wasn't just there for guests? I mean, I am a guest. No, I'm not really one. I'm a captive." She groaned and leaned against the wall and banged the back of her head against it. "Ignore me. I'm babbling."

She was, but he wasn't stupid enough to agree with her. Some of his tension let go. Valeriya was totally transparent. Every emotion she had was visible on her face. She was no more capable of subterfuge than a child.

"It's okay." He finally did what he'd wanted to do since he'd left her hours before. He leaned down and kissed her.

She made a sweet sound and went up on her toes to deepen the caress. His dragon roared inside him, wanting him to claim Valeriya as his own. Tarrant broke the kiss and frowned.

He wasn't quite sure what the creature wanted or was telling him to do. Even after all these years, the two parts of him had never fully integrated. That was the way of drakons. They were two halves of a whole, but each side didn't always understand the other. The creature worked wholly on instinct. The human part of him relied on instinct, but intellect as well.

"Are you hungry?" he asked.

Her eyes widened and she licked her lips. His pants grew extremely tight and uncomfortable. "You can't be hungry again. We just ate. Didn't we?"

He was hungry all right, but not only for food. "That was

hours ago." She'd managed to sleep for quite some time.

"Oh." She pushed away from the wall and wandered over to sit on one of the sofas. He followed, unable to be more than a few feet away from her.

"You obviously needed the rest. You've been under a lot of stress lately."

She snorted. "That's one way of putting it." She pulled her feet up on to the edge of the couch and wrapped her arms around her legs. It made her seem small and fragile.

Calculated move or natural reaction? Tarrant wished he could be one hundred percent sure. Instinct told him to trust her, but his intellect demanded caution. Even if she was innocent in the war, her sister was still Karina Azarov. And in his experience, when the shit hit the fan, people always sided with family, not matter what the circumstances.

Valeriya barely knew him. She could turn on him and give information to her sister. And the worst part of the situation was he couldn't really fault her for it if she did. Family was family.

He just had to make sure he never put her in a position to betray him. Cynical? Maybe. But better safe than sorry.

"What are you going to do with me?"

He could smell her fear and didn't like it. "What am I going to do with you?" He knew there was only one choice for him. "I'm keeping you."

Chapter Eleven

Valeriya stared at Tarrant. He was keeping her? "What exactly do you mean by that?" And why did his words make her feel all warm and fuzzy inside. She should be screaming, shouldn't she?

Strange as it was, she trusted Tarrant more than she'd ever trusted anyone in her life. Common sense told her everything was mostly likely a ruse and he was most likely working for her sister or another of the Knights. But her intuition was saying just the opposite.

"Just what I said." Tarrant sprawled on the other leather sectional and spread his arms across the back, taking up most of it with his big body. He might be living underground, but there was nothing basement-like about this place. It was gorgeous.

"I can't let you go. Your sister or one of the Knights would grab you in a heartbeat."

"So you took me in order to protect me?" She slowly released the grip on her legs and slid them back down.

He shook his head. "Wish I could say that was totally true,

but I can't. That's a side benefit. I took you in case you were working with the Knights and had information. If you didn't have information, I thought you might be valuable."

Wow, that was brutally honest and painful to hear. "I see."

Tarrant huffed out a breath and sat forward, resting his forearms on his legs. "No. No, you don't see at all. You're dangerous to me. I should take you back and let the Knights deal with you."

Her stomach dropped and she thought she might be ill. She hadn't realized how safe she felt here with Tarrant until he threatened to take it away. She swallowed before she could speak. "And will you? Take me back?"

"Never." The single word dropped between them like an anvil.

She licked her dry lips. "Never is a long time."

One corner of his mouth kicked up. "Time is something I have plenty of."

"Who are you? Who is the real Tarrant?" Valeriya needed to know more about the man she'd slept with, the man who was quickly becoming her entire world. "You're not a Knight, and you're not a mercenary."

"You sure about that?" He raised one eyebrow in question.

She was filled with a surety she was right. Her instincts were telling her to trust him. But more importantly, she felt no sense of danger. And her intuition, her gift, was never wrong.

She gave an emphatic nod. "Yes."

"Who do you think I am?"

She sat forward, mimicking his pose. "I'm not sure. You seem to have plenty of money. This place didn't come cheap."

He chuckled and shook his head. "No, it didn't come cheap."

This might make him angry. The last time she'd mentioned Darius Varkas, Tarrant had become furious with her. Still, there was only one way to learn more about the mysterious man sitting across from her.

"I think you're a friend of Darius Varkas. I read about him online. He's made a ton of money in mining."

Tarrant nodded thoughtfully. "You think I work for Varkas?"

She started to agree but stopped. "No. I don't think you work for anyone." Tarrant was too used to being in command to allow anyone to give him orders.

He cocked his head and studied her with his icy-blue gaze. "You're right. I don't work for anyone. And you're very observant for a children's author."

She shivered. "It's the artist in me. I notice details."

"Have you told me everything you know about the Knights and dragons?"

"Drakons," she corrected automatically. "They're called drakons."

"So they are."

"I've told you I don't belong to the Knights."

"And you left your home and flew across the country on the off-chance Darius Varkas might be hanging around that cabin I found you in, even though the Knights know about it."

Put like that, it didn't sound like the brightest of plans. "I acted on instinct." She flopped back against the sofa cushions and crossed her arms over her chest. She knew it was a defensive act, but she couldn't stop herself.

"Why?"

He already thought she was crazy. Why stop here? "I thought he might be a drakon, okay? Or that he knew one."

Tarrant moved so fast, he was a blur. One second he was on the other sofa, the next he was looming over her, his hands on the back of the sofa, caging her in. "Why do you care?" His voice was soft, but there was no disguising the menace beneath.

She tried to swallow but couldn't. "It's not right, what my sister, what my family has done for generations. I thought if I could warn one drakon, maybe save one…" She trailed off.

Tarrant seemed perplexed.

She gave a wry laugh. "Yeah, I know it was a dumb idea. What drakon would listen to me—the sister of the head of the Knights of the Dragon? Heck, I wouldn't believe me, either."

But she wanted Tarrant to believe her. "I've always felt drawn to drakons. I dreamed about them as a child. I even had one as an imaginary friend when I was small."

Tarrant eased back and sat beside her. "An imaginary friend? A drakon?"

She didn't care how silly it made her seem. "I was a lonely child. What better friend than a powerful creature who could be both playmate and protector, both human and dragon?"

• • •

Tarrant was stunned by her confession. He, possibly the most cynical man on the planet—although Ezra gave him a run for the title—believed her. It made sense that she wrote children's books about dragons. She was probably drawing on her childhood memories.

"Maybe it wasn't the brightest idea in the world." She rubbed her eyes. "No, scratch that. It was stupid. I know my sister keeps tabs on me, has people watching me." She gave him a pointed look. "Karina has spies everywhere. I can't trust anyone."

"Then we have that in common." He could tell from her expression that she didn't quite understand, so he elaborated. "I can't trust anyone, either." That wasn't quite true. He trusted his brothers, and now Sarah, but that was it. He'd trusted one human, Father Simon Babineaux, but now he was gone.

Valeriya inched away from him. His expression had gone

dark at the thought of his murdered friend. He raked his fingers through his short hair and shook himself. Best not to think about his friend, not while he was dealing with Valeriya.

"What would you have done if Darius had been here?" He was curious and also more than a bit jealous. Valeriya was his.

She smoothed out a small crease in her jeans. "I don't know. I would have told him that my sister and the Knights were searching for him. It's never good to be a person of interest with them."

"And what if he'd been a drakon?"

Her green eyes widened, and she bit her bottom lip. Possessiveness roared through Tarrant. He didn't like the thought Valeriya might be interested in his brother. Of course, she didn't know Darius was his brother. She didn't even know what his brother looked like. All she'd wanted to do was help. That calmed his dragon somewhat, but not much.

"I've always wanted to see one." Her whisper was so soft, he might not have heard it if it weren't for his preternatural hearing.

"Why? Do you want to capture one? Drink his blood?"

She shook her head emphatically. "No. I would never harm a drakon. They've been hurt enough over the centuries. But there's one thing I don't understand."

"And what is that?"

"They're more powerful than any human. How can the Knights capture them?"

"Potions and magic," he muttered.

"What?" Valeriya asked.

Tarrant wasn't about to talk about the Knights. That just drove his temper sky-high. He focused on the one fact that seemed most important to her. "So you want to see a drakon, do you?"

"Oh, yes." She breathed the words, sounding much like

she had when they'd made love. He didn't like the idea of her mooning after some unknown drakon. Or even worse, a known one, like Darius.

"What if I could give you that?" How far would she go to get what she wanted?

"You know a drakon?" She was practically vibrating with excitement. Then her enthusiasm dimmed. "Best not to tell me anything. If my sister ever finds me, I can't tell her what I don't know."

Tarrant was stunned. He'd offered her the one thing she wanted, and she'd turned it down. All to protect someone she'd never met. She didn't know he was a drakon.

Even if she did know about the tattoos they all had, he'd been wearing a long-sleeved shirt with a high neckline the entire time he'd been with her, and they'd made love in the dark. She'd never seen his markings. And in this day and age, a lot of men had tattoos all over their bodies. It wasn't such a distinguishing mark anymore.

Tarrant stood and held out his hand. "Come with me."

Valeriya slid off the sofa and slipped her much smaller hand into his. Almost immediately, his anger dimmed. She really did soothe the savage beast.

"Where are we going?"

He didn't answer as he led her down the hallway. He stopped in front of a large steel door. Once he did this, there was no going back. For either of them. If he did this, he could never let her go. His dragon coveted her. The man wanted her.

Tarrant shoved the door open and pulled her onto the metal landing.

• • •

Luther Henderson evaded the men trailing him before he made his way to Gervais Rames's bookstore. He'd exchanged his trademark tailored suit for jeans and a black leather jacket, allowing him to blend more easily with the general population. He had no idea if they were Temple's men or if they worked for another one of the Knights of the Dragon. This was a dangerous and risky business. No one trusted anyone.

That's what had led to this mess in the first place. Temple's son had taken Rames into his confidence, and the man had stolen a very valuable book from his boss's library. Now both Christian Temple and Gervais Rames were dead, and the book was still missing. Luther didn't think it would be here in the shop, and neither did Temple. But his boss wanted to make sure that if there were any other books of interest, he got them before the other Knights.

There was definitely little honor in this brotherhood, even among Temple's own men.

Look at Riggs. The men had been talking, and Luther had been listening. Seems their leader was sleeping with Karina Azarov. He'd even taken off to the West Coast on some errand for her. Luther knew that Temple wasn't happy with either Riggs or Karina. Riggs was playing a very dangerous game, one he couldn't hope to win.

The Knights of the Dragon took betrayal very seriously. They were also a suspicious and paranoid bunch, always posturing and jockeying for position within the organization. It had taken Luther two long years to work his way to where he was now. And he knew he was damn good at what he did. He was also cautious.

Luther stopped outside the back door of the old building and listened. He was a big man, but he knew how to walk silently, how to blend. He'd been doing it his entire life. When he was sure he was alone, he jimmied the lock. He'd disabled the security system when he'd found it earlier. The shop was a dark, dingy place.

He prowled through the narrow aisle toward the front of the store. The ambient light coming in through the large glass window was more than enough to allow him to see.

It was like walking through a tunnel. The small storefront was jammed with books. They were stacked everywhere—on the bookshelves, the floors, and the counter. A light layer of dust covered the desk that acted as both a workspace and a checkout area—a testament to the fact the owner hadn't been around for a while. Neither had anyone else.

There was no way of knowing how long the situation would last. Eventually someone would realize the shop wasn't opening again when the rent wasn't paid. The owners of the building might confiscate the contents or sell them outright. Then any chance of discovering anything would be gone.

There was little chance of finding anything interesting up front. Gervais Rames hadn't been a stupid man. He'd gotten a member of the Knights of the Dragon to share secrets and then had stolen a valuable artifact. Had Rames had a buyer for the book? That was the most likely scenario.

Luther wasn't fond of the most likely scenario. He wondered if Rames hadn't been playing a deeper game. Was he a friend of the drakons? He hadn't been a drakon. That much was obvious. He wouldn't have been so easy to kill. Nor would the older Temple have allowed him to be killed if that had been the case. He was desperate for a new supply of blood.

He made his way to the office and peered around. Too obvious. Still, he closed the door, turned on the small desk light, and made himself search. Sometimes men were stupid when it came to hiding secrets.

After an hour, he was convinced there wasn't anything there to find.

He stepped outside the office door and studied the small shop. It wasn't easy to get an idea of the layout with the high shelves and books stacked everywhere. He pulled up his mental files on the building. Luther was fortunate enough to have an eidetic memory. He could recall anything after seeing it only once. He never wrote things down. Ever. Unlike most people, he guarded his secrets.

The dimensions of the room were off.

He stayed in the shadows, in case a passerby glanced in the window, and paced off the space. The room was definitely shorter than the blueprints showed.

He walked back toward the office. Beside it was a large bookshelf that extended about five feet. The wall angled off after that, which meant there was a space five feet wide and about seven feet deep behind that shelf.

Luther studied the shelf. It had to open in a way that no one would accidently discover. He noticed a stool not far from the shelf. He retrieved it and stepped up. His height allowed him to see everything. He ran his fingers along the top and found a small indentation on one end. He pressed down, and the shelf began to slide.

He climbed down off the stool and entered the tiny room. It was a tight fit for a man his size. Unlike the store, this room was ruthlessly organized. A tiny table and chair took up one corner. Beside it sat a rather large safe.

Luther turned on the lamp on the table, lowered himself to the floor, and went to work on the lock. It was surprisingly easy to open, as it wasn't secured.

Why wasn't it locked? Had Rames been confident his secret room was secure enough? On closer inspection, he noticed the lock was broken. Had the safe always been like that or had someone been here ahead of him?

Frowning, he pulled open the door and found the safe was filled with books. He removed the first one. It was a first edition of Oliver Twist. This was Rames's stash of very rare books.

He pulled them out one at a time and studied them. He opened covers to make sure they matched what was outside and weren't a ruse to hide something more interesting.

There was a wooden box in the back corner of the safe. Luther pulled it out. It practically hummed with energy. Unlike most people, he knew there were things in the world that most people thought were myth. He also knew some artifacts, including books, had great power.

He set the box on the table and slowly opened it. There was a small book inside. The binding was leather. It was old and worn from being handled many times. He hesitated and then lifted the cover. It was written in Latin, but that was no problem for him. He'd taught himself many languages as a child. He had a talent for it. Having a photographic memory had allowed him to add even more languages to his repertoire as an adult.

When people didn't think you could understand them, they talked more freely. He'd picked up some very interesting information that way. Not even Temple knew he spoke more than English, and certainly nothing as obscure as Latin. He'd never have sent him to the bookstore otherwise.

"Secrets of the Dragon," he read. He carefully turned several of the yellowed and brittle pages. The little volume was filled with information about dragons. There was even the promise of a potion to control them. It gave their strengths and weaknesses. This was an extremely valuable book.

Luther closed the leather cover and then the lid of the wooden box. He finished his search, determining there were no more books pertaining to dragons or the Knights. There was, however, a small notebook containing business transactions—a list of buyers and books purchased and for how much. He tucked it in his pocket to examine more closely later.

He was just about to leave when another book caught his

eye. It was about three hundred years old and was a treatise about mythological creatures. He glanced through it and found a section on dragons. He tucked the book in his pocket. He'd give this one to Temple. No need to give him the other one.

He returned everything to the safe just the way he'd found it. He turned off the light and stepped out of the small room. The shelf pushed easily back into place, clicking when it was secure.

Luther left the same way he'd entered. Using stealth and skill, he made his way to a basement apartment in a not-so-good area of the Bronx and deposited the box and the notebook in a secret floor safe. Then he made his way back to Manhattan with the book he'd taken to give to Temple. He only hoped it was enough to convince his boss there'd been nothing else there of use. And if he sent someone else to look…well, Luther had already removed the most interesting book.

He wanted time to think and to examine what he'd found before he deciding if he would hand it over to Temple. It was risky to put his boss off, but it was a chance he was willing to take.

He picked up a new tail before he was back to his Manhattan apartment. Now that was interesting. He recognized one of the men before he could duck out of sight. Seems that Karina Azarov herself was interested in his comings and goings. Which meant that there was an internal war brewing among the Knights.

Chapter Twelve

Valeriya followed Tarrant down the winding metal staircase. She had no idea where they were going or what he wanted to show her. Her mood was all over the place. He'd taken her because he thought she might have information, and if she didn't, he might be able to use her for leverage.

Even though she'd known that in her heart, it still depressed her.

Did she want him to keep her, as he seemed determined to do? And what did he really mean by that, anyway? He was attracted to her. That much was obvious. But at times he seemed angry with her as well.

Their relationship, or association, or whatever it was, wasn't off to any kind of healthy start. A therapist would tell her she was making a huge mistake to even consider trying to have any kind of relationship with him. Not that they had a real relationship. It was more of a mutual need. She needed to help protect the innocent from her sister and the other Knights. As for Tarrant… Well, she wasn't quite sure what he wanted, other than to destroy the Knights and sleep with her.

"Where are we going?" Better to focus on the here and now. The staircase was well lit and went down, down, down.

"Almost there." His fingers were big and warm wrapped around hers. She took a deep breath and watched her footing until they reached the bottom.

She didn't know what she'd been expecting, but it certainly wasn't a huge, empty room. It was more like an underground warehouse. It had to be at least four stories high and was the length of several football fields.

"What is this place?" There was nothing stored here. It was just a big, empty space. The walls were rock, as though it was a natural cave.

"It's somewhere I come when I want to be alone." He released her hand and walked several feet away from her.

Valeriya's heart began to race, and goose bumps ran down her arms. She had no idea what was about to happen, but she knew it was going to be big. Tarrant was deadly serious about whatever he was about to reveal.

She didn't know if she should be flattered or scared to death.

Then he grabbed the hem of his long-sleeved shirt and pulled it up and off. She was momentarily distracted by the breadth of his chest and the ripple of his abs. She'd felt him, and seen him in shadows, but it was nothing compared to viewing him in full light.

His body was a sculpted masterpiece.

Then she noticed the tattoos. They bisected his body perfectly, covering the left side of his body from neck to waist. They also trailed down his arm all the way to his wrist.

It couldn't be. Her gaze flew to his, but he wasn't looking at her. He'd already removed his sneakers and was busy pulling his jeans down his legs. He wasn't wearing underwear and was quickly naked.

The tattoos continued down his torso. Beautiful swirls and patterns in a rich silver color. And all of them were outlined in the same blue color as his eyes.

She continued to look lower. His legs also carried the strange, hypnotic pattern. That tattoo ended at his ankles.

Her knees turned to jelly, and Valeriya sat down hard on the steps. She didn't think Tarrant had stripped because he wanted to have sex, even though his shaft was fully erect.

No, this was about his tattoos and what they meant. Lots of men had tattoos, but very few had ones that perfectly bisected their body, including the genitals.

"You—" She broke off and shook her head, unable to believe what he was showing her. "You're a drakon." Her voice was weak. It was difficult to breathe. It was as though he'd sucked all the air out of the cavernous room.

Tarrant simply raised his arms in the air. Thick, plate-like armor raced down his arms and legs and over his chest. It shimmered silver and bright, but each scale was outlined in blue. His head changed, growing larger and wedge-shaped, and flattening on top. His jaw was elongated, and his eyes seemed to glow.

God, his huge body was around fifteen feet or so, and his tail was just as long. Eight-inch claws tipped both his hands and feet.

And then he spread his wings. They had to span at least thirty feet.

He was perfect. Exactly what she'd imagined a drakon to be. He flapped his wings and the breeze made the tendrils of her hair fly away from her face.

Then something occurred to her. "Are you really Darius Varkas?" Had he lied to her?

He threw back his head and roared. Valeriya slapped her hands over her ears and lowered her head to her lap. The sound was deafening and hurt her eardrums.

She'd take that as a no.

Something nudged her head. She slowly raised it to find

a scaly muzzle right next to her. She took a deep breath and reached out, but stopped a few inches from his face. "Is it okay?" She didn't want to do anything that might anger him.

He could devour her as a snack.

He lowered his large, wedge-shaped head. Taking that as permission, she placed her hand on his muzzle. He was warmer than she'd thought he'd be. Much warmer. The scales appeared icy cold, but he was hot.

"You're magnificent. Just as I'd imagined."

He inclined his head in agreement before moving away. When he was a good distance from her, he spread his wings again. Then he took flight.

"Holy shit." He was fast. And she had a feeling he wasn't even exerting himself. He also had amazing agility. He dipped and spun, taking the corners at an enormous speed. She closed her eyes, expecting him to crash, only to feel the backwash of air as he zoomed by her.

She laughed. She couldn't help herself. It was all so wonderful. She jumped to her feet and clapped, feeling like a child who'd just been given the most perfect present. Drakons were real, and she was looking at one. No matter what else happened in her life, she'd have this one special memory.

Then reality came crashing back down.

Tarrant was still winging around the room. She stepped away from the staircase and waved her arms at him. "Hey." He didn't seem to notice her, lost in the wonder of flight. She couldn't blame him, but they needed to talk. Now.

"Hey, Tarrant." He turned when she called his name. He rocketed toward her, coming to a halt with just inches to spare. She'd jumped back onto the staircase, not sure just how agile he was when it came to landing.

He heaved a sigh and a slight plume of smoke trailed out of his nostrils. She bet he could breathe fire, too. As much as she wanted to see that feat, she wasn't about to ask him to show her.

"Did the Knights see you when you took me from the cabin?" The last thing she wanted was for Tarrant to get on the radar of the Knights of the Dragon. "You took a huge risk. You shouldn't have done that."

His forehead rose, and he tilted his head to one side. He seemed surprised she was so upset. The air around him began to shimmer. The dragon faded, leaving only the man behind. He was just as impressive, if not more so.

He grabbed his jeans and pulled them on, but didn't button them. Was there anything sexier than a guy wearing nothing but jeans? Especially a sexy, tattooed guy?

Valeriya shook herself. This was not the time to be thinking about sex.

He strode toward her and cupped her chin in his hand. "Worried about me, sweetheart?"

She ignored the fluttering low in her belly at the endearment. He probably didn't mean anything by it. "Of course, I'm worried. Do you have any idea how much power the Knights have?" When he continued to look more bored than worried, she pressed on. "They have people in governments around the world, in law enforcement, in banking. Everywhere."

He sat on one of the steps, taking up so much space she was shoved against the railing. Before she could be totally squashed, she angled her body toward him.

"You don't need to worry."

"Yes. Yes, I do. I've seen firsthand just how powerful they are. They obviously found me here, even though I paid cash for my plane ticket. They were behind me the moment I left New York. Normal people can't do those kinds of things."

"I'm not normal," he pointed out.

"No, you're a drakon."

"Meaning what? I'm not as smart as them?"

He was frowning again, not a good sign. She hadn't meant to insult him. "I'm sure you're very smart. It's just there are a lot more of them." She clutched his biceps and tried to shake him. He didn't even move an inch. She sighed and pressed her hands against his cheeks. "I don't want anything to happen to you."

Tarrant was one of the few precious drakons in the world. Her family had been enslaving and destroying them for centuries. It was her job to right some of the wrongs perpetuated by them. And the way to do that was to protect Tarrant and any other drakon out there.

"Do you know Darius Varkas?" He tensed, his warm body turning almost to stone beneath her. She shivered, suddenly feeling chilled.

"Why do you want to know?" he asked.

"You could call him and warn him that the Knights know about him."

"He already knows."

"Oh." Just like that, she felt deflated. There'd been no need for her to leave New York at all. She'd thought to fly out here to help somehow. Instead, all she'd done was possibly put Tarrant in danger. "I don't know if the Knights know about you or not." She didn't mention her sister. It was easier for her to just use the generic term "Knights"—that large group that clung to the shadows but wielded great power.

• • •

Tarrant was still buzzing with power from having shifted into his dragon form. Having Valeriya watch him, seeing the delight in her eyes and hearing her praise, had made him feel good. It had also made him incredibly horny.

She was so serious, so set on protecting the world. He didn't like hearing her talk about his brother. Darius could look after himself. But he understood it. Darius meant nothing to her except a chance at redemption.

Because whether or not she realized it, Valeriya was trying to atone for the actions of her family. And that was impossible. The Knights had been hunting his kind since they'd first discovered a way to enslave them. But before that, in times long gone, they'd been friends and allies.

All that men craved now was power and wealth. Friendship and honor had little meaning in this modern world. They were destroying the planet and themselves along with it, and were too shortsighted to notice. Either that or they didn't care. Tarrant didn't know which was worse.

It was no matter to him. As a drakon, he'd be here long after the human race was nothing but a memory. His kind were tough and could survive almost anything. The problem was many of them no longer wanted to survive. Not alone.

"Tarrant?"

He'd been lost in thought, but now he brought his attention back to the amazing woman sitting beside him. "I don't know if the Knights know about me or not, but I'm quickly learning everything there is to know about this latest group."

"How?" She was so earnest, so worried. Still, a small part of him urged caution.

"Let's just say I have resources."

"I hope so, because the Knights have very deep pockets." She sighed and rested her head on his shoulder. That easily, he relaxed and pulled her closer. "How do they trap drakons?" she asked. "My grandparents never told me, and Karina never speaks of it, at least not around me."

He tensed, wondering why she wanted to know. But it was common enough knowledge among both the Knights and the drakons. "They have potions that render a drakon weak. They can then chain the creature. As long as they keep feeding it the potion, it can't shift back to human form, either." It had happened to far too many of them before they'd gotten wise and gone into hiding. "There are supposedly incantations and artifacts that can do the same thing." He'd lived a very long time and knew certain items had great power. So did words.

"That's horrible." Tears swam in her eyes. "How can they do such a thing?"

"Power. Wealth. Longevity. Freedom from disease. Men have been killing for less since the dawn of time.

"I know." She sighed and lowered her gaze. "That doesn't make it right or easier to bear."

He rubbed his hand up and down her delicate spine. "They'll never get a drakon's treasure. A drakon will die before giving it up." The words slammed down on him almost like a vow, like a spell of some kind.

He knew his words to be true. A drakon would die before relinquishing his treasure. Up until this moment, his greatest wealth had been the information he'd gleaned from the airwaves. He'd used it to build an empire.

He'd give it all up in a heartbeat to protect Valeriya.

She was now his greatest treasure. He'd never felt more vulnerable in his life. Even as a child, he'd known how to protect himself. And if he faltered, his brothers had come to his aid.

He had no defense against what Valeriya made him feel. God help them both if she ever betrayed him.

"What's wrong? You're so tense. I'm sorry if you're worried about the Knights. I know you must have lost friends over the years. I'm sorry for that, too, and for bringing up bad memories."

Tarrant knew he could never tell Valeriya what she meant to him. He would never give her the opportunity to betray him.

A little voice in the back of his head reminded him that Darius had trusted Sarah.

And look where that had gotten them. Father Simon was

dead because of it.

No, that wasn't fair. It was Tarrant's fault for asking his friend to help. And the ultimate blame lay with the Knights of the Dragon.

He would never risk Valeriya. He'd keep her safe.

He stood and lifted her into his arms. She gasped but didn't ask to be put down. Her trust in him settled some of the anger and confusion swirling around inside him.

"Where are we going?" she asked as he climbed the stairs.

He didn't want to talk. He needed to feel her bare skin against his, to claim her as his own, to mark her with his kisses. The dragon inside him wanted more, but Tarrant didn't know exactly what. Whatever it was, it would have to wait.

When he reached the top of the stairs, he pushed the door open. It slammed shut behind him. His phone chimed, and he paused.

"I have to take this." He carried her toward the kitchen and set her down on one of the stools. Only his brothers had his number.

Valeriya leaned her elbows on the counter and edged closer, making no pretense of giving him privacy. She was obviously going to try to hear every word.

He pulled his phone out of his back pocket and answered it. "Yeah?"

"Anything new to report?" Darius's deep voice boomed over the line.

"The Knights are after you." His brother already knew that, but he was curious to see Valeriya's reaction.

"I already know that," his brother replied.

Her eyes widened, and she mouthed the words, "Is that Darius Varkas?"

He nodded and kept talking. "I know, but Valeriya Azarov went to a lot of trouble to warn you, so I'm warning you."

"She's there in the room with you, isn't she?"

Always astute his brother. "Yeah."

"You need to be cautious. This isn't like with Sarah."

"No, it's not. Karina Azarov, Valeriya's sister, is the leader of the Knights of the Dragon."

"What!" Darius roared.

Tarrant pulled the phone away from his ear. Valeriya jerked back, her eyes wide. He put the phone back so he could continue the conversation. "I'm looking into it." That was all his brother needed to know. "I'll call you when and if I know something. In the meantime, stay safe." He couldn't say more, not with Valeriya sitting there.

He might want her more than anything else he'd ever coveted, but he would not put his brothers' lives on the line. After thousands of years of keeping secrets, he couldn't just start sharing. It went too much against his nature.

He ended the call and tossed his phone on the counter. It was locked and couldn't be opened without a password. Even if she could open it, she'd find nothing. He didn't keep any contact numbers on his phone and had created an app that wiped his history after each use. And since he was also the owner of the carrier company, it was easy to ensure that there was no physical record of any of his calls to be found.

His brothers were as safe as he could make them.

"That was him, wasn't it? That was Darius Varkas. Is he like you? I have so many questions to ask you. You must have lived a long time and seen so much."

Tarrant didn't like her interest in his past. He didn't want to be suspicious, but couldn't seem to help himself. "I'm more interested in the here and now."

He stalked toward her. She glanced down, and her eyes widened when she saw the bulge in his pants.

"There's something to be said for the present," Valeriya agreed as she slid off the stool and ran her hands up his bare chest.

Chapter Thirteen

Valeriya's thoughts were whirling with everything that had unfolded in the past hour. Tarrant was a drakon, one of those rare, elusive creatures she'd been obsessed with her entire life. He was big and beautiful in his dragon form—dangerous, too. But she'd been drawn to him before she'd ever known what he truly was.

Now she understood why he'd kept the lights off when they'd made love. It had kept her from seeing his distinguishing tattoos. There were plenty of big men walking around with colorful markings on their skin. But a drakon's tattoos were unique in the depth of their color, and their sheer beauty, as well as their placement.

Tarrant also knew Darius Varkas. Did that mean that Varkas was also a drakon? It seemed likely, even though she hadn't been able to learn a whole lot from their phone call.

And none of that mattered, not with Tarrant standing in front of her with his hands on her butt. Her palms rested against his taut abs. She felt positively tiny beside him, even though she wasn't a short woman. He was just so much bigger.

He pulled her close until her belly was pressed against the rather large bulge in the front of his jeans. Her drakon was aroused.

Her drakon.

Letting herself get more deeply involved with Tarrant wasn't smart. He was a drakon. The implication of that sunk in. He would be alive hundreds—no, thousands of years after she was dead. He'd already lived a very, very long time. Just trying to wrap her brain around it all was enough to make her dizzy.

He put the edge of his hand beneath her chin and tilted it upward. "What are you thinking?"

She clutched at his waist for support. His skin was so very warm. "You've lived for thousands of years, haven't you?"

The expression in his eyes went from warm to blank in a heartbeat. "You already know?"

She nodded. "Yes, I do, but I still can't quite reconcile it. You're four thousand years old."

He nodded. "I am."

She hated the tension thrumming between them. She much preferred the sexual heat. She cocked her head to one side and grinned. "You look pretty good for an old guy."

His jaw dropped, and then he threw back his head and laughed. It was a large booming sound that echoed throughout the space and made her smile.

He shook his head and the uncomfortable tension quickly dissipated, leaving behind a much different kind. "You're a dangerous woman, Valeriya."

"Me." She snorted. "They don't come any less dangerous than me." Her sister was the one to be afraid of. Valeriya was just a regular, ordinary woman.

He ran his hand up the length of her spine. "I don't know about that."

She shivered at his touch. There was no doubt where

this was leading. They'd made love before, but this was somehow different. She wasn't stupid enough to think there were no more secrets between them. Tarrant was a drakon. He probably had more secrets than a hundred people put together. But he'd shared his biggest one with her.

It made this seem more special somehow, more like they had a real connection.

"Where do you keep disappearing in that active mind of yours?" he asked. He didn't seem impatient or upset, just interested.

She lifted her arms and linked them around his neck. "I'm sorry. It's just a lot to take in."

He nodded. "I imagine it is. Much like finding out the sister of the woman you're sleeping with is your mortal enemy."

She winced. "I guess." This was worse than some Shakespearean drama. "This probably isn't a good idea, is it?"

He shook his head. "Probably not. But that's not going to stop me." He leaned down and kissed her. His lips were soft and warm, and Valeriya forget every reason why they shouldn't be together.

She went up on her toes to deepen the kiss. Her entire world had exploded, but she'd landed in the safest place possible. She honestly didn't think Tarrant would do anything to hurt her. She couldn't say the same about her sister.

Tarrant sucked on her tongue, drawing a moan from deep within her. The outside world could just leave them alone. All she wanted right now was to be with the man currently kissing her senseless.

"Bedroom," she muttered when he trailed kisses down her jawline and neck.

He shoved his hand under her top and pushed it up and over her head. "Too far away."

She had to agree. It was too far away.

He undid her bra, whisked it down her arms, and tossed it

aside. She helped him with that and then rubbed her breasts against his chest. Her nipples tightened. Tarrant had no chest hair. There was nothing but a broad expanse of warm skin and hard, rippling muscles.

And her earlier question had been answered. His skin was naturally bronze in tone, not tanned.

He bent and caught her around the back of the thighs and lifted. She wrapped her legs around his waist and hung on as he carried her over to one of the large sectional sofas. She thought he'd lay her down on it. Instead, he set her back on her feet.

His gaze was hot as he went down on one knee in front of her and undid her jeans. He unzipped her slowly, as if opening a present. She shivered with longing. No matter what happened, she could never regret her time with Tarrant. He was special in so many ways, and not just because he was a mythical creature, although that did add another layer to her already out-of-control attraction.

She shimmied her hips as he tugged the fabric down, taking her underwear along with her jeans. She put one hand on his shoulder for support as she stepped out of her clothes. He pulled off her socks at the same time, leaving her totally naked.

She wasn't the least bit cold. How could she be? The room was nice and toasty, not to mention Tarrant's heated gaze was warming her from the inside out.

"Your turn," she told him. He was only wearing jeans, but that was still way too much clothing. She wanted him naked.

She eased the zipper down and slid her hands into the opening of his jeans, spreading them wide over his hips. Tarrant groaned, and his erection sprang free from the confining fabric.

She ignored his jeans and traced a finger over a long blue vein running the length of his shaft.

"Valeriya." There was a wealth of warning in his tone. She ignored it.

Since the sofa was right there, she knelt on the cushions. Tarrant growled, more of a rumble actually, deep in his chest, but he didn't stop her.

She was fascinated with the silver tattoos swirling over the left side of his chest, down his flank, and ending at his ankle. Even the left side of his penis was tattooed, not to mention one side of his scrotum. It was incredibly sexy.

His shaft was long and thick with a broad head. She wrapped her fingers around him, feeling the pulse beat against her palm. She licked her lips and lowered her head.

"Fuck."

She ignored his unspoken plea to hurry. She wanted to take her time. His cock jerked toward her as she lapped at the slit on the top. He muttered something and then his fingers were nimbly undoing her braid. When he was done, he spread her hair over her shoulders.

She dragged her tongue around the broad head, circling it, licking it like she might an ice cream cone. He tightened his fingers in her hair and tugged lightly on her scalp.

Her drakon was exerting a tremendous amount of control.

Deciding she'd had enough of that, she opened her mouth and took him inside. His roar of pleasure made the dishes in the kitchen rattle. She shivered at the reminder of the primal power contained inside him.

He palmed the back of her head and guided her into a rhythm he liked, slowly gliding in and out of her mouth. With her hand wrapped around the base of his shaft, she controlled how deep he went.

He tasted salty and musky. Touching him, enjoying his obvious pleasure, was having an effect on her. An ache grew between her legs, deep in her core, and her breasts felt full.

"Enough," he told her. When she didn't immediately stop,

he stepped back.

She looked up at him and frowned. "I wasn't done." She'd barely gotten started. She reached out and gave his balls a light squeeze.

He toppled her back onto the sofa and dropped to his knees beside it. He had her legs draped over his shoulders and his face buried between her thighs before she could protest his heavy-handedness. But she really couldn't complain. Not when he was bringing her such intense pleasure.

• • •

Tarrant's dick was close to exploding. For all his years of experience and control, having Valeriya's sweet mouth on him had almost been too much.

She was fascinated with his tattoos. He'd seen her looking at them. He had a vision of lying on the bed while she ran her tongue over every swirl and line painting the left side of his body. Oh, yeah. That was his idea of a good way to spend an afternoon.

Maybe once he'd had her a couple of hundred times he wouldn't feel such a sense of urgency, a deep-seated need to mark her, to claim her before someone took her from him.

Having her mouth on him had been incredible. The wet heat surrounding him while her tongue teased, the slide of her hand up and down his length, and the little murmurs of pleasure she'd made had pushed him close to the edge.

Now it was his turn. He had her sprawled on the sofa with her legs over his shoulders. She was open to him in the most vulnerable way a woman could be. He wanted to bring her pleasure, to chain her to him with mind-blowing sex…and the promise of more.

He wanted her to choose to stay with him. What he didn't want to do was admit to any kind of tender emotions.

He might feel them, but it was safer to keep them to himself. Maybe if she stayed with him for a decade or two, he'd be able to finally declare them. In the meantime, he could bind her to him using sex.

He had plenty of money, but he didn't think using that as leverage would work with Valeriya. In fact, he knew it would only piss her off. He'd managed to learn something about women over the course of his long life. Some of them might be attracted to his wealth, but those weren't the kind he'd ever want in his life on a full-time basis.

He inhaled her arousal before dipping his tongue into her sweet core. She was wet and ready. He could take her now, but it wasn't enough. He wanted to hear her cries of release before he lost himself in her warmth.

Whether she knew it or not, he was hers, body and soul. It had been more than three thousand years since he'd shown his dragon form to a woman. Back in those days, humans had treated them more like gods, to be respected and feared. That had changed over the centuries. Plus, he'd gotten tired of women wanting him only because he was a powerful drakon.

Valeriya had slept with him before she'd known what he was. But if his being a drakon enthralled her and kept her with him, he wasn't too proud to use it. Darius would never let him live it down if he found out. Come to think of it, neither would Ezra or Nic. Best to keep his mouth shut.

She cried out as he ran the flat of his tongue over her clit. He felt the sting of her nails digging into his shoulders. He wanted to imprint himself on her body so she'd know who she belonged to. That might not be modern thinking, but he wasn't a modern man. He was a drakon, which meant half of him was a wild creature that lived by instinct.

He teased his fingers over her slit before sinking one inside. She gasped and raised her hips to take him deeper. Her eyes were closed, her lips parted. Her cheeks were flushed a lovely rose color. He liked her hair tumbling around her shoulders like a black cloud.

Her breasts were firm and full. He kept his hand between her legs as he levered up so he could capture one pert nipple between his lips and suck.

"Tarrant." She jerked upward and then fell back against the cushions. Her inner muscles rippled around his finger. He released her nipple and dove back between her thighs, licking and sucking her clit to prolong her orgasm.

She moaned and pleaded and gasped, and still he didn't stop. He loved the taste of her, like a succulent peach ripened by the midday sun.

He finally stopped and sat back. Her arms were over her head, half covering her face. She was panting hard, her breasts heaving with every lungful of air she pulled in.

He had to have her.

Tarrant stood and pulled Valeriya off the sofa. Her gaze was unfocused and she was frowning. He didn't have time to explain. He placed her behind the sofa and bent her over the cushioned back.

His need for her was like a living thing, driving him, pushing him. He used his own legs to spread hers wide. She moaned and leaned forward, tipping her ass more toward him.

He eased his cock between her damp folds, letting her essence coat him. He closed his eyes and gritted his teeth to keep from spilling himself before he got inside her.

Tarrant pressed the head of his cock against her opening and pushed. Just like before, there was resistance. He kept going, and her slick channel rippled and stretched to accept him.

He didn't stop. Couldn't stop. He kept up a steady pressure until he was buried to the hilt. He leaned forward, covering her with his larger body. She had her arms spread out along the back of the sofa. He linked their hands together and remained still while he caught his breath.

When he thought he could move without coming right away, he eased his hips back an inch or two and then pushed in again. Heaven. It was sheer heaven when she squeezed his dick, surrounding it in wet heat. He did it again and again. Each stroke got faster and deeper, harder and more desperate, until he was pounding into her.

He let go and allowed the pleasure to take him. His dragon roared inside him. Tarrant yelled as his release rocketed from the depth of his balls all the way up his shaft. Valeriya cried out and her warmth flooded him.

He kept pumping until she started to shake. He released her hands and pulled away. It was not an easy thing to do. He wanted to stay buried in the warmth and welcome of her body.

When she started to fall, he scooped her into his arms and all but fell on the sofa. She snuggled against his chest and wrapped her arms around his waist.

"Are you okay?" He'd gotten a little rough there at the end.

"Mmm." She nodded and rubbed her nose against his shoulder. He closed his eyes and enjoyed a rare moment of peace. It wasn't often that he wasn't thinking and planning, using the information that was his life's blood to expand his empire in some way that would protect him and his brothers.

Since Valeriya had arrived, she'd taken all his attention. He frowned when he realized he hadn't checked the stock markets or any of his usual news sites in hours. She hadn't been here long, and already she was changing him.

Tarrant wasn't sure he liked that. Since the alternative was not having Valeriya, though, he'd have to find a way to deal with it. Rules. He'd lay down some ground rules. They both had things they needed to do. She could work on her books, and he'd spend his time in his computer lab. Simple.

Not to mention, he could keep an eye on her from there.

Satisfied he'd found a solution to the problem, he was about to lay it all out for Valeriya when he felt the soft puff of her breath against his skin. She'd fallen asleep. He'd obviously worn her out.

Before he could get too pleased with himself, a low buzzing sound interrupted the moment. He eased away from Valeriya. She frowned and curled into a ball.

He grabbed his jeans and pulled them on before heading over to the security panel and turning off the alarm. Someone was on the property.

Tarrant detoured to his bedroom long enough to pull on a dark shirt and boots. He also grabbed the comforter off his bed and went back to the living area and draped it over Valeriya.

Her clothing was still strewn about. He smiled at the reminder of their passionate lovemaking. It quickly became a frown. Whoever was out there had interrupted their time together. He should go to his computer room to check things out. For that matter, he could even use his phone or tablet to access the security cameras. But he wanted to see for himself just what was going on. He'd just take a quick peek outside.

If it were just himself, he probably wouldn't bother, but he was protecting Valeriya. Both his human and dragon sides insisted he handle this matter personally.

He stepped over her bra and put the code into the panel. As the door opened and he stepped into the hidden staircase, he kicked the thin garment toward the door. He was so intent on finding out who'd disturbed them, he didn't realize the door hadn't click all the way shut behind him.

Chapter Fourteen

"We're here." Riggs opened his eyes as soon as the driver spoke. They'd turned off the main road and had been bumping along for some time. This cabin was about as isolated as one could get.

He opened the door and stepped out of the vehicle. He took the small communication device that was offered from one of his men and slipped it into his ear. "Spread out. I want the place surrounded."

"Yes, sir." They all took different directions, disappearing into the thick woods. These were his men, handpicked for the assignment. He'd been cultivating the small team for some time now, and they answered only to him. He didn't trust anyone that either Temple or Karina would assign to help him. He knew he was playing a dangerous game, but it was one he planned to win.

His men all had rifles, but he had a Sig Sauer P226. The weight was familiar, the weapon an extension of his hand. They were looking for a woman, not a dragon. Darius Varkas was long gone from here and would likely never return. Why

Valeriya Azarov chose to come here was something Riggs wanted to find out.

His men faded into the surrounding woods. The cabin was just around the bend. Riggs decided to take the fastest route—straight down the dirt road. He kept to the edge, though, in case he needed to hide.

His booted feet made little noise, and his tension grew with every passing second. He stopped when the cabin came into view. It looked deserted, but as he well knew, looks could be deceiving.

It was made of logs and had a front porch. There was no smoke coming from the chimney. Small piles of dead leaves had blown onto the steps. It looked like any rustic cabin. There was nothing special to distinguish it. Except for its isolation, this particular site had no defensive advantages.

Its effectiveness as a hiding place depended on no one knowing about it. Since Varkas had to know it was compromised, it was useless to him.

But where was Valeriya Azarov? And how had she managed to evade her sister's men? How had she even known they were watching her?

Riggs listened intently but heard nothing. Then it hit him. He heard nothing. No birds, no animals. Nothing.

Maybe one of his men hadn't been as quiet as they should have been. It was fall, and there weren't as many birds and animals around. But Riggs had been in this game too long. Something told him they weren't alone.

"Report." He whispered the word and quickly got three clicks in return. His men were out there. Everyone was accounted for.

More cautious now, Riggs approached the cabin. He took his time and circled the perimeter, peering in each window. There was no sign of anyone inside.

He rounded the front of the building and went up the

stairs, keeping to the side of the tread where it was less likely to creak. The hair on the back of his neck rose on end, and he whirled around.

The wind blew through the trees, shaking what few leaves remained. Something or someone was out there. Maybe it was nothing more than a wild animal. Either way, his men would have to deal with it.

Riggs put his hand on the doorknob and turned. Not surprisingly, it wasn't locked. There really wasn't any reason to do so all the way out here. If someone wanted to break in, they'd simply kick the door open or smash a window. Wasn't like there was anyone around to hear.

The door gave a low creaking sound as he pushed it inward. He stepped away from the opening and put his back against the wall. No one called out. No barrage of gunfire erupted.

Still, he waited.

After about five minutes, he moved, quick and low, into the space, gun up and ready to fire. He sniffed the air and caught the faintest hint of wood smoke and a touch of perfume or soap. Both were faint.

He took nothing for granted and searched both the bedroom and bathroom, finding nothing. When he knew for certain he was alone, he began a methodical search of the place. Other than the boxed and canned food in the kitchen area, the place was empty. Wherever Valeriya had gone, she'd left nothing behind.

He stood in the center of the living area. "Where are you?" he muttered. She hadn't had a vehicle. According to Karina's men, that had been picked up by the rental company. There was nowhere out here she could be, unless she was camping in the woods. That didn't seem likely. Valeriya was a city girl. He couldn't picture her roughing it in the wilderness. Not alone.

And that was the kicker. Maybe she wasn't alone. Maybe

she had help.

He slipped out the front door of the cabin, closing it behind him. If she'd left the area and there was a clue to be found, he'd find it.

And when he found her, he planned on keeping her with him. He didn't trust Karina. It might be useful to have an ace up his sleeve.

• • •

Tarrant watched from his perch high in the trees. From his research, he recognized the man going into the cabin. Matthew Riggs worked for Herman Temple. Tarrant had spent hours piecing together the comings and goings of all the major players. He knew that Riggs and Christian Temple had been the two men to visit Father Simon. There hadn't been any flight records, but there was camera footage of the two men leaving together. And since the younger Temple and a local had died along with Tarrant's friend, Riggs was the only person who really knew what had happened.

The urge to swoop in and grab him was great.

The only thing stopping him was that his instinct to protect Valeriya and his brothers was greater than his burning need for revenge.

The last thing Tarrant wanted was the Knights taking a closer look at this area. It wasn't likely they'd discover his lair, but he didn't want to tempt fate. Not the way things were going these days.

Matthew Riggs could leave here, but there was nowhere he could hide. Tarrant could afford to wait for a better time to question him. Time was on his side.

His preternatural vision and hearing allowed him to track all the men surrounding the cabin. There were four of them. As far as he could tell, they'd all arrived together.

They'd obviously been sent to look for Valeriya. Once again, doubt reared its ugly head. Had Valeriya expected to meet with Riggs? Was she working with another member of the Knights instead of her sister?

He shook his head. No, he couldn't believe that about her. Wouldn't believe it. She was too honest, too open for such subterfuge.

He settled in to watch and wait. He probably should have stayed inside and monitored them from his computer room, but the threat had been too great to allow his dragon half to remain safely inside while someone was threatening his woman.

He needed to be outside in case he had to defend her.

It comforted him to know she was safe in his lair right below their feet. They'd never find her. She was safe.

• • •

Valeriya was cold. Tarrant was no longer snuggling her, and she missed his big body wrapped around hers. He'd obviously covered her, because there was a comforter draped over her.

"Tarrant?" She sat up, shoved her hair out of her eyes, and looked around. There was no sign of him.

She pushed off the sofa and started to gather her clothing. It was awkward because she didn't want to drop the comforter. She sat back down long enough to pull on her socks. Since she also had her underwear and jeans nearby, she shook them out and tugged them on.

She had a vague memory of losing her shirt over in the kitchen area. Sure enough, it was lying in a heap on the floor. She padded over to the eating area and grabbed it. All she needed was her bra.

Tarrant had removed the garment and tossed it over his shoulder. She grinned as she scanned the room. It had to be around here somewhere. She could just leave it and go get a shower, but she didn't have that much clothing with her.

She caught sight of it over by the wall. A red light flashed on the security panel, but it made no sound. When she got closer, she realized the band of her bra was caught in the doorway. Was this really the way out?

She stopped a few feet away. What should she do? Had Tarrant gone outside? Here was her chance to find out exactly where she was.

Why was she so hesitant to leave this place?

Because she felt safe here. Because she didn't want to do anything that might hurt Tarrant.

She nibbled on her lower lip and continued to stare at the crack in the doorway. She could take a quick look just outside. That surely wouldn't hurt. They had to be safe here, didn't they?

If she was going outside, she'd need shoes.

She dumped the comforter on the sofa and pulled on her shirt. At this point, a bra was the least of her worries. She hurried to the room where her things were and dragged on a hoodie and yanked on her sneakers instead of her boots. She wasn't going far.

There was still no sign of Tarrant, and that worried her. He seemed super security-conscious.

Why had he gone outside? Was someone sneaking around? Had one of the Knights found them? If Tarrant was in danger, she couldn't just stay inside and do nothing.

"Don't jump to conclusions," she muttered. Her instincts began to tingle, but she couldn't be sure if it was because there was real danger outside or because she was so worried about Tarrant. Or maybe it was because she was considering going outside, something she knew Tarrant wouldn't want her to do. Her overactive imagination was an asset to her writing, but it did get her in trouble sometimes.

The door hadn't miraculously closed while she'd been

gone. The choice was hers. Go or stay.

She took a deep breath, eased her fingers into the crack, and pulled the door open. She wasn't sure what she'd expected to find, but there was an ordinary staircase in front of her. Made sense, since they were obviously underground.

Up it was. She put her hand on the rail, but at the last second made sure her bra was still draped across the opening. The last thing she wanted was to get locked out of the place.

If she was quick, maybe she could be out and back in again before Tarrant discovered her missing. Her stomach clenched. She didn't like the idea of lying to him, but she knew he wouldn't be happy she'd left the safety of his hideaway.

There was still time to turn around and go back. She could close the door, wait for Tarrant, and pretend this had never happened.

Her shoulders slumped forward. That wasn't going to happen, and she knew it. She had to know where she was. Most of all, she needed to know where Tarrant was.

Valeriya cautiously crept up the staircase. It was dimly lit, but her eyes adjusted to the light. When she reached the top, she was faced with another door. She listened intently but didn't hear anything.

Go or stay?

There was no choice, not really.

If there was a threat outside these doors, she couldn't allow Tarrant to face it alone. And if he was angry with her, well, he'd just have to suck it up and get over it.

Decided, she started searching for a lever or knob, some way to open the door. She ran her hands over the thick panel. Her fingers brushed a small indentation by the edge. She pressed it, and the door soundlessly slid open.

Valeriya blinked. Then she blinked again, not able to fully believe what she was seeing. It was the kitchen in the cabin. She'd been underneath the cabin the entire time. She didn't know whether to be angry at Tarrant for not telling her or amazed by his ingenuity. The Knights had no idea they'd literally been standing on top of a drakon.

She stepped out into the kitchen and listened intently but heard no sound. Her hip bumped the counter area that had slid away to reveal the opening. It glided shut before she could stop it. She heard the slight click and knew it was locked.

Panic threatened and she forced herself to take a deep breath. She ran her hand over the side of the cabinet but didn't find a lever. She knew the door was there, so she could find a way to open it. Or at least she hoped she could.

Before she could continue her search, a quiver went down her spine. Danger. There were no doubts this time, and she didn't question her instincts. Her talent had never let her down. Someone was nearby, and whoever they were, they weren't a friend.

The smartest thing for her to do would be to figure out how to open the secret door and make her way back to Tarrant's bunker. She'd be safe there.

But Tarrant was out here somewhere. The fact he hadn't discovered her missing and stopped her meant he was already outside. It didn't matter that he was an immortal drakon and could take care of himself.

She loved him.

"Oh God." She bent over and took several deep breaths. She was in love with a drakon. It had happened so fast that most people wouldn't believe what she felt was real. They'd think it was brought on by her dependency on him and his skills as a lover. And they wouldn't be totally wrong. But it went much deeper than that.

He was strong and caring and intelligent. Most of all, he touched something deep inside her, and for the first time in her life, she didn't feel so alone. Every instinct she possessed told her she'd never find a man who suited her as well as Tarrant did. It didn't matter that any relationship between them would not be an easy one, considering both their backgrounds, and the fact that he was still keeping secrets from her.

She was a fool to want to stay with him, but she knew she could no longer walk away.

In the meantime, nothing had changed. There was still someone out there besides Tarrant. Cognizant of the danger, she crept to the window and peeked out. She didn't see anyone, but she could sense them. There was more than one. She felt surrounded.

Her survival instincts warned her to return to safety, or at least to hide. She glanced around, but there really was nowhere. The closet in the bedroom had no door. The bed was too low for her to slip under. And time had run out. Her gift was practically screaming at her to move, to get out of the cabin.

She needed to get outside where she could find a place to hunker down until whoever was here left. And if she could catch a glimpse of them, she might be able to help Tarrant identify them once they were gone. He kept saying he had resources, but he was vague about that. She really had no idea what he knew or didn't know about the Knights. They had more power than he could imagine.

Or maybe he knew everything.

Valeriya rested her forehead against the cool log wall. She was working blind here. She might love Tarrant, but she was under no illusions he felt the same way. He wanted her and talked about keeping her, but a part of her didn't trust he wasn't just saying that to keep her cooperative.

Trust wasn't easy for either of them.

There was no time to second-guess her actions. She was here now and had to deal with it.

She glanced at the wall containing the secret doorway. There was also no time for her to fumble around searching for a way to open it. There were people too close to the cabin, and they'd hear her for sure. She needed to get outside and hide. It was her only option.

The front door was too obvious, too open. She went to the back of the cabin and listened with all her senses, using her talent for detecting danger. Long seconds ticked away. Her heart beat louder until she was sure whoever was outside had to be able to hear her. Sweat made her shirt cling to her, in spite of the cool temperature inside the cabin. She rubbed her palms up and down her thighs and waited for the right moment to move.

Now. She didn't hesitate. She opened the door and swiftly moved through it, making sure she silently closed it behind her. It made more sense to head right, into the thickest part of the surrounding forest, but she went left, because that's where her instincts were telling her to go.

The wind whipped around her, nipping at her bare skin and sliding up the cuffs of her hoodie. It really was bitterly cold.

She put her head down and kept going.

Then she felt a tug from the left. Someone was coming from that direction. She turned right but knew that way wasn't safe, either. She hurried straight ahead, hoping she could slip between whoever was out there.

Because she was so distracted, she missed the telltale sign she was heading straight into danger.

"Well, well, well. Thank you for making my job so easy. I didn't expect to run into you out in the woods."

She didn't recognize the man walking toward her, but she knew his type. He was a big man in dark clothing, and he carried a gun in his hand like he knew how to use it.

She eased her shoulders back and gave him the haughtiest expression she could muster. It was one she'd seen her sister use a hundred times. He halted, tilted his head to one side, and studied her.

"You look like your sister."

Obviously, Karina had sent him. But why? "Who are you and why are you here?" Better to go on the offensive. She hoped he couldn't hear the quiver in her voice or see the trembling in her body.

"I'm here to bring you home, of course." He stalked toward her like a tiger tracking prey—slowly and with great menace. "Your sister is not happy with you."

That was probably an understatement. Karina did not like to be inconvenienced in any way. Valeriya didn't want to go, didn't want to leave Tarrant, but she couldn't allow them to find him. "Fine. Let's go."

She turned to leave, but he caught her arm. "Not so fast, sweetheart." He studied her intently. She kept her expression as blank as she could. "You and I are going to have a little chat first."

He dragged her back toward the cabin. She thought he might take her inside, but he pulled her onto the front porch instead.

She swallowed her fear and stood facing him. "Tell me who you are first."

He shook his head. "Not important. I need to know why you're here and how you managed to evade the men your sister sent to watch you." He pointed the gun at her in a casual gesture. "That was quite the feat. You upset quite a few people coming out here on your own."

Valeriya would tell him everything. Everything that had nothing to do with Tarrant. She'd protect her drakon to her last breath.

"Fine. I'll tell you what you want to know. But not until I know your name." It was important. It would allow her to talk to him on a more personal level and maybe keep him from hurting her. It wasn't much but it was all she had.

He shrugged. "Riggs."

Chapter Fifteen

Tarrant looked down at his chest, certain his heart had been ripped from his body. There was no other way to explain the pain coursing through him. Valeriya was not only outside, but she was talking with Riggs.

How had she gotten out of the bunker? Was she more technically savvy than she'd let on? Had she been waiting for Riggs all along?

Smoke billowed from his nose, and he had to drag himself back under control before he compromised his location. Valeriya had betrayed him, and she knew his biggest secret. Worse, she would tell Riggs, and her sister, about this place. About his brothers.

He would have to destroy it. After he dealt with them.

His dragon roared inside him. Even after this obvious betrayal, the creature still wanted Valeriya. So be it. Maybe he wouldn't kill her, but she'd never see the outside again, and he'd never trust her.

He kept all his senses open and listened. He needed to know what she told Riggs.

"We should leave here. We can talk on the way." Valeriya huddled near the end of the porch with her arms wrapped around her. She had to be cold.

Tarrant didn't like that. He shook his head in disgust. What did it matter when the woman had betrayed him?

Riggs leaned against the railing, his gun still in his hand. "Why are you in such a hurry to leave?"

"You caught me. There's really no reason to hang around here. I'm tired of roughing it."

Tarrant frowned. This wasn't right. Why wasn't she telling Riggs everything she knew? Did she know he was out here? She had to, he supposed. If he'd stayed inside, she never would have found a way out.

"Not so fast," Riggs told her. "I want to know why you're here. How did you find out about this place?"

Tarrant narrowed his gaze. Valeriya was trembling. From the cold or from fear, he couldn't say. His nails turned to claws and dug into the tree he was hiding in.

"What does it matter?"

Riggs stirred from his position and pushed away from the railing. "Call it my need to know." There was an underlying threat that had Tarrant fighting to keep his beast in check.

"Fine." Valeriya looked out over the yard. "When I last visited Karina and she left to get ready, I went into her office. There was a pad of paper on the desk. I ran a pencil over it and got an impression of numbers." She turned her gaze back to Riggs. "They were coordinates that led me here."

Riggs chuckled. "So much fuss because of this. Why did you bother to come here?"

Valeriya shrugged. "I overheard part of a phone conversation as well. I knew Karina was looking for a man and that he'd been here. I thought I could warn him if he came back."

Tarrant's heart began to beat faster. She was telling Riggs

exactly what she'd told him. Was she what she seemed to be in all this—a courageous, innocent woman?

But if that was the case, how had she gotten outside and why?

Riggs shook his head. "I'm not buying it. Oh, I don't doubt that most of the story is true. Karina will be pissed when she finds out you were spying on her."

"She shouldn't be surprised. She spies on me all the time. She spies on everyone." Valeriya canted her head to one side. "You sound very familiar with my sister. Are you sleeping with her?"

"None of your business," Riggs told her.

"She likes strong, useful lovers," Valeriya continued as though Riggs had never spoken. "She doesn't keep them long."

Tarrant inwardly swore. What was she doing provoking Riggs? Was she trying to make him angry? If so, it was working.

Riggs strode to Valeriya, grabbed her by the arm, and yanked her closer. "You don't know anything about me and Karina."

The look Valeriya gave him was filled with pity. "No, it's you who doesn't know anything about Karina. Power is everything to her. She'll crush you as easily as she has the rest. Who did you betray to come to her attention?"

"How did you evade the men she'd sent to watch you?" Riggs shook her. Tarrant growled, not liking another man touching his woman.

"I just did. I'm good at that kind of thing. I did grow up in the home of the leader of the Knights of the Dragon. While I want nothing to do with them, it was impossible not to learn something."

Everything inside Tarrant stilled. She hadn't mentioned him or his bunker at all. She wasn't going to betray him. He was still mad as hell at her for leaving the protection of his home. They'd hash that out once he got rid of Riggs and his men.

"There's something you're not telling me." Riggs ran the muzzle of his gun over the curve of her jaw. "What are you hiding?"

Tarrant had seen enough. He released the branch he was holding and dropped down to the ground, landing lightly on his feet. He raised his head and sniffed the air. There was a man off to his right. Tarrant smiled and began to hunt.

• • •

Valeriya was scared, but she was determined, too. She would protect Tarrant to her dying breath, which, unfortunately, might be a lot sooner than she'd anticipated. She'd seen men like Riggs before, men desperate for power and wealth. She didn't think it was money driving Riggs, but the need for power, for strength.

"I'm not hiding anything."

"Then where are your belongings? Where's your clothing? Where have you been living? Because it's not in the cabin. The stove is cold, and so are the ashes in the fireplace."

She was momentarily at a loss. Then her imagination kicked in. "I took everything out into the woods, but a bear attacked my campsite. Everything was destroyed. I was coming back here when I saw one of your men." There was no way she'd tell Riggs she could sense his men. Better to say she'd seen one.

She held her breath as he considered her words. He looked like he believed her. Then he shook his head. Her heart sank. "I'm not buying it."

"Whether you buy it or not, it's the truth." It was the only truth she was willing to tell him.

The smile he gave her sent chills slithering down her spine. "We'll see about that. There are ways to loosen your lips."

"My sister won't like it if you hurt me." She wasn't sure that was true, not anymore, but it was the only hope she had.

Riggs leaned so close their lips were almost touching. "The only thing Karina will mind is not getting to kill you herself, so I'll leave that for her. There's a lot of room between healthy and dead."

Valeriya's blood ran cold. He was going to torture her. Furthermore, she thought he might actually enjoy himself. "What kind of man are you?" She hadn't meant to ask that question aloud.

His slow smile made her shudder. "The kind who gets what he wants." He dragged her toward the front door and opened it. Before he shoved her inside, Valeriya glanced toward the woods, hoping Tarrant was far away and safe.

The door slammed behind them with a finality that made her jump. Then a sense of calm settled over her.

Riggs hauled her across the room and shoved her down onto one of the kitchen chairs. He went into the kitchen and set his gun on the counter. "Don't even think about running," he told her, "or I'll shoot you in the leg."

There was nowhere for her to run. He had men waiting outside. She had no idea how many, but at least two more. She tried to think of what she could do to escape. If she could get outside, she had a chance.

Riggs was busy lighting the kitchen stove, and she didn't think it was because he wanted a cup of tea. She glanced around the room searching for anything she could use as a weapon.

There was an iron poker by the fireplace, but that was on the other side of the room. And a poker was no defense against a gun.

She had to do something. She couldn't just sit here and let him hurt her.

Better to make a run for it and be shot than meekly sit here like a lamb waiting to be slaughtered.

Adrenaline pumped through her veins. It was now or never. She surged up off the chair, grabbed it by the back, and swung. Riggs was already turning around, gun in hand, when she brought the edge of the chair down on his arm. He swore, and the gun clattered to the floor.

He batted the chair out of her hands and lunged. Anticipating such a move, she was already in full flight. She raced for the door. She heard Riggs swearing behind her. She had the door open and was on the deck when the loud retort of a gunshot echoed in her ears.

She stumbled and fell down the two stairs, landing heavily on the ground. Her right calf stung, and she'd skinned her palms catching herself. She rolled back to her feet and pushed off the ground. The trees—she had to get to the trees.

Another gunshot rang out. It was as though someone had shoved her forward. Valeriya jerked and fell face down in the dirt. He'd really shot her. The bastard.

The only comfort she had was the fact he didn't know anything about Tarrant.

"You stupid bitch." Riggs shoved his foot under her stomach and rolled her onto her back. The pain was agonizing, and her vision began to dim.

"Oh, no," he told her. He reached down and dragged her to her feet. "You're not going to die. At least, not yet. Not until you've told me everything you know."

Valeriya felt herself drifting away and absently noted the trail of blood she was leaving on the ground behind her.

A loud sound reverberated around them, shaking the branches in the surrounding trees. She thought it might be thunder. She peered up at the sky. It was cloudy, but there was no sign of a storm. The woods around them went strangely silent, as though the entire world was holding its breath.

Riggs swore and released her. She crumbled to the ground in a heap.

"Varkas is here, isn't he?" Riggs demanded.

At least she could tell him the truth. "No, he isn't."

• • •

Tarrant had dispatched the last of the three men in the woods when he heard the first gunshot. He raced back toward the cabin, moving faster than he ever had in his life, praying Valeriya hadn't been shot. Her sister was the leader of the Knights. He'd never dreamed Riggs would really hurt her, but he should have. The Knights had no sense of honor or loyalty, not like drakons did.

Before he could get there, another gunshot echoed through the trees.

No! No! No!

He couldn't be too late. Not this time. He hadn't been able to do anything to save his friend. Father Simon had been murdered by the Knights. That had been painful enough. He didn't think he could live if Valeriya died.

She was his heart and his soul.

The wind began to whip up around him. He roared, the booming sound ripping through the woods like thunder.

When he reached the cabin, Valeriya was lying on the ground, and there was a trail of blood behind her. Over her stood Matthew Riggs.

"You're not Varkas." He seemed surprised by that.

"No, I'm not." He took a step forward but stopped when Riggs lowered his gun and pointed it at Valeriya's head. She was wounded and hurt, but she was still alive. He could hear the low beating of her heart.

"One step closer, and I'll shoot her."

"Shoot her, and you're dead."

"I'm the one with the gun," Riggs pointed out. He touched the communication device on his ear. "Where are you?" he demanded of his men.

Tarrant crossed his arms casually over his chest when what he really wanted to do was rush at Riggs and tear him limb from limb. But Riggs was too close to Valeriya. If he shot her at such close range, he wouldn't miss.

"I don't think you'll be getting any help from that quarter."

Riggs sneered. "So her job was to distract me while you took care of my men. Who are you? Do you work for Varkas?"

He shook his head. "Why are you all so interested in Darius?" He paused and smiled. "When I'm right here in front of you."

Tarrant shifted. His clothing ripped as his dragon leaped forward. Familiar plate-like armor raced down his arms and legs. His body expanded and his limbs changed shape and size. His jaw lengthened and his head flattened. But it was his tail he needed, and he employed it like the deadly whip it was. He snapped it out and hit Riggs's body, driving the man twenty feet in the air. He'd held back because he wanted him incapacitated, not dead. Not yet.

Riggs yelled as he flew through the air. He smashed into the trunk of a large oak tree. The crack of bones was loud and satisfying.

Tarrant stalked toward his prey. He might have miscalculated slightly. Riggs's chest was caved in and his breathing was labored. Blood bubbled around his lips and ran from his nose. This was Tarrant's one chance to find out what had really happened to Father Simon.

Then Valeriya's breathing changed, becoming shallower. Tarrant forgot all about Riggs, no longer caring if the man lived or died, and hurried to her side. He shifted as he went, and was back in his human form when he fell to his knees beside her. She was bleeding from her upper right shoulder and her right calf.

The bastard had shot her twice.

"Valeriya." He put his hands down to move her, but was almost afraid to touch her. He didn't want to hurt her any more than she already was.

Her eyelids fluttered open, and she frowned. "Get away."

Pain struck him like a sledgehammer. Had she seen him attack Riggs? Was she afraid of him now? It didn't matter. She'd just have to get over her fear. After this incident, he wasn't letting her out of his sight.

She licked her lips, her expression one of fear and worry. "Not safe." She pushed at his arm. "Go."

If he'd thought his heart had broken when he'd believed she'd betrayed him, it was nothing compared to what he was feeling now. She was trying to protect him. She was human, a female, and injured, and she was protecting him, a male drakon.

He split the leg of her jeans and sighed with relief when he discovered the calf injury was only a flesh wound. He ripped off a piece of the garment so he could wrap a makeshift bandage around her leg. Then he went to work on the more serious wound in her shoulder.

He worked quickly and methodically to make padding from the thicker hoodie material and then bound it with the thinner fabric from her shirt. It got more difficult to see what he was doing as he worked. Something wet flowed down his cheek and landed on her chest.

He ignored the distraction and kept going until the wound was covered. It would do until he got her inside.

"It's safe," he promised her as he finished. "There's nothing for you to worry about." He brushed the hair out of her face. "I've bound your wounds, but I need to get you inside."

She nodded. "Okay." She blinked and looked beyond him to where Riggs was lying. "Is he—" She swallowed and didn't finish.

"He's not dead. Not yet. The men who came with him are." Tarrant refused to lie to her. This was war, and people would die. It was the choice the Knights had made when they started hunting his kind.

She frowned as she reached up and touched his face. "You're crying."

"I'm not." He'd never cried. Not once in his entire existence. It was ridiculous to be starting now. Valeriya was injured, but he'd take care of her and make her well.

Drakon tears were too rare and precious to shed indiscriminately. Each type of dragon was unique. The tears of an earth drakon became the most perfect diamonds. For fire drakons it was rubies, and for water drakons it was sapphires. But as an air dragon, his tears turned to the most exquisite emeralds.

And a drakon cried for only one reason—his heart was breaking.

To distract her, he lifted the precious green gems from her chest and held them in his hand. "These are for you."

Her eyebrows furrowed as she stared at the glittering stones. "Are those emeralds?" She went to reach for one and gasped again, closing her eyes as pain rocked her.

Tarrant had to heal her, but he couldn't leave Riggs alive. He wasn't about to take any chances. "I'll be right back," he promised.

He strode over to Riggs. The man was still clinging to life. His eyes were wide open, but there was no fear there, only regret. "You're—" he managed to gasp.

"A drakon," Tarrant finished for him. "Yes, I am." He crouched beside the man. "We left you alone for centuries, but you wouldn't leave us in peace. This time we're fighting back."

He glanced over at Valeriya, who was watching and listening to every word.

"What happened with Father Simon?"

Riggs's gaze widened. "You know." The words were faint gasps.

"He was my friend. I think you killed Christian Temple and Father Simon."

Riggs struggled for breath and then exhaled one final time. Tarrant knew the answers he needed had just died with the man.

Anger and regret tore through him. He clenched his hands and blew out a deep breath. He had to let it go. It had to be enough that Father Simon's murderer had been brought to justice. Whether it was Christian Temple or Riggs who had killed him, both men were dead now. That had to be justice enough. It was all he was going to get.

He left Riggs lying in the dirt and went back to Valeriya. He calmly collected the large gems scattered around her and held them out. "Here, take them, they're yours."

She held out her left hand and he poured the dozen perfect emeralds into her palm. She looked at them and blinked. "Where did they come from?"

Tarrant carefully slipped his hands beneath Valeriya and lifted her off the ground. He carried her up the stairs and into the cabin. He didn't speak as he activated the staircase and walked down. His gaze widened when he noted her bra was jammed between the door and the frame to keep it from closing.

He kicked it aside and the door slammed shut behind him. He carried Valeriya into his bedroom and laid her on his bed. Her fingers were clenched tightly around the gemstones he'd given her.

He manually turned on the bedside lamp to supplement the dim glow coming from the baseboard lighting. He captured her hand and slowly uncurled her fingers to display the fortune in emeralds she held there.

He sighed and bowed his head. "Those are drakon tears. They're rare and precious and they belong to you." He removed them and placed them on the nightstand.

He leaned down and kissed her sweet lips. "We have a lot to talk about. First and foremost, about how and why you left the safety of the bunker."

When she glanced guiltily away, he caught her chin between his thumb and forefinger and turned her face back to him. "I'll take care of your injuries first. Then I need to go back outside and take care of the evidence. I can't afford to have anyone discover the bodies or their vehicle."

Valeriya nodded. Her eyes closed and she sighed. He was an idiot. She had to be in a lot of pain, even if she wasn't saying so. She'd also lost a significant amount of blood. Not enough to be life threatening, but more than enough to weaken her substantially.

He could take the old-fashioned route and clean and stitch her wounds. Or he could take a drastic measure that would signify another step forward in their relationship.

He rose from the bed and walked into the bathroom. There was a glass sitting on the vanity next to the sink. He retrieved it and went back to the bedroom.

Valeriya's eyes were closed. It was just as well. She probably didn't need to see this part. Exercising great control, he allowed one claw to emerge and raked it over his forearm. When blood began to flow, he held it over the glass until it was less than a quarter full. She wouldn't need much.

The wound was already healing, so he licked the excess blood from his arm.

"Valeriya." He gently pushed one arm beneath her back

and raised her up. Her eyelids fluttered open. Her eyes were more unfocused than they'd been, and that worried him. "I have some medicine for you to drink." He was more certain than ever that this was the right way to heal her.

He held the glass to her lips and tilted it up. She parted her mouth and his blood flowed into her. When she'd swallowed it all, he gently pressed his lips to hers.

Then he waited.

Chapter Sixteen

Valeriya was exhausted, not just physically, but emotionally. In spite of growing up in a family steeped in the work of the Knights, she'd never been subjected to such violence. Riggs might have killed her. And if he hadn't, her sister probably would have when he'd finally taken her in.

Then there was Tarrant. He'd swooped in like a hero and rescued her. She didn't like being the damsel in distress, but she didn't mind her drakon stepping in to help. He'd been magnificent. A brutally efficient fighting machine.

And who was Father Simon? Obviously, Tarrant believed Riggs was somehow responsible for the man's death. There was so much she didn't know about Tarrant. So many secrets.

The medicine he'd given her tasted slightly sweet, and his lips were warm. She sighed and felt herself drifting off again.

Her eyes flew open as a blast of heat shot through her. It felt as though her internal organs were on fire, as though she were burning from the inside out. "What's happening to me?" She cried out as the pain grew deeper and harder to bear.

Tarrant stretched out on the bed and dragged her into

his arms, holding her immobile. "I've got you," he promised. "Everything will be fine."

But she wasn't so sure. She could barely feel his arms around her. Fire blazed through her limbs and into her core. It snaked through her body, consuming everything in its path.

Had the bullets hit something vital? Was she having some kind of allergic reaction to whatever medicine Tarrant had given her? Sweat coated her skin, and breathing was becoming almost impossible.

She was dying. There was no way she could live through this, whatever it was. After everything they'd been through together, she couldn't die without telling him the truth. He deserved it. They both did.

"Love you," she whispered.

Then she was lost to the fires raging within her. This was what hell must feel like. The thought came and went in a heartbeat. The flames roared through her. Just when it seemed they would consume her, the fire went cold.

She sucked air into her starving lungs. Her fingers hurt. She looked down at them only to discover they were gripping Tarrant's hands so hard they were stark white. She had to be hurting him. She made herself ease her grip, when all she really wanted to do was hold on.

He hadn't replied to her confession. Had she even said it out loud? She honestly didn't know if she'd managed to speak or if she'd only thought the words.

Exhaustion ate at her. Valeriya was more tired than she'd ever been. She had no idea what was happening to her, but she no longer felt in danger of burning to a crisp.

She had so many questions to ask Tarrant but was too darn tired to ask them.

He kissed her temple and gently released her. She immediately missed the heat from his body. The sheets were like ice against her skin, and she flinched. Then the shivering began. She'd been burning hot only moments before, and now she was chilled to the bone. It was like the worst flu she'd ever had, but times a thousand, maybe even a million. And that wasn't an exaggeration.

Tarrant swore and tucked the blankets around her, then cradled her against his large body once again. She might not have known him for long, but it felt so right to be lying together like this. The heat he gave off seeped through the biting cold. She snuggled closer and buried her nose against his bare chest. The man was better than a furnace.

He stroked her face, gently pushing aside several strands of her hair. Her shoulder no longer hurt, and her calf had stopped throbbing. Strange, but she actually felt pretty good, especially for a woman who'd been shot twice. Whatever Tarrant had given her was potent stuff.

"Sleep." His deep voice seemed to echo inside her. She closed her eyes and sighed. She'd rest for a bit, but they needed to talk.

• • •

Tarrant knew the second Valeriya fell into a deep sleep. The amount of blood he'd given her was just enough to heal her injuries, but she'd still need rest and food to replenish her blood loss. Maybe he should have given her more, but he hadn't wanted to risk it. There was no telling how a person would react to drakon's blood. It would help in the long run, but it could be brutal while it was working, especially if the person ingesting it had an injury or disease.

He'd hated having to put her through even more pain, but it was worth it. She was sleeping peacefully. He hadn't removed the makeshift bandages he'd fashioned, but he knew her wounds would be healed.

He waited as long as he dared, not wanting to leave

Valeriya alone.

She loved him.

The words echoed in his mind even as he warned himself not to take them to heart. She'd been hurt and out of her mind with pain when she'd uttered them.

It was a monumental task to make himself ease away from her. He wanted to stay by her side and protect her. He stood beside the bed and stared down at her small form huddled beneath the blankets. The emeralds glittered on the bedside table. He swore under his breath and turned off the lamp.

There was work to be done. She probably hadn't meant what she'd said, anyway. It was just reaction to everything that had happened.

But oh, how her declaration made his heart soar.

Realizing he was still naked, he detoured to the closet long enough to grab a pair of jeans. He stepped outside the room, closed the door, and yanked on his pants. It took everything in him to walk away. Every instinct he had was screaming at him to stay. But the way to protect her best was to deal with the mess he'd left outside.

He strode down the hallway. He didn't give himself time to think and went straight to work. His phone was outside. Not good.

This time, he made sure the access panel to the stairwell was closed behind him. He took the stairs two at a time and didn't hesitate when he reached the top. Everyone outside was already dead. The secret door slid open and he stepped out into the cabin. The stove was still warm from the fire Riggs had started earlier. The shattered pieces of a chair littered the floor.

He didn't want to think about what had happened. He'd have to ask Valeriya, since Riggs was dead. Or better yet, view the security footage so she didn't have to relive the event.

He gathered the pieces of the broken chair and fed them

into the stove. Better to burn them than to leave them lying around. If someone came looking, it would make them ask questions.

He walked around the cabin, making sure everything else was in place. When he was satisfied all was as it should be, he stepped out onto the porch. The October air was chilly in the mountains. His feet and upper body were bare, but the cold didn't bother him in the least.

He left Riggs where he was and made a circuit around the cabin, collecting one body at a time. No predators had approached them yet. They no doubt scented Tarrant and were wary about encroaching.

He carried each body back to the clearing in front of the cabin. He methodically searched each one but didn't find anything to identify them, which wasn't surprising. These men were pros.

Thankfully, they'd been careful and quiet while moving through the woods and had left little sign of their passage. That cut down on the amount of work Tarrant had to do, and it wasn't long before what little trace there had been was erased.

Tarrant went in search of what remained of his clothing. He didn't care about the garments, but he wanted the phone he'd tucked in the back pocket. He drew it out, turned it on, and smiled when it still worked. He strode back to the dead men and took pictures of them all. They might not have any identification on them, but he'd find out who they were.

He piled the bodies and the remains of his tattered clothing in a pile. Then he went over to Riggs. Searching him was a long shot. A man like Riggs didn't make mistakes. Or at least, not many. He'd certainly made one in coming here, and it had been fatal. He was almost finished when he found a secret pocket in Riggs's jacket. It contained a cell phone. Now that could be interesting. He quickly went through the contacts list and call history. Not surprisingly, it was sparse. There was only one number. He memorized it and then put the phone back where he'd found it.

He grabbed Riggs by the ankle and dragged him over to the pile. He couldn't afford to leave any sign that the men had been here. That meant he couldn't bury them. He had no choice but to burn them.

Tarrant removed his jeans and set them aside, making sure his phone was safely tucked inside the pocket. He could breathe fire in his human form, but it was much hotter and more effective as a dragon. Easier, too. He raised his arms and shifted. His dragon burst forth, more than happy to help with this part of the cleanup. These men had attacked Valeriya. For that, they deserved to burn.

He had to work to control the dragon half of him. The beast wanted to lay waste to everyone and everything. But that would only bring more attention to them, and to Valeriya. That would put her in danger.

Keeping a tight rein on his dragon half, he opened his mouth and flames shot out. It was hotter than anything in the human world, more akin to the molten core of the earth. The bodies ignited and were turned to ash in under a minute. When nothing remained of the four men, Tarrant let the flames die out.

As an air drakon, he controlled the wind as easily as he breathed. He gathered the cool air around him and blew gently. He only wanted to disperse the ashes, not start a hurricane. Ash and dust swirled into the air before taking to the currents and flowing in every direction. When Tarrant stopped, the only thing remaining was dirt.

He shifted to his human form, then pulled his jeans back on, grabbed his phone, and placed a call. He didn't give his brother time to speak when he answered. "I had visitors."

Darius swore. "What the hell happened?"

"I had a visit from Riggs and his crew. I'm not sure who sent him, Temple or Karina Azarov."

"They didn't find anything, did they?" He hesitated long enough for his brother to start swearing again. "What aren't you telling me, Tarrant?"

"I went outside to keep an eye on them." He started walking down the road. He had to find the vehicle the men arrived in.

"Why the hell would you do that?" Darius demanded.

"It was the right thing to do." And he wasn't about to justify himself to his older brother. He knew Darius was going to lose his mind, but he couldn't hold back the truth. "Valeriya left the bunker."

Complete silence. He'd actually stunned his brother. He couldn't help but grin as he rounded a turn in the road.

"How. The. Hell. Did. That. Happen?" Each word was enunciated slowly and precisely.

"Not sure yet. Haven't had time to look into it." The SUV was parked on the side of the road. Since none of the men had been carrying the keys, he hoped they were inside.

"You haven't had time. Then what the fuck have you been doing?"

Tarrant growled and had to shake himself before he spoke and said something he'd regret. "Since Valeriya was shot trying to protect me, and you, by the way, I was busy taking care of her."

"I'm sorry man." He could hear the sincerity in Darius's voice, and it calmed him. "How is she?"

"Sleeping." He opened the door and slid into the driver's seat of the SUV. As he'd hoped, the keys were there. He started the vehicle and began to back it down the road.

"Did you have to—" Darius broke off, but Tarrant knew what his brother was asking.

"Yes, but only a small amount. Enough to heal her

injuries. She's still weak." When he reached a small opening in the trees, he turned the vehicle around and headed down the road. There was a pond not far from here that would do for what he had planned.

"How do you feel about her?"

That was the big question, wasn't it? He sidestepped it. "I can't let her go." That was enough for now. He didn't want to love a human woman. Valeriya would die unless he fed her his blood. He wasn't sure it was something she'd want. She'd be tied to him for eternity. That was a lot to ask of any woman.

Darius sighed. "I know you're driving. I can hear the engine. What's going on?"

"I burned the bodies and destroyed all the evidence. I'm getting rid of the vehicle now."

"You should come out east."

Tarrant heard Ezra muttering in the background, "I'm not running a damn hotel. Fuck, tell him to come. And he can bring the woman."

He knew his brother would open his home, even if he didn't fully trust Valeriya. That meant a lot to him.

"Tell Ezra thank you for his heartfelt invitation, but I'm sticking around for now. I want to know if anyone else is going to show." Plus, he really didn't want to share Valeriya with anyone else. It was his possessive drakon nature.

"Is that wise?"

He shrugged away Darius's concern. "It's what has to happen." He couldn't just abandon his home, not if there was a chance he could gain more information about what the Knights were up to.

He also wanted to spend more time alone with Valeriya. There were so many things they needed to discuss. Not the least of which were her feelings for him.

"Gotta go. I'll call later."

"You do that," Darius replied.

Tarrant knew his brothers were worried about him, but he was fine. He ended the call and tucked his phone safely in his pocket. He'd already been away from Valeriya for far too long. He pushed the gas pedal to the floor. It took him under ten minutes to reach his destination.

He climbed out of the vehicle and took several minutes to thoroughly search it. There was no identification in the glove box, and he left the weapons where they were. There would be no evidence that Riggs and his crew had been anywhere near here.

He shifted into his drakon form and set the vehicle on fire. This time, he used his mastery of the wind to create a protective bubble around the flames so when the gas tank blew it wouldn't destroy the surrounding area. It was the reason he'd moved the SUV to the lake to destroy. Better to be safe than sorry.

When the gas ignited, it exploded in a fiery plume of ash, smoke, and flame, and threatened to send debris raining everywhere. But Tarrant contained it all within his bubble of wind, incinerating every piece of metal, every shred of plastic and wire. Nothing escaped.

It took a little longer than he'd hoped, but he had to be certain not one piece of the vehicle remained. He'd have been done in seconds if he'd only had to explode it.

When nothing remained but fine ash, he shifted the winds, softening them. The ash blew onto the pond and sank beneath the water. The surrounding woods were quiet and then he heard the trill of a bird.

Satisfied there was nothing left of the men or their transportation, Tarrant shifted back to human form, dressed, and began to run. He'd been gone for far too long. He needed to see Valeriya, to know she was safe. His body blurred as he shot through the trees, moving faster than any mortal man ever could.

Chapter Seventeen

When Valeriya woke, she was alone. She reached out, found the bedside lamp, and turned it on.

Green fire glinted from the stones sitting on the nightstand. She picked one of them up and held it to the light. "Beautiful." There were a dozen of them. What had Tarrant called them? Drakon tears. What did he mean when he'd told her they belonged to her?

One of them alone had to be worth a fortune, and there were a dozen. She carefully set it back down and took a moment to assess her injuries.

She cautiously rolled her shoulder and frowned. It didn't hurt. She tentatively touched the bandaged area. When excruciating pain didn't shoot down her arm, she poked it a bit harder. Nothing.

Frowning, she eased her legs over the side of the bed and bent down to check out her leg. She straightened the limb and then bent it. It moved easily and without pain. She reached down and shoved the makeshift bandage down her calf. The skin was normal. Except for the dried blood covering the area, there was no indication she'd ever been shot.

She pushed off the bed, taking a minute to ensure she was steady on her feet before making her way to the bathroom. She turned on the light and studied her reflection in the mirror. Her hair was a rat's nest. Dirt and dried blood dotted her torso. She was a mess.

But it was the bandage around her shoulder that interested her most. She worked her fingers under the binding and managed to loosen the fabric enough that she could remove it. "Impossible." She turned and peered over her shoulder. Her shoulder looked perfect. There wasn't even a scar.

She picked up the bandage and examined it. She recognized the fabric from her shirt and hoodie. It was covered in blood. Her blood. She swallowed hard. No doubt about it. She'd been shot.

How had she healed so quickly?

She swallowed hard and caught the slightest metallic taste from the medicine Tarrant had given her.

It hit her like a bolt of lightning. It hadn't been medicine at all. It had been drakon's blood. His blood. There was no other explanation for her miraculous healing.

What did that mean, if anything? It was the last thing she'd expect him to do, especially since the Knights hunted drakons for just this reason. And she'd left the bunker, snuck out when he hadn't been around. Surely he would be angry with her about that.

She had so many questions, and only Tarrant could answer them.

She stripped off what remained of her clothing and stuffed it in the trash can. Then she turned on the water in the huge walk-in shower and stepped beneath the spray.

She was shaky and rested one hand against the tile for support. Probably not the smartest idea to be taking a shower, but she wanted to be clean. There was dirt and dried blood all over her skin and in her hair.

She tilted her face up and let the water cascade over her. It rolled down her skin, washing away the filth and grime. She wished it could take the memories just as easily.

By the time she wrapped herself in a towel, her legs were quivering. She knew she had to sit before she fell down. Every muscle was trembling with fatigue. She left the bathroom and made her way back to the bed. The urge to just climb under the covers and stay there was great. She sat on the edge and took a deep, slow breath. She did it again and again until she felt more grounded.

Clothes were the next hurdle. Digging up clean ones meant going back to her room, but Tarrant's closet was right across from her. It wasn't snooping, not really. He shouldn't have left her here if he didn't want her looking around.

Feeling justified, she walked over to the closet and opened it. Jeans were stacked on one shelf and T-shirts on another. There were shelves with sweaters. Shirts and several expensive suits were hung neatly on a rod. She touched one dark gray jacket. It would look amazing on Tarrant with his dark hair and blue eyes.

She chose a cheaper cotton flannel shirt, dropped the towel, and slid it on. It fell nearly to her knees. When she buttoned it, it was almost like wearing a dress. The sleeves were long and she had to roll the cuffs a couple of times before they hit her wrists.

Then she rummaged around the built-in dresser and found socks and a pair of sweatpants. Even after tightening the drawstring on the pants all the way, the waistband slid down around her hips. She cuffed the legs and tried walking. She might look ridiculous, but she was warm, and that was all that mattered.

Whether it was from shock, blood loss, the adrenaline crash, or a combination of all three, she felt chilled to the bone. She needed something to eat. She felt as weak as a three-day-old kitten.

Putting off leaving the room a bit longer, she looked around. It obviously belonged to Tarrant, but there were no personal touches in the place. Other than his clothes in the closet and his toiletries in the bathroom, this could be a guest room. There were no pictures on the walls, no books on the nightstand. No wallet, keys, or spare change on top of the dresser. Nothing.

Why did that depress her so much?

Deciding she'd put off the inevitable long enough, she left the bedroom. The place felt empty. She walked down the hallway to the kitchen and living area, but Tarrant was nowhere to be found.

She had no idea where he was or when he'd be back. Not that he needed to keep her informed of his whereabouts. They didn't have that kind of relationship. "Suck it up," she ordered herself. "You're alive. That's all that matters."

Since she knew where things were, she filled the kettle and set it on the stove. She dug around and found the tea and got a clean mug from one of the cupboards. While she was waiting for the water to boil, she padded to the refrigerator and opened the door. She wanted something fast and nutritious.

She pulled open the fruit drawer and found some apples—Golden Delicious, her favorite kind. She also found a block of cheddar cheese. She took both and used her hip to shut the door before placing the food she'd gathered on the counter.

"Crackers." She really wanted some kind of crackers. She opened the large bottom doors on the pantry cupboard. Mostly canned and bottled goods down there. She opened the top doors and hit pay dirt. There were three different kinds of crackers, including a wholegrain organic brand she favored.

She grabbed the box and set about fixing a plate. By the time she was done, the water had boiled, and she filled her mug. She slid onto what was becoming her seat at the counter and began to eat.

She'd managed one slice of apple and two crackers when she muttered a curse, slid off the stool, and carried her meal into the living room where she could watch the door. If Tarrant wasn't around, it meant he had to be outside. The door was more easily visible from the living area.

She sipped tea and cleaned her plate. Her stomach settled, and she was feeling steadier now that she'd eaten something. She was considering her next move when the panel slid open and Tarrant walked in.

• • •

Tarrant was sweaty and anxious as he hurried down the stairs. The urge to get back to Valeriya was great. Knowing she was safe inside his home didn't ease his anxiety. He had to see her.

What he didn't expect was to see her the moment he opened the door. He stepped inside and made sure the panel was securely closed behind him. He wasn't taking any chances. He'd even changed the security code, since he wasn't certain how she'd managed to get out in the first place.

She set her mug down on the coffee table and rose. "Is everything okay?"

He hated the echo of fear he heard in her voice and saw in her eyes. "Everything is taken care of." He walked toward her, needing to touch her.

"You were outside like that?"

He frowned, not sure what she meant.

"You're hardly wearing any clothing," she pointed out. "It's October in the mountains."

He ran his hands down her arms and up her back in an effort to reassure himself she was whole and healthy. "Don't need much. I don't feel the cold. Not the way you do."

"Oh." When she kept her hands by her sides, he took a step back, trying not to take it as a rejection. She'd been through a lot.

He caught sight of the plate on the table. "You've eaten." He'd meant to cook her something when he came in.

"Some cheese and crackers, and an apple."

"That's not much." She needed meat and vegetables to build her blood and strength.

She shrugged. "I didn't think my stomach could handle anything heavier." She sat back down on the sofa. "What did you do outside?"

He pushed her plate out of the way and perched on the coffee table in front of her. She looked so worried that he wanted to reassure her. "The bodies are gone and so is their vehicle. There's no trace they were ever here."

She nibbled on her bottom lip, and his jeans got a whole lot tighter. He forced himself to watch her eyes instead.

"You're sure there's no sign of them?"

He nodded. "Drakon fire burns everything to ash."

"Wow."

"It takes effort, and isn't sustainable at such an intense rate for long periods of time, but it works well for short blasts." Unless you were a fire drakon. They could sustain their fire indefinitely.

"Okay." She nodded and then picked at the hem of the shirt she was wearing. It was one of his, as were the pants and socks. She looked adorable as hell in the too-large clothing with her damp hair hanging around her shoulders. "You gave me your blood."

It wasn't a question. She had to know that was what he'd done. There was no other explanation for her healing so quickly.

"I did."

She tilted her head, studying him. "Why?"

"Why?" he echoed. "What kind of question is that? You'd been shot. Twice. And were bleeding."

"But I would have healed given time," she pointed out. "Your blood is precious. Men and women through the ages have killed to obtain it, and you just gave it to me."

Why was she questioning him about this? "It's mine to give. Would you rather I'd left you in pain?" Not that he would have. It had hurt him to see her injured.

"No, of course not." She hesitated and then pushed onward. "But considering everything—"

"Everything?" he prompted when she abruptly stopped. "Like the fact your sister is the head of the Knights? Or that you left the safety of this place?"

"Yes." She gave a defiant nod. "All that and more."

He didn't want to talk about his reasons. "It's done, and you're healthy once again. That's all that matters.

He had questions of his own, and there was no point in putting them off. It was best to get everything out in the open. She had no way of knowing he'd be studying the security feed later to corroborate her story. He needed to know if he could trust her.

"How did you get out of here?"

The corners of her full lips turned up in a hint of a smile. "My bra."

He must not have heard her correctly. "Your bra?"

She nodded. "When you left, you must have accidently kicked it or nudged it. It was stuck in the door."

"I'll be damned." All this because he'd been careless. Who would have thought one tiny scrap of fabric could compromise his security system so easily? Something to think about so it didn't happen again. Maybe he needed a heavier door.

"Okay, we've established how you got out. But why did you leave?" He kept his tone level when all he wanted to do was yell at her and demand to know why she'd left his home.

Again, she nibbled on her bottom lip. A man could only take so much. Explanations could wait. He groaned, leaned forward, and kissed her.

She tasted like tea and crisp apple—sweet and fresh. He slid his tongue into her mouth, and she welcomed him. He canted his head to the side and deepened the caress. All his fears came crashing down around him.

He'd almost lost her.

Riggs would have killed her as soon as he'd learned everything she knew. Tarrant had no doubt about that. He'd been paid to kill any enemy of the Knights, regardless of who they were. Being Karina's sister wouldn't have saved her.

Valeriya gave a small cry and surged forward. He caught her as she wrapped her arms around his neck. The position was making it difficult for him to touch her as he wanted. He stood and strode toward the bedrooms. He went to her room this time. His bed had bloodstained covers. She might not be able to smell her blood on them, but he could.

She wrapped her legs around his waist and clung to him. Their lips never parted as he carried her to the bed and took them both down to the mattress.

• • •

Tarrant obviously had more questions, and so did she. But all that paled when stacked against her need to reconnect with him on the most basic level. She'd been shot. She could have died. Now she wanted to reaffirm life in the most primitive way. She wanted to make love with the man she loved.

She had no idea if he felt the same, but she knew he cared deeply. Why else would he risk his life for her, put his home and everything he'd built in jeopardy by confronting Riggs and his men when he could have let them take her? Why else would he make her drink his precious blood?

He'd cried for her. Drakon tears, rare tears that turned to gemstones. That had to mean something, didn't it? She'd never ask him. Tarrant was a proud man and would abhor any sign of weakness.

No, he might not have told her he loved her, but actions spoke much louder than words ever could. And his every action told her he considered her precious, someone to be protected.

Giving free rein to her heart, she kissed him. Their tongues tangled. The muscles of his back rippled beneath her hands. When he'd walked inside wearing nothing but a pair of jeans, she'd wanted to jump him then, but had managed to restrain herself. At least until he'd kissed her first.

Then all bets were off.

He was on top of her with most of his weight resting on his forearms. He kissed her again and again, stealing her breath. He left a hot trail of kisses down her neck and over her collarbone.

He started to unbutton her shirt, swore, and then ripped it open. Buttons pinged off the walls and floor.

He made a low growling sound in his throat as he peeled back the fabric. The expression on his face was hard. She'd have thought he was angry if not for the heat smoldering in his eyes. His jaw was like granite, and a muscle pulsed just below his eye.

He nuzzled the undersides of her breasts one at a time before lapping at the distended nipples. "Are you sure you're up for this?" he asked.

Was he nuts? "Don't you dare stop," she warned him.

One corner of his mouth kicked up into a sexy smile. "I won't. Not unless you tell me to."

She caught his hair in her hands and dragged him back to her breast. He chuckled and then captured the nub between his lips and sucked. This was what she needed. His touch. His heat. Just him.

She raked her fingers lightly over his shoulders and down his back. He arched his spine as if seeking her touch, silently asking for more. She stroked him wherever she could reach him, but it soon became apparent it wasn't enough.

Valeriya thumped on his shoulder. He immediately raised his head. "Am I hurting you?"

She shook her head. "No. But we're both overdressed."

He laughed, rolled off her, and kicked off his jeans. This certainly wasn't the first time she'd seen him naked, but each time it was such a visceral impact. The swirling silver tattoo that covered half his body seemed to pulse with life. It seemed deeper in color than before, especially the blue outline.

She'd never seen a man as sexy as Tarrant. There was something primal in him that spoke to that part of her.

Admitting she loved him had added another layer to the passion he stirred within her.

"Now you." He dragged the flannel pants over her legs and skimmed off the socks she wore. Now they were both completely bare.

He knelt beside her and ran his gaze over her from head to toe. He paused on her shoulder, and again on her calf.

"I'm fine," she assured him. "I need you." As if those were the words he needed to hear, he straddled her and covered her breasts in his large hands.

"I'll be gentle," he promised.

"I know you will."

Chapter Eighteen

Tarrant prayed he'd be able to keep his promise. He wasn't a gentle man by nature. He wanted to fuck Valeriya until she'd never think about leaving him. He wanted his scent on her skin and the marks of his possession on her body.

Darius would tell him he was being an idiot, that he shouldn't trust her. But Darius had been an idiot over his Sarah. Tarrant knew that trust had to start somewhere. She'd had the chance to give him up to Riggs in order to save herself and hadn't.

His blood ran cold thinking about how close she'd come to being killed.

She belonged to him. He'd waited for thousands of years to find a woman who made him feel the way Valeriya did. Yes, she was dangerous to him, a weakness that could be exploited, but she was also a gift. And right at this moment, she was waiting for him to make love to her.

Her breasts were full and firm, her nipples hard kernels that dug into his palms. Her eyes put the emeralds he'd given her to shame. The expression of longing and need shining from them was more valuable to him than a million gemstones.

The dim baseboard lighting was the only illumination in the room, but the door to the hall was open, filtering light in from out there. There was more than enough for her to be able to see him, and he certainly didn't need the light to see her perfectly.

He kissed her, loving the small, sexy sounds she made. She skated her hands over his chest and shoulders, down his arms, and over his back. He loved the hint of desperation he sensed in her touch.

She really wanted him.

Her lips were moist when he broke their kiss. Their mouths were so close they were almost touching. Her breath puffed against his skin.

Valeriya touched the side of his face with her fingertips. It was a tender, poignant moment that made him catch his breath.

His heart was racing, his muscles quivering with the restraint he was exercising. He licked her bottom lip, and she sighed. He kissed her jaw, her throat, and her shoulder, drawing a gasp. It was music to his ears.

He could spend hours licking and sucking her breasts, but only gave himself a taste before kissing a trail down her slender rib cage. His restraint would only last so long. He stroked his hands over the curve of her hips and around to her full ass.

She didn't object when he lifted her and buried his face between her thighs. He tasted her with his tongue. She moaned his name and dug her fingers into his hair. He found the tiny nub of nerves and sucked. She bucked against his face, moaning and whispering his name over and over.

He knew he'd never get enough of her like this. Never.

He eased one finger into her slick channel. She was wet and ready and sucked him into her body. He withdrew and inserted two fingers.

Valeriya tensed and then her core rippled around his fingers and coated them in her release. She cried out and quivered beneath him. He didn't push her, not this time. He withdrew and lay down beside her, pulling her into his arms.

His cock was pulsing hard, straining for release. His balls felt as though they were about to burst.

She snuggled close, throwing her leg over his thighs. It was the most exquisite torture. Finally, she raised her head. "What about you?"

"I don't want to hurt you." The more primal part of his nature wanted to claim her, but it wanted to protect her more, even if that meant protecting her from him.

"You won't." She pushed upright and eased herself onto his thighs. He gripped her hips to help support her. His dick flexed, as if trying to get closer. "That has to hurt." She pointed at his erection. He shrugged, not about to lie to her.

"We can't have that," she continued. She wrapped her hand around his shaft and pumped. His hips came off the bed so fast she almost toppled over and would have, if he hadn't had such a tight hold on her.

She licked her lips and then rose up onto her knees. Tarrant stopped breathing. She scooted forward and fit the head of his shaft to her opening. Bracing her hands on his chest, she lowered herself over him.

He wanted to be gentle, wanted to let her lead, but he was too far gone. He pulled her down until she was seated to the hilt. They both groaned as their bodies fit together the way nature intended.

It was perfect.

Valeriya was panting for breath. So was he. She ran her fingertips over the tattoo that swirled over his chest and left arm. "This is so beautiful."

He wasn't sure he liked her description. "It's fearsome.

Barbaric." Those were both words that had been used over the centuries to describe it.

"That, too," she assured him. She squeezed her inner muscles and robbed him of breath. "But beautiful, too. Like you."

God, she was going to destroy him. He dragged her down until their mouths melded together. He used his hands to guide her into sliding several inches up and down his shaft while they kissed.

He loved the feel of her lips on his, and her full breasts rubbing against his chest as she rode him. This was what he wanted, what he needed.

He swallowed her small cry of pleasure. Then he pulled his mouth from hers and roared as his release shot through him. Valeriya buried her face against his shoulder. He felt the nip of her teeth as she bit him. He roared again and pumped his hips against hers.

He surged upward, clamped his mouth on the vulnerable curve of her neck where it met her shoulder. He paused, forcing himself to be gentle as he returned her biting caress. She cried out his name, and her wet channel rippled around his shaft. He released her and fell back against the cushions, barely swallowing another roar.

Valeriya's heart was racing and her breath was coming in hard pants against his neck. He held her as they both calmed. Her entire body relaxed and melted against him.

He was content to simply lie there and hold her. The immediate threat to them was neutralized. There would be more trouble, but at this particular moment in time, they were safe.

Finally, she raised her head. "We haven't been using protection." He could see the concern glowing in her eyes and hurried to reassure her.

"You can't get pregnant unless I allow it."

She shook her head in disbelief. "What?"

"In dragon culture, they decide when they procreate, so it's ultimately up to the female dragon. As drakons, we're a bit different. Since there are no female drakons, we decide if and when we get a woman pregnant. I've never personally known of a drakon who's gone that far."

She nodded and rested her head back on his shoulder. "I can understand that. Trust is a big thing."

He trailed his fingers up and down her delicate spine. "Yes, it is. Our fathers always knew they could leave this world and go back home. This was just an experiment for them, an adventure."

"But they left you all behind."

He thought he'd controlled his bitterness, but obviously not. "Yes. They thought their genetics would override that of the humans they impregnated, but we are only half dragon. Our base form is human. The dragon half of us lives inside us, a part of us, but not fully integrated. Our fathers' base form is that of the dragon. They used their powers to assume the form of a human for a short time. They saw us as inferior."

"That's not right—"

"That's life." There was no point in going down that road. It was over and done. Now he had more important things to discuss than his past. "Why did you leave?"

She sighed and the small puff of breath tickled his skin and made his cock jerk. He was still semi-erect inside her. She shivered, and he grabbed one edge of the comforter and yanked it over her. It didn't totally cover her, but it would keep her from getting cold.

She dragged the tip of her index finger over his chest in a random manner. "I woke and you weren't there. I realized the door had been opened, because my bra was stuck inside. I figured I could take a quick look around to see where I was."

"You planned to be back inside before I discovered

you'd left." That made his heart ache, but he appreciated her honesty. It made perfect sense from her point of view. He'd kidnapped her, after all. They'd come so far in such a short time it was hard to remember how she'd happened to be there in the first place.

She nodded, her hair brushing over his skin. "Yes. I was shocked when the door at the top of the stairs opened." She sat up so she was looking straight at him. "I had no idea your home was under the cabin."

• • •

Valeriya wished she could see Tarrant better. His chest was visible, lit by the glow filtering in from the hallway, but his face was in shadow.

She wanted to make him understand. It wasn't easy to order her thoughts, not with his cock still throbbing inside her. She'd come twice and was sated, but it probably wouldn't take much to get her wound up again.

They needed to talk first. There were too many secrets between them. She couldn't expect him to tell her everything—he had lived for thousands of years. But there needed to be honesty between them.

"I know," he told her. He tightened his grip around her hips. She wondered if he was going to pull her down and kiss her. It was almost disappointing when he didn't.

"When I realized where we were, I got worried about why you went outside." She didn't like remembering the fear that had swamped her. She peered down at him, trying to see him better. His eyes glowed, a reminder he wasn't quite human.

"All the more reason you should have stayed inside," he informed her.

She thumped her fist against his chest. It was like hitting a rock. She pulled her hand back to her chest and fought the urge to shake it. "All the more reason for me to look around," she corrected. "If I'd known we were still at the cabin, I doubt I would have ever climbed the stairs. I truly only meant to see where I was." It was important to her that he believed her.

"I was just going to take a peek, but I was already in the cabin when I realized there was someone out there, someone dangerous."

"So you left anyway, instead of going back where it was safe."

She raised her chin and gave him a nod. "I accidently closed the door behind me. Besides, I couldn't let you face whatever danger there was alone."

He nodded and shifted enough that she could see his jaw and mouth in the light. He was frowning. Not a good sign. "What did you think you could do?"

"I don't know." She was human and he was a drakon. That meant he was stronger, faster, and more powerful than she could ever hope to be. But none of that had mattered when she'd thought he might be facing his enemy alone. "I just wanted to help."

Tarrant swore and dragged her back down. He kissed her forehead. "Promise me you won't ever do that again."

She wanted to give him what he wanted. Truly, she did. But she wasn't about to lie. "I can't."

He stilled. "And why not?" She though she caught a thread of hurt in his voice, but she was probably mistaken.

"Because if I think you're in danger, I'm not going to stay locked inside the tower like some princess from a fairytale while you face the enemy alone."

"You're protecting me." He rolled her onto her back and loomed over her, managing to keep their bodies joined as he did. She could see the incredulous expression on his face. From his perspective, she supposed it did seem a bit ridiculous.

But she was determined. "Yes." Whether he accepted it or

not, she loved him. That meant doing everything in her power to protect him. "I thought maybe I could lead the men away."

"You'd have gone with them." The words came out as a low growl. Her drakon wasn't happy about that.

"If it meant they'd leave and never know you were here, yes, I would."

He framed her face between his large hands. "They would have tortured you, killed you."

"I know." Her sister had obviously decided she was too much of a risk to have running around on her own, especially since it was apparent now whose side she was on in this war.

He groaned and pressed his forehead against hers. "What am I going to do with you?"

She wanted to suggest he love her, but managed to keep her mouth shut. It was bad enough she'd admitted she loved him and he hadn't responded. From now on, she'd do what he did—let her actions show she cared. It didn't make her any less vulnerable when it came to Tarrant, but it did make her feel as though her heart had a slight bit of protection.

Who was she kidding? Her heart was already his. But at least if she didn't say the words again, she could pretend to have some distance. She'd put her heart on the line. It was his turn to say the words, or not.

The memory of the drakon tears flitted through her mind. Maybe he had told her he loved her in his own way.

They were obviously done talking, as Tarrant began to flex his hips. His shaft was full once again and stretching her in the most wonderful way. It was just as well. She'd had enough talking for now, too.

She opened her legs wider and took him more firmly into the cradle of her hips. He slid deeper.

"Valeriya."

She loved the way he said her name. There was a hint of possessiveness in the tone that should rankle her independent soul, but she couldn't deny she loved it. And why not? She was possessive about Tarrant.

Whether he believed her or not, she was willing to die for him. She would have gone with Riggs, but she would have taken her secrets to the grave. Her family and the Knights had done enough harm to the drakons. She'd do anything to help balance the scales of justice.

She'd have done that much for any drakon.

But Tarrant was special. He'd kidnapped her heart. That might not have been his intention when he'd taken her from the cabin, but it's what had happened.

He began to move, and she forgot everything but what was happening between them.

• • •

Tarrant plunged in and out of Valeriya's hot depths. He had to have her again. She'd been protecting him. She would have died for him.

He believed her. How could he not? She'd been roughed up and shot in an attempt to get Riggs and his men away from the cabin. She hadn't given Riggs any information about him, not even when Riggs had shot her.

He could still see her lying face down in the dirt, blood seeping from her wounds.

Tarrant was thankful Riggs had been such a good shot. He'd aimed to incapacitate, not to truly injure. He'd wanted Valeriya to be able to talk. A shudder rolled up his big body as he imagined just how Riggs would have gone about that. He was glad the bastard was dead. It was too bad he'd died so quickly. He'd deserved to suffer for what he'd done.

"Tarrant, what's wrong?"

He'd stopped moving, lost in his thoughts. "Nothing," he assured her. He halted any further questions by kissing her.

He began to thrust again, losing himself in the pure pleasure of her body.

Both their lives had been irrevocably changed when he'd made the decision to kidnap her. There was no going back. Whether she truly understood it or not, Valeriya could not return to her normal life. She would never live in her New York apartment again.

He'd find a way for her to keep her writing career. He was a tech wizard. He could get her manuscripts to her agent and funnel all communication in a way that the Knights would never uncover.

He could give her that much.

He moved faster and harder, wanting to imprint himself on her very soul. He wanted to give her everything she desired, but knew that was impossible. By taking her, he'd destroyed her world. Now all he could do was try to replace it with something that would make her happy, make her want to stay with him.

Tarrant plunged his tongue into her mouth, drinking in her sighs of pleasure while trying to push her over the edge. She arched her hip against his pelvis, grinding her clit against him.

He slipped an arm beneath her thigh and lifted it high, allowing him deeper penetration. She cried out, and he followed her into pleasure.

He had enough presence of mind not to collapse on top of her. He eased out of her silken depths and rolled her so she was facing away from him. Before she could object, he spooned her from behind.

He couldn't look at her. Not now. He'd stolen her life and her home. She'd be forced to spend the rest of her life in hiding. If the Knights ever found her…

He growled low in his throat. If they ever took her from him, he'd lay waste to the world, starting with the Knights headquarters in New York.

Chapter Nineteen

Tarrant was too wired to sleep, but he stayed with Valeriya for almost an hour, enjoying having her in his arms. He hated to leave her, but there was work to be done. He needed to check out the computer feeds from when Riggs and his men had arrived. He needed to run facial recognition on the men he'd killed. There were always threads, money trails to help him find out more about the Knights.

The enemy was getting bolder.

He eased out of bed and grabbed his jeans on the way out. He yanked them on once he'd closed the bedroom door behind him. He didn't bother with food, even though he was hungry, or a shower, even though he could use one. There was too much to do.

When he reached the end of the hallway, he spread his arms wide so his hands landed on the security palm-plates on either side. When the green light came on, he then input the twenty-four-digit code into the keypad. Only then did the door to the elevator slide open.

"Down," he ordered.

The elevator moved swiftly and quietly downward until it reached his computer lab. He put his eye against the retinal scan in the heavy titanium door at the bottom. When it verified his identity, the door slid open.

Long counters spanned two walls. There were multiple computers and screens, all engaged in different tasks. He sat in his chair and rolled over to the computer that handled his home security. It didn't take more than a couple of seconds to pull up the surveillance feed for the time in question.

Before he started viewing it, he hit several buttons until he had the live feed of Valeriya sleeping in bed. He couldn't help but smile. She looked so peaceful snuggled beneath the thick comforters.

His stomach growled, reminding him he hadn't eaten in a long time and had expended quite a bit of energy. He rolled his chair over to a dark cabinet in the corner. He opened the door to reveal a refrigerator below and storage above. He pulled two protein drinks from the fridge and three boxes of granola bars from the cabinet. It was only a light snack, but it would have to do.

What he really wanted was a couple of large steaks and about a dozen potatoes. He'd cook later, when Valeriya woke. She needed more than cheese and crackers to regain her strength.

With his stash in his lap, he rolled back over to the computer with the security footage. He ripped open the first box of bars and started the security feed playing. He decided to view the outside one first. Once he'd watched that, he'd cue the inside feed so he could see if things unfolded the way Valeriya had told him.

He didn't have any doubts, not really, but his thirst for information needed to be quenched, even more than his real thirst and hunger did. But this way, he could feed both at once. He ripped open a granola bar and ate it in two bites while the feed started to play.

The first box of bars disappeared, then the second, as he carefully reviewed the replay, watching Riggs and his men arrive and spread out around the cabin. It was important to learn how they worked in such situations, how they set up a perimeter. He wanted to know how they thought, how they worked. There was no telling when such a piece of information might prove valuable.

He retrieved his phone from his back pocket and used his thumb to scroll through the pictures he'd taken. Keeping one eye on the security feed, he uploaded the pictures and began running them through every database on earth. If the men had ever been entered into any of them, he'd find them.

He didn't need to watch himself dispatch the men that had been with Riggs, so he went to the camera facing the front of the cabin. Tarrant grabbed the last box of bars and ripped into it. He was tossing the final wrapper into the garbage just as the video replay reached the part where Riggs shot Valeriya. Fear was etched on her face as she ran, but also determination.

He clenched his fists to keep from roaring. Even all the way down here, he might wake Valeriya, and she needed to sleep. He growled as she stumbled down the stairs and then pulled herself back up and ran. His hands clenched into fists when the second bullet knocked her off her feet.

He forced himself to focus on Riggs as he strode toward her. There was no mistaking the anger on Riggs's face. No doubt about it, he'd been ready to kill Valeriya.

Tarrant viewed the footage until the bitter end. He saw himself race to her side and try to help her, but tried not to look too closely at his own expression. He watched dispassionately as Riggs died. And he finally sighed in relief as he picked Valeriya up, carried her inside the cabin, and closed the door behind him.

He raked his fingers though his short hair and took a deep breath. He swiveled in his chair so he could watch the live feed of Valeriya sleeping and know she was safe. He half wished she'd wake so he'd have an excuse to put off viewing more of the footage.

But it had to be done.

He started with the camera inside his home. He fast forwarded the images until he got to the part where he left. He zoomed in low. Sure enough, he had kicked her bra and it had caught in the door, keeping it from closing behind him.

He would have laughed if it hadn't almost been a fatal mistake. Valeriya could have died because of him. She shouldn't have left the safety of his home, but it was human nature to do so.

His phone rang. He answered, not because he particularly wanted to, but because he knew it was one of his brothers. "Yeah?"

"Have you reviewed the security footage yet?" While Darius's voice boomed over the line, Tarrant could hear Sarah in the background reminding him to ask about Valeriya.

"You can tell Sarah that Valeriya is sleeping." He leaned back in his chair and kept watching the security footage. He could run it faster than normal and still see everything. Valeriya woke alone on the sofa and looked around for him. He saw her call for him. There was no mistaking her curiosity when she saw the door was open. She'd hesitated, though. Hadn't made a mad dash for the exit. That was something.

Darius huffed out a breath. "Okay, now that we know she's fine, have you found out anything yet?"

Tarrant wanted to be mad at his brother, but he knew it was fear making him sound so callous. "I'm reviewing it now. So far, nothing I didn't already know."

"So Valeriya's story is checking out?"

Worried or not, if Darius had been standing next to him,

Tarrant would have given him a shot in the jaw. "Yes."

"Damn it, Tarrant. You can be pissed all you want," Darius told him, "but my first priority is your safety."

He knew that. It was a stark reminder that he'd been a bit of an ass about Sarah when his brother had first brought her here. "Let's just say we're even now."

Darius swore and then collected himself. "What do you know?"

"Oil stocks are down. It's a good time to buy." He couldn't help himself. He had to needle his older brother.

"Fuck you," Darius shot back, but there was no real heat in his voice. "Tell me what you know."

Tarrant sighed. "I'm running facial recognition on the men who came with Riggs. So far, no hits, but I'll find them. When I do, I might be able to backtrack and find some other members of the Knights. Even if it's their foot soldiers, I can work my way forward from there.

Everyone left a trail in life. They shopped certain places, spent time with certain people. It all told a story. Where did they go? What did they spend their paychecks on? All Tarrant needed was a starting point. He could access information all over the world. Who knew where it would lead?

"You'll need to talk with Valeriya," Darius reminded him. "She may know things she doesn't realize she knows."

Tarrant swallowed a growl. At least his brother was no longer accusing her of being a spy. "When she wakes up."

He flinched when he got to the part in the feed where she and Riggs fought. He'd wondered how she'd managed to get away from him. She'd been smart to try to incapacitate Riggs long enough to run.

Even though the sound volume was low, he could hear the echo of the first gunshot. Valeriya stumbled and fell. She dragged herself up and kept going until Riggs shot her again.

"Tarrant? You still there?"

He'd been so consumed by the video replay he'd stopped paying attention to Darius. "I'm here."

"Is there anything I can do? Do you need me to come to you?"

As much as he loved his brother, the last thing he needed was company. Three would definitely be a crowd. "You're safer where you are. No one knows we're here."

"You're sure?"

"Yes." If there was one thing Tarrant was sure of, it was that. "If the Knights suspected anything, the area would already be overrun. It's all quiet out there." The perimeter alarms were all running, and everything was normal. To be on the safe side, he did a quick review of the live feed from each camera.

"What are you going to do?" Darius asked.

Two of his searches pinged at once. "I've got something."

"What is it?"

He brought up two files. "Two of the men are former military. They left a few years back and went to work for a private security company. You'll never guess who."

Darius growled. "If I already knew, you wouldn't need to tell me, would you?"

"Fucking Knights Security." Tarrant's fingers flew over the keys as he started to search for every crumb of information about the company. "Surely they can't be that bloody arrogant?"

"This is the Knights of the Dragon we're talking about," his brother reminded him. Darius's dry tone drew a laugh from Tarrant.

"Have I told you lately how much I fucking hate knights of any kind?"

"Beat up any armor lately?"

It was a running joke how Tarrant bid on and purchased some of the finest pieces of medieval armor ever made and then beat the crap out of it before melting it into a heap of metal. Nicodemus often outbid him to save the artifacts. His brother loved to collect art of all kinds and considered armor to be just that.

As Nic had told him many times, "All armor was worn by medieval knights, but not every knight was a member of the Knights of the Dragon." It was a distinction that really didn't matter to Tarrant.

He scanned the information scrolling down the screen. "They actually have it set up as a legit business," he told his brother. "They work for politicians and celebrities. Those who have the bucks to afford them."

"It helps to finance their other interests. Just as their pharmaceutical companies do." Darius might act like a Neanderthal at times, but he knew business.

"That makes sense. It's going to take me a while to get through all this information. I need to start compiling it into some sort of useful intel."

"I know you reached out to other drakons, those you know about, and told them the Knights of the Dragon are back and stronger than ever. Any of them reach back to you?"

Tarrant kept scanning and absorbing information as fast as he could. "No. And I didn't expect them to. Drakons are a mistrustful bunch."

Darius laughed. "They certainly are."

Something flickered in his peripheral vision. Tarrant halted the feed he was reading and glanced to his right. Valeriya was stirring.

"I've got to go."

"Sleeping Beauty about to wake?"

Before he could growl at his brother, Darius grunted. "Ignore him." Sarah's sweet voice came over the line. "Go and take care of her, Tarrant. If there's anything we can do to help, just let us know."

"Will do. You keep the big guy in line."

"Oh, I will."

Tarrant was grinning when he hung up. His big brother was about to get an earful from his woman. Valeriya rolled onto her side, and her eyes fluttered open. She pushed her hair out of her face and slowly sat up in bed.

He was out of his chair and halfway across the room before he'd made the conscious decision to leave. Valeriya needed him. She hadn't slept as long as he'd hoped, but that was okay. She'd had some rest. Now he'd feed her.

He accessed the elevator and stepped inside. "Up." The rest could wait until they'd eaten. Then it would be time to show her his world.

• • •

"What is wrong with you?" Sarah tossed the phone down on the kitchen table and then smacked Darius in the shoulder.

He didn't dare grin, but Ezra didn't show that much restraint. It was rare to see his brother crack even that much of a smile. "Yeah, Darius, what's wrong with you?" Ezra echoed. The bastard was enjoying himself a little too much.

"Tarrant isn't thinking straight." When Sarah frowned, he knew he probably wasn't taking the right tack, but it was the truth. "He's thinking with his hormones."

Sarah leaned back in her chair, slowly lifted her coffee, and took a sip. "So what you're saying is he's thinking with his small brain and not his bigger one?"

Ezra had just taken a mouthful of coffee. He choked and half of it sprayed over the table.

Darius ignored his brother. "Yes, that's what I'm saying." He really didn't want to be having this conversation. There was no way for him to win. "The Knights can't be underestimated. Do you have any idea what they'd do to Tarrant if they found him?" It was enough to make him break out in a cold sweat.

Sarah pushed out of her chair and came to him. She cupped his face in her small, capable hands. "I know you're worried, but you have to trust him." She shook her head before he could object. "He was forced to trust you about me," she pointed out.

He hated when she was logical. He was completely rational about everything, except when it came to the safety of his family. Then logic flew out the window.

"That was different," he pointed out.

"Oh." She eased away and propped herself up against the edge of the table. "How is that?"

Screw logic. "Because it was you and me."

Ezra snorted, grabbed a cloth from the kitchen, and mopped up the coffee he'd spewed.

Darius ignored him and focused on Sarah. "You came to me with information about the book."

"I could have been sent by the Knights to ensnare you. Isn't that what you thought at first?"

Darius dragged his fingers through his hair. He didn't like being away from Tarrant at a time like this. He was the oldest, the head of the family. It was his job to take care of his brothers. "You don't understand."

Sarah sighed and brushed her hand down the side of his face. He immediately felt calmer. "Unfortunately, I do. I know you want to protect him, but you have to trust him, too. If he gets in trouble, we'll rescue him."

God, he loved this woman. He palmed her hips and yanked her onto his lap. Ezra tossed the damp cloth into the sink and quietly let himself out the back door. Darius would have to remember to thank him later. They were guests in his home, but his brother was astute enough to realize he and Sarah needed some alone time.

"I worry." He nuzzled her temple, drinking in her sweet

scent.

"I know you do." Sarah ran her palms over his chest and shoulders. "I didn't spend a whole lot of time with Tarrant, but he strikes me as a man who isn't impulsive."

"He's not. Usually. But this situation is different." And that was what worried him.

"How? Help me understand." He could get lost in her brown eyes. They were so sincere, so kind and giving.

How could he phrase this so she'd understand but not get pissed at him? "It's like I was with you." He opted for blunt honesty. "When I met you, something inside me shifted." He lifted one of her hands from his shoulder, kissed it, and placed it over his heart.

"After a certain point, it wouldn't have mattered if you were there to harm me, because there was no way for me to protect myself. I would've done whatever it took to make you happy. Do you understand?"

She curled her fingers into his shirt. "You're saying he's in love with her?"

Darius nodded. "He might not realize it yet. Or, knowing Tarrant, he might not be willing to admit it. But he's there. That makes her dangerous. He'll protect her no matter what. Do whatever it takes to make her happy."

She sighed and leaned forward, resting her forehead against his. "We have to trust him. Trust the dragon inside him. If she's lying and means him harm, he'd know it. Wouldn't he?"

He tightened his arms around her. "I hope so."

"There's nothing we can do, is there?"

Darius rose with her in his arms. "There is something we can do. It won't help Tarrant, but it will help me."

"Really? Now?" She shook her head, but he could hear the smile in her tone.

"Always." He carried her up the stairs and into their room.

• • •

Ezra was down on the dock but heard the upstairs door being kicked shut. He'd known that's where they'd end up. He loved his brother, truly he did. He loved Sarah, too, because she made Darius so happy.

But it was hard having them here, watching them together. They fit. Ezra couldn't quite explain it, but it was true nonetheless.

He stripped off his clothes and tossed them onto the dock. It didn't matter that it was late October and the Atlantic Ocean off the coast of Maine was freezing. He needed the water.

He dove in, barely raising a ripple, in spite of his large body. He cut through the water faster than a dolphin and more dangerous than a great white shark.

He shifted, allowing the dragon inside him to come out to play. He was a water drakon. As such, vast areas of unexplored territory were his. Man hadn't conquered the seas yet, and never would.

He dove deep and the darkness embraced him.

Chapter Twenty

Valeriya knew Tarrant was around somewhere. He wouldn't have left her alone, not after what had happened. She was feeling much better, even though she sensed she hadn't slept all that long. She was hungry again, too.

She was back in her room and not in Tarrant's. She tried not to read anything into that. Maybe her room had been closer.

"Stop it." She padded to the bathroom, used the facilities, and washed up. At least she had access to her own clothing. She dug through what remained in her suitcase and found her last set of clean underwear, a pair of leggings, and a long-sleeved sweater that went all the way to her thighs. It was warm and comfortable.

She either needed to do laundry or get more clothes. Some of hers had been destroyed, and what remained was dirty. She gathered her clothing into a pile and added the flannel pants and socks she'd "borrowed" from Tarrant. The shirt was ripped and missing buttons. She dropped that into the garbage can in the bathroom before leaving the room.

Valeriya heard movement in the kitchen as she walked down the hallway. Tarrant was standing in front of the large stove. Each burner had a pan on it, and an electric grill was plugged in. He was also only half dressed. His jeans hung low on his hips, cupping his firm butt. His torso was tanned and ripped, his shoulders incredibly broad. She'd have thought she'd be used to seeing him like this by now, but Valeriya didn't think she ever would.

She cleared her throat. "What are you cooking?"

He flipped a large steak that sizzled when it landed back on the grill. "I thought about steak and potatoes but didn't want to wait that long. I'm doing eggs instead."

Sure enough, three of the four pans were filled with eggs, the forth with onions and mushrooms. "Think there's enough?" She was only half joking.

"Maybe." He picked up the spatula and scrambled the eggs in each pan. "I can always dig up something else to eat if I'm still hungry."

She couldn't help but smile. "Just how much do you eat?" She leaned against the counter next to him, wanting to be close.

"A lot." He leaned down and nuzzled her neck. "But don't worry, there's plenty of food." He caught her earlobe between his teeth and tugged, sending a jolt of desire rushing through her. Honestly, the man should come with a warning label. She had to be careful or they'd end up back in bed before they managed to eat a bite.

She put her hands on his chest and pushed. When he frowned, she added, "Your eggs are going to burn."

"Shit." He went to work quickly and rescued the eggs, transferring them into a large bowl.

Valeriya was pleased to find the kettle already boiled. She made a mug of tea and poured Tarrant a coffee from the full pot on the counter. She set his mug beside him. Making herself useful, she pulled out cutlery and plates before she took her usual seat.

"Did you learn anything?" She knew Tarrant had mostly likely been busy while she'd been sleeping, but she really didn't expect that he'd discovered much yet. It was way too soon.

She was sorry he'd left her. Just once she wanted to wake with his arms around her. Was that too much to ask?

He put the steaks on a large platter and then made sure the stove and grill pan were turned off before he joined her at the counter. "Take what you want."

She cut one of the large steaks in half and added a couple of scoops of eggs. Tarrant frowned. "Is that all?"

She motioned to the piece of perfectly cooked meat. "This is more than I'd usually eat."

He still didn't look convinced, but he dragged the platter over in front of him, dumped what was left of the eggs onto it and added the onions and mushrooms. He had a mountain of food, but she knew he'd eat it with no problem. His appetite was enormous.

"What have you been up to while I was sleeping?" She cut a bite-size piece of steak and popped it into her mouth. It was perfectly seasoned and cooked to perfection. She made a small moaning sound. Tarrant stopped eating. When she glanced his way, he was staring at her mouth, and his eyes were glowing.

She carefully swallowed and took a sip of tea. "Well?"

Tarrant slowly and carefully picked up his fork and knife and started eating again. "I reviewed the security footage."

"Was there much to see?" She had no idea just how much security he had around the place.

He nodded and swallowed. "Yes. I learned a lot about how they deploy in such situations. It could be useful down the road."

She toyed with the small mound of eggs with her fork. "What about Riggs?" She hated saying his name, but she couldn't bring herself to ask Tarrant directly if he'd watched her being shot. She gave an involuntary jerk as phantom pain seared through her shoulder.

"Yes." There was a finality in Tarrant's voice that kept her from asking more questions on that front. He'd seen her fight with Riggs, seen the man shoot her.

She shivered and tried to put that particular event out of her mind. "Okay. So, is there anything else?"

Tarrant sighed and emptied half his coffee mug in one swallow. "Two of the men with him were ex-military. They worked for a security company." He paused and studied her intently. "Knights Security."

She knew her jaw had dropped, and she forced herself to close her mouth. "You're not kidding, are you?"

He shook his head and cut another chunk off his steak. "No." He popped it into his mouth and chewed.

"Knights Security," she repeated. "Never heard of them."

Tarrant swallowed. "They don't exactly advertise. They're elite and discreet. The rich and powerful use them."

"Oh." That made sense. She mulled it over as she ate more of her eggs. "How did you find out about them so quickly? You didn't even know their names." She set her fork down and looked pointedly at him. "Wouldn't their military records be confidential?"

He flashed a smile. Her breath caught in her throat, and her heart stuttered before beginning to race.

"Nothing is confidential, not to me. I had their pictures. It was enough."

There was so much she didn't know about the man she was sleeping with, the man she was in love with. It was time to learn. "Just who are you, Tarrant?" She rubbed her fingers over her forehead. "I don't even know your last name. That's not fair, since you know pretty much everything about me."

He looked at her so long and hard it was all she could do not to start squirming. He either trusted her, or he didn't. It hurt. More than she wanted to admit. But there was nothing she could do about it.

"Forget it." She couldn't eat another bite. Not with the huge lump stuck in her throat.

"Cooper. I go by the name Tarrant Cooper."

He said the last name like it had some significance. She studied him over her mug and raised one eyebrow in question. "And that means what exactly?"

He pushed the half-empty platter of food aside and rested his elbows on the stone countertop. The tension grew thick around them. A muscle worked in his jaw. He grew more and more remote by the second.

"Tarrant?"

"I'm Cooper Communications."

Valeriya was shocked even though she knew she shouldn't be. He was a drakon. He'd had centuries to build an empire. Heck, he'd been around at the dawn of technology. He'd seen the world go from the firelight to the lantern to the electric light.

"Wow." Not exactly the most articulate response.

One corner of his mouth quirked up. "Yeah. Wow."

"You're Cooper Communications," she echoed.

He nodded. "I know."

His tone was so dry she couldn't help but smile. "So you have resources."

Tarrant smiled, and his icy-blue eyes warmed. "You have no idea, baby." He yanked the platter back over in front of him and began eating again. "Eat some more," he ordered.

She grinned back and managed to finish her eggs and about half the steak. She was done. Her curiosity was also overflowing. "So you what? Hacked into military records?"

Like most people, Valeriya knew her way around a computer. She could do what she needed to in order to conduct business, but that was pretty much it.

"Yes."

That was it. Just "yes," like it was no big deal. "Wasn't it difficult?"

He finished his meal and leaned back on his stool. "No."

Frustrated, she pushed her plate away. "Could you maybe be a little more forthcoming?"

He shook his head and stood. "Best to show you." He started clearing the table. She hurried to help him. The quicker it was done, the sooner she'd hopefully understand more about him. Cooper Communications. That was still blowing her mind. His company was the largest communications empire in the world. It was synonymous with communications.

The implications were enormous. He probably owned and controlled the cell towers and internet providers for a good number of the Knights. If she remembered correctly, his company was also involved in military contracts.

He was also loaded.

When Tarrant took the dirty plate from her hand and popped it into the dishwasher, she realized she'd simply been standing there. She glanced around, but he'd already cleaned up the mess while she'd been lost in thought.

"I'm sorry."

"No problem. It's a lot to take in." He started the machine running.

"It really is. I mean I'm a children's author, and you're—"

He started to laugh. She loved the deep full sound, even though he was laughing at her. When he finally stopped, he reached down and took one of her hands in his. "You accept that I'm a drakon with little problem, but finding out I own a communication company throws you for a loop."

"You don't just own a communication company, Tarrant.

It's an empire. You practically own the airwaves. And you're rich. Extremely rich." The last came out almost as an accusation.

"That a problem?" he asked as he tugged on her hand to get her to follow him down the hallway.

"Not a problem. I mean I don't care how much money you have. It's just…" There was no way to say this that didn't make her seem foolish. "Forget it." She should have just kept her mouth shut.

"No, it's just what?"

She huffed out a breath. "It's intimidating okay. On top of the fact you're gorgeous and smart and a fricking drakon, you're also a bloody billionaire."

"So you think I'm gorgeous, do you?"

She could see smug pleasure reflected in his eyes and in the curve of his mouth, and she wasn't sure if she wanted to kiss him or smack him. She did neither. "If that's all you heard out of what I just said, we really need to work on your listening skills."

They'd reached the end of the hallway. There was a huge door constructed of some kind of metal. It reminded her of a door to a bank vault. There was a keypad in the center of it. "What's this?"

Tarrant released her and stood right in front of the door. He spread his arms wide and placed his hands on two scanners mounted on the walls. A light flashed on the keypad, and he input a long code. The light turned green and the door opened to reveal an elevator.

He stood back and motioned her inside. The second she was beside him, the door slid shut. There was no way out. Valeriya was so nervous she was sweating. The elevator space was small. Assuming it was an elevator.

"Down." His deep voice echoed in the enclosure and they began to move. Valeriya held her breath and counted. Before she could become lightheaded or pass out, the machine came to a halt.

Tarrant leaned in close to another panel. One she hadn't even noticed until now. The light scanned his eyes. A retinal scanner? She'd only seen those in movies. She didn't think her bank was this secure.

The door slid open to reveal a large room covered in computers and other electronic devices. "Welcome to my control center."

She stepped out of the elevator, cognizant of the huge step this was in their relationship. There was no way to unsee what he was about to show her. Either he trusted her or he planned to kill her. She was almost certain it was option number one, but there was still a tiny part of her that worried.

"You have your own Batcave." It was just like something out of a superhero movie.

"No."

She jumped at the thunder in his voice. His face was set in hard lines, and his hands were curled into fists. He was truly pissed.

"You're both billionaires and secretive," she pointed out.

Tarrant stalked toward her, and she backed up until she hit the wall. He slammed his hands on either side of her head and leaned down. She wasn't afraid to admit she was a little scared. She had no idea why he was so upset. "Tarrant?"

He closed his eyes and leaned forward until their foreheads were touching. "He's the damn Dark Knight. I hate knights."

She could certainly understand that, but it was a little funny, too. If she hadn't been so scared only seconds before, she might have been able to hold in the chuckle. But her emotions were all over the place, and she giggled.

His head jerked back. "You think that's funny?" His brows lowered and his jaw tensed.

"No. Yes." She closed her eyes and swallowed back a laugh. "You have to admit it is a little funny. You're real, and a drakon to boot, but you're upset about a fictional character."

He pushed away. "Knights are no laughing matter." He turned from her.

Suddenly, it wasn't so funny anymore. She stepped forward and wrapped her arms around his waist from behind. "No, the Knights of the Dragon are no laughing matter." She sighed and rested her head against his back. Her drakon was wounded in so many ways.

He stood like a statue, stiff and unmoving, for several long minutes. Then he sighed and tugged her around so he could hug her. "I'm sorry. My brothers are always telling me I overreact."

That was another bombshell. "You have brothers? As in multiple?"

"One thing at a time." He kissed the top of her head and turned her to face all the computers. "Welcome to my world."

• • •

Tarrant knew he was acting like an ass, but he couldn't help it. Hearing Valeriya compare him to a knight of any kind, even one only fictional, hit him hard. They were his enemy. It was a stark reminder her sister wanted him captured or dead.

He didn't want Valeriya on their side. He wanted her on his. That meant she had to hate all knights, as he did. It wasn't rational or logical, but emotions seldom were.

He cursed himself for mentioning his brothers. She was curious, but she let the subject drop for now and turned her attention to what he was showing her.

"This is incredible." She ran her gaze over the long counter filled with computers.

Pride had his chest puffing out. It was ridiculous for a

man of his age and experience to get so much pleasure out of a couple of words, but that didn't negate it. He wanted to impress her.

"How do you run your business from here?" She looked up at him, worry etched on her face. "You can't be away from your empire for long, can you?"

He wrapped his arm around her shoulders and pulled her close. "I can be anywhere I want or need to be," he informed her. He motioned to the array of machines. "I have people in place to handle the day-to-day running of things. I only leave here when I have to."

"How is that possible? I mean, if you're not around, wouldn't someone try to take advantage of that?"

"Some have tried and have found themselves in huge trouble." He took her over to his chair. He sat and pulled her onto his lap. "Look." He pointed out three computers. "Those are set up so that every transaction for every business I own runs through here every single day."

"That's a lot of information." She watched the information scrolling quickly over the screens. "Makes me slightly sick to my stomach just watching it move so fast."

Tarrant settled her more snugly against his chest and tried to ignore the erection pushing against the front of his pants. Having her so close made concentrating on work a hell of a lot more difficult.

"How much do you know about drakons?"

She glanced up at him, surprised by his change of topic. "The basics." She pushed a lock of hair away from her face. "Why?"

"Drakons, like dragons, like to collect. Some would say hoard."

"But you wouldn't?" Valeriya grinned.

He tweaked her nose. "No, I wouldn't."

"What do you collect? Computers?"

He shook his head. "Something infinitely more valuable. Information."

He saw the growing comprehension in her eyes. "You're able to read all that information every day, aren't you?"

"It's a skill. I can scroll several days' worth of work, world news, and events in a matter of hours. If anything jumps out at me, I delve into it." Valeriya sighed and rested her head on his shoulder. "What is it?" he asked. Did she think he was a freak for having such a skill? It shouldn't matter what she thought of him, but it did.

"Just when I thought you couldn't get even more impressive."

He put his hand beneath his chin and tilted it up. "Why should that bother you?" He was completely baffled. He'd lived a long, long time, but he still didn't understand women.

"I'm so ordinary." It came out as a plaintive wail. Then she looked disgusted with herself. "Ignore me. I'm not myself."

She looked so disgruntled he couldn't resist leaning down and brushing his mouth over hers. The sound of pleasure she made shot through him, arrowing down to his dick.

"You're not ordinary," he told her. "You managed to capture a drakon."

She made a gurgling sound, part choking, part laughing. He muffled it as he kissed her. She stroked her hands over his chest and around his neck. He slid his tongue past her parted lips to taste her heat.

She delighted him in every way possible. He'd shared aspects of his life with her that only his brothers knew. She was firmly in his life now. There was no going back for either of them.

But she was human and would die unless he fed her his blood. He tensed, and she felt the change in him and pulled back. "What is it?" she asked.

He wanted to keep kissing her, but he wanted matters

settled between them. It was his nature to want to have things laid out in an orderly fashion.

"I fed you my blood to help you heal."

She nodded. "I know. And I appreciate it. It saved me a lot of pain and recovery time, even if it was a little uncomfortable."

She put her hand on his cheek. Only she touched him like this, like he was precious and special. "You're human," he pointed out.

"Yes, I know." He could tell he was confusing her.

"You'll age and die unless you drink my blood on a regular basis." There. It was out there. No more secrets between them.

"I will, but hopefully not for decades."

"I don't want you to die." He finally spoke aloud what he'd been thinking. He didn't want her to leave him, didn't want to lose her.

"It's inevitable." The smile she gave him was sad and resigned.

"No, it's not. Not if you drink my blood."

"You want me to drink your blood, even when I'm not injured?" She said it slowly, as though she wasn't quite sure she'd understood him.

Tarrant nodded.

"Why?"

He could tell she was honestly confused. Her sister would kill for the opportunity to keep him continually drained. So would the rest of the Knights. Yet not only was Valeriya not jumping at the opportunity, she seemed at a loss.

What little armor he had left around his heart cracked and shattered as he gave her the blunt truth. "Because I can't lose you."

Chapter Twenty-One

Valeriya wasn't sure how to react to Tarrant's pronouncement. He had to care deeply for her, maybe even love her, at least a little bit, if he wanted her to drink his blood to keep her alive. But she didn't want to be like the Knights and use him to prolong her life. She chewed on her bottom lip while she considered how to best handle the situation.

"Well?"

Her drakon was impatient. "I'm thinking," she told him.

He turned away, but not before she caught a fleeting glimpse of hurt in his eyes.

"It's not because I don't want to be with you. I do," she confessed. She felt at a distinct disadvantage having this conversation while sitting in his lap. "I just don't want to use you. I don't want to be like the Knights."

"What?"

She shrugged and twined her fingers together in her lap. "They want you for your blood. If I drink it, how am I any different?"

He placed his large hand on the side of her face. "Because

I'm offering it freely. Because I want you with me."

This was what she wanted—to be with him. She'd be a fool not to take advantage of his offer. "Okay, but only as long as you want me with you." She didn't want to think about leaving him, but she was realistic. "Forever is a long time. We can try being together for a couple of years, and then if you still feel the same way, I can drink your blood on occasion to stay young." It was a compromise.

"Done." He looked pleased with himself. Valeriya had done what she thought was right. They could take some time and see where their relationship was going before they made any drastic decisions.

"What now?" They needed to be cautious. Valeriya knew her sister and the Knights had tentacles everywhere. "How do we proceed?"

Tarrant reached his arms around her and began to type on the keyboard.

"Umm, wouldn't this be easier for you if I wasn't sitting on your lap?"

"No." He kept typing and brought three pictures up onto the screen. "Do you recognize any of these men?"

She studied each one intently. As an artist, she generally had a good memory for faces. "No, I don't. Are these the men that came with Riggs?" Just saying his name made her stomach churn. He might be dead, but she'd be a long time getting over what had happened.

"Yes." He pointed out the two on the right. "These two are former military. I'm still searching for this one." A low ping came from a machine off to the left. "Got it." He rolled his chair over to the screen. She gave a small yelp and clung to his shoulders so she didn't topple over.

"I need my own chair," she muttered.

Tarrant frowned but simply typed something onto the keyboard. A driver's license with the man in question pictured on it popped up.

"Do you think it's really him, or an alias?"

"Maybe. Maybe not. But it's a starting point." His fingers were a blur on the keyboard as he typed in more commands. He finished that and rolled back to what seemed to be his main computer. This time she was prepared and hung on as he rolled.

"What can I do to help?" There probably wasn't anything, but she hated feeling like such deadweight. There had to be something she could do.

"I need you to think back to everyone who ever came to your parents' home. Anyone you ever met. And work forward to present day. Who did your sister meet or talk about?"

"It won't be a long list," she warned him. "Neither my parents nor my sister talked much about the Knights around me after it became apparent I didn't approve of what they were involved in." Too soft. Too weak. She'd heard them say that about her more than once as a child.

She had to move. She pushed off Tarrant's lap. He let her go, but with obvious reluctance. "I need paper and pencils if you have it. I can make sketches as well as lists. Some of the people are dead now, but I can still give you pictures and names."

He nodded and pointed at a metal cabinet. "Office supplies are in there. You should find everything you need."

"I have a sketchpad and pencils in my knapsack," she reminded him.

His gaze softened and his normally icy-blue eyes warmed significantly. "I don't want you to leave."

"I'd only be gone a couple minutes," she pointed out. It wasn't like she was leaving his home.

But when he didn't budge, she relented and went to the cabinet, very aware of Tarrant watching her every step. She opened both upper doors and looked inside. There were pencils and pens of all sizes and colors, pads of lined and unlined paper, notebooks, sketchpads, and more. Heck, he even had an unopened set of watercolors and another of oil paints. It was like shopping in her personal stationary and art supply store.

"I think you'll find everything you need." He was smiling, the smug devil.

There was so much to choose from she almost didn't know where to begin. "Pencils," she muttered. She selected several pencils of different hardness, some for drawing and others for shading. She grabbed a medium-size sketchpad and closed the cabinet before she spent too much time checking out the selection.

Tarrant didn't have computer desks here, but long countertops running along two walls. They were mostly covered with computers. There was a lone empty space on the far end with a computer chair in front of it. She carried her supplies there and took a seat.

She opened the cover of the pad, picked up one of the pencils, and thought back to her childhood. Then she decided it was probably best to work backward from present to the past. Anyone she'd seen around her sister would have more relevance to what was happening with the Knights right now.

Tarrant was watching information scroll by on several screens at once. She could only marvel at his ability. What was nothing but gibberish to her made perfect sense to him. He could read and comprehend at a phenomenal rate.

She wondered how many languages he knew. Man had gone from painting on cave walls and writing on papyrus to the computer age over the course of his life. It was incredible. He would be able to tell archaeologists so much about the world. Too bad humans had alienated drakons with their greed and lust for power.

Sensing her attention, he turned and cocked one eyebrow.

"Is there something you need?"

You. She shook her head before she could answer aloud.

He patted his lap. "Plenty of room for you."

"I need space to sketch." Not totally true, but true enough. If she sat on his lap, she'd be so distracted by him she'd never get anything done.

She was finally able to catch her breath when he nodded and turned back to his work. They both needed some time to process everything that had happened. The attraction between them had been immediate and intense. Not to mention she'd discovered Tarrant was a drakon, been shot, and then healed by his blood. It was a lot to come to grips with. This was more normal, more like their everyday life would go—him working on computer and her sketching. Granted, she'd usually be working on her books. She'd get back to that as soon as the latest threat from the Knights was handled.

That is, if she still even had a career. She hadn't been in touch with her agent or publisher in days. She was between projects, so she probably wasn't missing too much. But that wouldn't last forever. What would happen when their emails went unanswered for too long?

Would anyone even realize she was missing? It was more likely that her sister would make it seem as though she'd just packed up and left. Or worse. She wouldn't put it past Karina to somehow hack her email account, write to her publisher, and tell them she was quitting. Then there would be no loose ends, no one questioning her disappearance, no one looking for her beyond the Knights.

She thought back to her apartment in New York, the one place she'd lived that felt like home. It had all her personal belongings, her books and clothes, the little mementos collected over the course of her lifetime.

Tears filled her eyes, but she blinked them back. She swallowed hard and shoved those thoughts away. There was no point in wanting what she couldn't have. Her plan had always been to go back home, but that was no longer an option.

She didn't know what the future held or where she would go. All she could do was take one day at a time.

Valeriya picked up a pencil and began to sketch the face of the man who was always by her sister's side. She knew him only as Birch—didn't know if he even had a last name. She drew with deft strokes, and his image appeared on the pad in front of her.

• • •

Tarrant was very aware of Valeriya working diligently not ten feet away from him. A sense of contentment filled him. She'd agreed to drink his blood. Not right away. That had hurt, but he understood her reasoning. Didn't mean he liked it, but he understood.

She needed time to be sure about him. He wanted her forever, knew she belonged to him, with him, but she didn't have the same instincts he did. Or maybe she did. She'd told him about her gift, but he wasn't quite sure how it worked. Did it only alert her when there was danger around, or did it guide her in other areas of her life?

She also hadn't told him she loved him again. Only that one time.

He tried not to read too much into that.

He got into his work, reviewing reports for his businesses, searching databases for more information about the Knights, and generally catching up on the news of the world. He hated being out of touch for as long as he had been.

He was vaguely aware of Valeriya poking around the cabinets in the room. He heard her go into the bathroom once, and at some point she set bottle of water beside him. He thought he remembered to murmur his thanks but couldn't be sure.

Other than that, they both worked in silence.

When he finally raised his arms over his head and stretched, he knew many hours had gone by. How many, he had no idea. He often lost track of time.

He swiveled his chair around and smiled. Valeriya was slumped over the counter with her head resting on her arms. He had no idea when she'd fallen asleep.

He went to the bathroom, and when he returned, she was stirring. He went to her and crouched down beside her chair. "Hey, sleepyhead." He'd have to remember that she was human and needed much more rest than he did. He needed a sofa down here. And blankets. Maybe a comfy pillow. Somewhere she could curl up and sleep while he was working.

Or he could let her sleep upstairs in a bed. That made more sense, but he'd want her with him sometimes. He'd have her check out some online shopping sites with him later so he could figure out what she liked.

Her eyelids fluttered and then opened. Her eyes were glazed over, but when she saw him, she smiled. It was so open and so loving it made his heart hurt.

She reached out and touched his face. "Hey, yourself. How is work going?"

He captured her hand and kissed the center of her palm. "I'm caught up on work and still running searches on the Knights. You?" He wanted to see what was in the sketchbook but didn't want to open it without her permission.

There were rules in relationships. He freely admitted he didn't know them because they'd never mattered before. They mattered now. *She* mattered.

She sat back in her chair and rubbed her hands over her face. "I've made a start." She took a sip of water from the almost empty bottle and made a face at the tepid drink.

"Have a look." She motioned to the pad.

He retrieved it and opened to the first page. Written neatly on the top of the page was the name Birch. The sketch showed a man in his mid to late forties, maybe even early fifties. It was hard to tell. He was a tough-looking bastard. "Who is he?"

Valeriya leaned forward so they were both studying the sketch. He tried not to notice how warm she was and how the lemony scent of the soap she'd used earlier mixed with her natural perfume. She was so close. It would be easy to pull her into his arms and take her on the floor.

She's tired and still recovering, he reminded himself. She didn't need to be fucked on a cold, hard floor.

"He's Karina's bodyguard. He's been with her since she was a teenager. I figured it was better to start with the people I know about in the present and work backward, since they'd have more impact on what's happening right now."

"Smart." He flipped another page. There were no names, but there were two smaller sketches. "Who are these men?"

She shook her head. "I don't know. I've seen them with Birch." She pointed to the one on the left. "He drives Karina. The other man sits up front with him sometimes in the limo."

He was about to turn the page again when his phone rang. He slid it out of his pocket, not surprised to find out Darius wanted to talk with him. "I want a face-to-face," Tarrant told his brother as soon as he answered the phone. "Get Ezra's laptop." He ended the call before Darius could start asking questions. It was time to introduce Valeriya to his family.

"You want me to leave?" She ran her hands over the black leggings she wore. He could tell she was nervous.

"No." He stood and pulled her chair over next to his. "It's time you met Darius Varkas."

Chapter Twenty-Two

Valeriya was nervous and trying desperately not to show it. She was about to meet Darius Varkas, the reason she'd started on her wild quest. She was almost positive he was a drakon, even though Tarrant hadn't confirmed it. They were most certainly friends.

She was glad Tarrant hadn't insisted she sit on his lap. That would have been too intimate, too telling. She wanted to make a good impression on these people. They were obviously important to Tarrant, and she had no idea what he'd told them about her.

"Ready?"

She wasn't, not really, but she nodded. Tarrant clicked some keys and a screen popped open. It showed a large man with straight black hair that fell to his shoulders. His features were rough. He looked tough and dangerous. But it was his eyes that caught her attention. They were green and looked as hard as the emeralds Tarrant had given her.

This had to be Darius Varkas.

After his first glance at her, he gave his entire attention to

Tarrant. "Is this wise?"

Well, that was certainly blunt enough. He obviously didn't trust her, didn't want to talk to her. "Mr. Varkas." He turned back to her, confirming her suspicion that he was indeed the man she'd come to find.

Even though Tarrant had already warned him, it was important for her to follow through on what she'd come here to do. After all, that one decision had put into play everything that had happened since. Like a row of dominos falling one on top of the other, her life had spiraled out of control. If she was going to lose her home and possibly her livelihood because of him, she wanted to have her say. It might not be of great consequence to him, but it was to her.

"I know Tarrant has already told you this, but the Knights of the Dragon know about you and are looking for you. They want you quite badly." She stood and her chair rolled back a couple of inches. "That's what I came here to tell you. What you do with the information is up to you." She wanted to stalk off but knew she couldn't get through Tarrant's security system. Her plan was to go back to her sketching, which was out of view of the screen.

She wished speaking with Darius had made her feel better, but it hadn't. There was a gnawing emptiness in her stomach that left her feeling slightly ill. Her mission, such as it was, was over. She had no idea what to do next—what she *could* do. With her sister and possibly the rest of the Knights looking for her, it wasn't as though she had many options.

Tarrant wanted her to stay with him, at least for now. And she wanted to be with him. But she hated feeling dependent on him. She didn't want him thinking she was only here because she had nowhere else to go. She wanted to be more of his equal.

Not that such a thing was even possible. After all, he was a drakon and a billionaire, while she was a homeless, possibly unemployed, children's author. Yeah, not equal at all.

She'd taken one step when Tarrant snaked one of his long arms around her waist and pulled. Valeriya stumbled backward and landed in his lap. "Kill me now," she muttered. She'd never been so embarrassed. So much for making a grand exit.

"Why would I do that?" Tarrant playfully nuzzled her neck. If his friend didn't know they were sleeping together, he did now.

"Tarrant." Impatience tinged Darius's voice.

"What?" he shot back. "You wanted to talk, we'll talk. I'm compiling a dossier on all the men who were here with Riggs."

"You identified the third man?" Darius leaned closer and looked so angry that Valeriya instinctively leaned back. He was such a commanding presence, she wouldn't have been surprised if he'd reached right through the screen. It was a silly thought, but it didn't stop her reaction.

Of course, Tarrant noticed. He frowned at her and then scowled at Darius. "Ease up," he ordered him. "Yes, I indentified the third man. While I was busy with that, Valeriya spent her time sketching and listing other people of interest she's seen with her sister."

"Why?" Darius leaned back in his chair and pinned her with his gaze. She was glad she was in Tarrant's arms. She wouldn't want to face this man alone. He was capable of anything.

She hadn't forgotten that Tarrant was cut from the same cloth. He had kidnapped her, after all, but she'd never felt threatened with him, not like this. "Why what?" Her voice squeaked a little, but there was nothing she could do about that.

"Why warn me? Why are you betraying your sister?" She heard the implication. If she'd betray her sister, she could betray him, too. It hurt, but it was also a valid question.

Tarrant closed his arms around her, lending her his strength. She straightened her spine, determined to show confidence she wasn't really feeling. She didn't owe Darius or anyone else an explanation, but she gave one anyway.

"Because what she and the Knights do is wrong. It's always been wrong. My family has been a part of the Knights since their inception. The obsession with drakons goes back even longer. I can't make up for what they've done, but I can try to stop the madness."

Her stomach was in knots just thinking about the centuries of harm, the insanity that had led her ancestors to chain and harm another person. She knew the Knights and her sister thought of those like Tarrant as creatures, but he was a flesh and blood man. He had just as much right to live as they did.

It sickened her that her legacy was one of violence and subjugation.

Darius said nothing for the longest time. "Do anything to harm him"—he pointed at Tarrant—"and I'll end you."

It was a promise, not a threat. Strangely, it made her feel better. She liked the idea of Tarrant having someone who'd look out for him.

Her drakon swore and glared at Darius. She caught his chin and turned his face so he was looking at her. "Don't be mad with him. He cares." She wished she had a friend or family who cared as much. If Riggs was to be believed, and she had no reason to doubt him, her sister wanted her dead because of her betrayal.

She faced Darius. "You have my word. I won't do anything to harm him."

He nodded and then turned his attention to Tarrant, once again dismissing her from his thoughts. She recognized it for what it was. Karina did the same thing to her all the time. It didn't hurt her feelings.

Tarrant, however, was through holding back. He pointed

his index finger at Darius. "Don't you ever threaten Valeriya again. Are we clear?"

Some of her tension melted. No one had ever stood up for her like this before. Only Tarrant.

She peeked at the screen. Darius was scowling, but he also appeared resigned. "We're clear."

Tarrant immediately changed the subject. "How's Sarah?"

Valeriya was immediately alert, aware that there were more people listening to their conversation. Who was Sarah, and why was Tarrant asking about her? She felt…jealous. It was an unfamiliar emotion. She immediately felt petty, not liking her reaction at all.

"Sarah is fine." There was a note in Darius's voice that made her look at him more intently. He seemed uncomfortable, but there was possessiveness in his tone that she found intriguing.

Suddenly, a woman appeared in the screen. She had short brown hair, brown eyes, and a friendly smile. She leaned on Darius's shoulder and waved at them. "Hey, Tarrant. And you must be Valeriya. Thank you for everything you've done. How are you feeling now?"

Valeriya was taken aback by the woman's kindness. It was a deep contrast to Darius's suspicion.

"I'm Sarah," she added.

Valeriya licked her dry lips. "It's nice to meet you, Sarah. You're welcome. And I'm doing very well, thank you." Her words were a little stilted. She never did well in situations like this. She wanted to be friendly but had a hard time. She blamed it on the fact she'd never really been able to have friends growing up. It had made her socially awkward.

Something else to pin on the Knights and her family.

But she was an adult now. She knew what her problems were, and she was trying to grow past them. Darius took the hand Sarah had rested on his shoulder and brought it to his lips. They were obviously a couple. She decided she liked the woman after all.

"I hope you're somewhere safe," she blurted.

Smoke came from Darius's nostrils and mouth. Real smoke. She glanced at Tarrant. He had a half smile on his lips. What was she to make of that? Darius was a drakon.

"And do you want to know our location?" he asked.

So that was his problem. "No." If he could be blunt. So could she. She was done with this conversation. She dragged her chair back to the corner and opened her sketchpad. She pretended to draw, but couldn't manage to actually work.

• • •

Tarrant missed having Valeriya in his lap, even though she'd just left. She was an addiction, one he wasn't interested in breaking.

Sarah sighed and tipped his brother's face toward her. "Why did you have to ask that?"

"It's a legitimate question," he insisted. Darius faced the screen. "It was a legitimate question," he reiterated.

"It was," Tarrant agreed, "but you only get to ask it once. Ask it again, and we'll have a problem." He wanted his family to embrace Valeriya, but it didn't matter whether they did or not. She was staying. He needed her in his life.

"You blew your cover, too, bro." It was too good an opportunity not to tease his big brother. "You had smoke coming out your nose and mouth."

"I didn't." He looked up at Sarah. "Did I?"

She nodded. "Quite impressive. I'm sure you made quite an impression on Valeriya."

Darius growled, but Sarah just laughed. Tarrant glanced over at Valeriya. She had her sketchbook open, but she wasn't using her pencil. She looked so alone over there by herself.

He had a flash of understanding. She'd spent most of her

life alone. Apart. Maybe that was why she was so fascinated with drakons. She understood them. Yes, she'd had her grandparents. From everything he'd learned, they'd been good to her. But it wasn't the same. She had a sister who would send someone like Riggs after her, and parents who'd virtually ignored her.

Tarrant knew that no matter how much his brothers aggravated him at times, they'd come to his aid in a heartbeat. They'd always have his back.

"Valeriya is mine." He made the announcement, daring his brother to object. Valeriya dropped the sketchbook on the counter and stared at him. Her mouth was open and her eyes wide. He wanted to kiss her.

Now.

He ended the transmission. He was through talking to his brother. He turned in his chair and crooked his finger at her. "Come here."

She shook her head. "Why did you say such a thing to them?"

"Because it's true."

She rubbed her hands over her thighs. "But they're important to you. What if things don't work out between us? You don't want to alienate them."

He knew he had his work cut out for him. She couldn't seem to believe that anyone would put her first. He patted his lap. "Come here and we'll talk."

She cocked her eyebrow and gave him a knowing look. "I come over there and we'll do more than talk."

That was his plan. "And what's wrong with that?"

She rubbed her face and transferred a smudge of lead from the pencil to her skin. "I didn't like hearing you ask about Sarah. Not at first."

Tarrant frowned. "Why not?" Sarah had been nice to her. Much more accepting than his grumpy brother.

She nibbled on her bottom lip and sighed. "I thought she might be someone you were interested in her."

Tarrant was stunned. Valeriya had been jealous. Of Sarah. A huge smile split his face. He couldn't help it and didn't want to. "There's no need to worry about that," he assured her.

"I know that. Now." She stressed the last word. "Anyone can see she's into Darius." She shrugged. "It was the way you said her name when you asked about her."

She looked disgruntled, but it was the hurt he sensed that moved him.

He stood and went to her, since she wouldn't come to him. He waited until she finally looked up at him. "I care for Sarah because she makes Darius happy."

Valeriya nodded. "She seems very nice."

"She risked her life for him." Tarrant couldn't stand the separation any longer. The dragon inside him wanted her, and so did the human part of him. That made her more special than she could ever know.

He scooped her into his arms. "Just as you risked your life for me." As he let that sink in, he carried her to the elevator. Once it opened, he stepped inside. "Up," he commanded.

"Where are you taking me?"

She didn't seem worried, since she twined her arms around his neck. "To bed." She needed to understand and accept him as he was. He wasn't the kind of man to give her poetry and candlelight dinners, but she'd never doubt that he wanted her.

It seemed to take forever for the elevator to reach the top. The door silently slid open, and he walked out. It slammed shut behind him. He hesitated, not sure which room to take her to.

"Shower," he decided. They could both use one. He veered into his room. He liked the idea of her there.

She sighed and rested her head on his shoulder while she

ran her fingers over his chest. "You know, I have no idea what time it is, or even what day it is."

"It doesn't matter." He carried her into the bathroom and set her down on the vanity. He didn't leave her, but stepped between her legs and crowded against her. "This matters." Then he leaned down and kissed her.

• • •

Darius scowled at the blank screen. Sarah reached around him and closed the laptop. "That went well."

He knew when she was being sarcastic. "I suppose you think I shouldn't have said those things to Valeriya."

Surprisingly, she shook her head. "You had to say them, to ask those questions. Tarrant is your brother."

She rubbed her hands over his shoulders, and he leaned back to rest his head against her chest. He inhaled her sweet scent, and it automatically relaxed him.

"But Valeriya is a part of his life now. I see it, so surely you can, too."

He could, that didn't mean he was thrilled with the idea. "Her sister is the leader of the Knights," he pointed out yet again.

"And I worked for the man who wanted to capture and cage you."

He couldn't refute Sarah's logic. Didn't mean he had to like it. "You're saying I'm being unreasonable."

"No. You're being a brother. You want to protect Tarrant. I get that. But look at it from his perspective. Valeriya betrayed her sister and her family to warn you. Since then, Tarrant kidnapped her, and her sister sent a man who shot her. She must be totally confused. And if she's developed feelings for Tarrant, she has to be questioning them. In some ways, we had it much easier."

"Easier?" He turned and captured his woman, dragging her into his arms. "We were on the run for days. We had teams from the Knights chasing us. Hell, they tried to blow you up." Just the thought had smoke billowing from his nose. His dragon was close to the surface.

Sarah waved the smoke away from her face, and he forced himself to get control. "But we didn't have years of family history between us. I had no idea who the Knights were before I went to work for Herman Temple. Valeriya has had to overcome her entire family history." Sarah rested her head on his shoulder. "I can't imagine how that poor woman must feel knowing her own sister sent a man after her, a man who shot her."

As much as it pained him to admit it, Sarah was right. "Okay. I get it."

"Do you? Because if Tarrant has his way, Valeriya will be with him forever. I saw how he looked at her."

"And how it that?"

"The same way you look at me."

Darius glanced at the backdoor. Ezra was still gone. He'd been gone for hours. He could be gone for days. As a water drakon, Ezra had more freedom than the rest of them. The water was his natural home. He could spend his entire life beneath the waves if he chose.

He felt guilty for driving the man out of his own home. But he wasn't here right now, and Sarah was. He didn't have to say anything. Her eyes went soft and she nodded. He picked her up and headed toward the stairs.

He wondered what Tarrant was doing then immediately scrapped that thought. If his brother was anything like him, and he was, he was making love to his woman. That was an image Darius didn't need in his head.

• • •

Karina was forced to admit that something was wrong. Either Riggs was dead, or he'd betrayed her. Neither was acceptable, but she had to deal with it.

She picked up her phone and tried Riggs's number one final time. Nothing. She hit the first number in her contacts list. "I need you," she told the man who answered. There was nothing more to be said.

A few minutes later, there was a knock on the door before it opened. Only Birch would be so forward. "What is it?" he asked. He knew her so well.

"Either Riggs is dead, or he double-crossed me." She was grateful he didn't say I told you so.

"What do you want me to do?"

That was Birch, always dependable. "We need to send a team to that cabin in the Cascade Mountains." She sighed and tried to order her thoughts. She was tired. Keeping on top of her business interests as well as the Knights was exhausting. And adding Valeriya's betrayal on top of it only dragged her down even more.

"I want that cabin destroyed. Burn it to the ground."

"Why?" She knew Birch wasn't questioning her decision or trying to change her mind. He wanted her to clarify her thoughts, not only for him, but for herself.

"If it's a safe house for Varkas, I want it gone. If my sister thinks to hide out there at some point in the future, I want it gone. I need to send a message to my enemies. There is nowhere they can hide. Nowhere they'll be safe from me." They all thought her ruthless, and she was, but it was time to step up her game.

She wanted Varkas.

"I'll send a team. It will be done within hours."

Being the head of the Knights gave her access to all their resources. "Make sure it's a team loyal to us." She'd had enough betrayal. First her sister, and now her lover. "Have them scour the area first. I want to know if there's any sign of Riggs and his crew or my sister. I want to know everything that cabin has to tell me before they destroy it."

She pushed out of her chair and walked around to the front of her desk. "I want it all recorded. I want to see this place for myself. I want to watch it burn." She needed that.

Birch's expression never changed, but she'd known him too long to be fooled. "What?"

"You have to let her go. You did everything you could for her."

She briefly closed her eyes. Only Birch would think that. Only he would believe it. "I should have been harder on her. I should have made her more aware of her duty to the family." It was her fault Valeriya had betrayed her. She'd been too lenient when her sister was a child.

Birch shook his head. "It was your father and mother's decision to allow Valeriya to go her own way. You were so strong they didn't think they needed anyone else. You were born to rule the Knights."

It was the truth, but didn't make her feel any better. "Just get it done. And keep looking for my sister. If she's still out there, I want her before one of the other Knights finds her."

Chapter Twenty-Three

Tarrant rested his hands on the stone countertop as he kissed Valeriya. He knew she was confused about their relationship. She had deep feelings for him. Hell, she'd said she loved him. And they'd only known one another for a short time. Then there was his history and identity to muddy the waters.

The wonder was she wasn't demanding to be released. But she was kissing him back, sliding her tongue between his lips, drawing a groan from them both. They'd both been working for hours and hours. He was used to it, but she wasn't. She'd fallen asleep at her desk.

He had to keep reminding himself she was human and therefore much more fragile than he was. She was still recovering from the blood she'd lost and the trauma to her body. Yes, his blood had healed her injuries, but she'd been pushed hard since the moment she'd met him. Stress could take a huge toll on the body.

And she was dealing not only with physical stress, but emotional as well.

He placed hot kisses along the line of her jaw and worked

his way up to her ear. There was a little silver hoop there. There was a matching one in her other ear. He noticed she never removed them. He caught it and lightly tugged.

"I'm going to start the shower running," he whispered. She nodded and tilted her head to give him easier access. He obligingly ran the tip of his tongue over the whorls of her ear.

Valeriya gasped and gripped his biceps.

Fully aroused, he put one hand on her lower back and dragged her right to the edge of the vanity. His erection pressed against her stomach. It was more torture than relief. If he didn't move soon, he'd end up taking her on the damn counter. Not a bad idea for another time, but right now they both needed to get clean. Valeriya also needed to rest.

He pulled away and stalked to the large shower stall. He felt her eyes on him the entire time. Her attention made his jeans even tighter. It was damn uncomfortable.

He swore and unzipped them. The relief was instantaneous, but it didn't last more than a second. If anything, it was worse now that the warm air in the room brushed his swollen shaft. He gritted his teeth and started the water running.

When he turned back around, Valeriya was still sitting where he'd left her. Her fingers were wrapped around the edge of the counter. Her knuckles were white.

He prowled back toward her, feeling every inch the beast on the hunt. She was such a tender morsel he wanted to eat her up in one bite. Her gaze fell to the opening in his pants. His cock was standing at attention.

A tiny smile played around the corners of her mouth. "Are you always this horny?"

She would think so, since he was always hard around her. He gripped the hem of her sweater and dragged it over her head. She raised her arms to make it easier for him.

"No," he told her. "It's you."

Her eyes widened, and she swallowed. He lifted her off

the counter and then stripped the remainder of her clothes off before removing his own. When they were both naked, he picked her up and carried her into the shower.

"Before you say it, I know you can walk," he told her. "But I like carrying you." He set her down in front of him. She raised her face to the warm spray and let the water cascade over her.

"I wasn't going to say it," she teased. He wasn't so sure about that, but he enjoyed their banter. Valeriya relaxed him in a way he'd never felt before.

She raised her arms and shoved her hair out of her face. It was still braided, so he took care of that. He tossed the elastic onto the built-in tiled shelf and threaded his fingers through the silky mass. He loved her hair.

She glanced over her shoulder and smiled.

Tarrant had to have her. He felt his dragon rising to the surface and forced him back. He couldn't have her if he shifted. That reminder was enough to have his beast subsiding.

So far, he'd rushed every time he'd taken her. Not this time. He grabbed the bottle of his body wash and squirted a dollop onto her back.

She jerked and then laughed. "That's cold."

"I'll warm it up," he promised. He placed his hands on her shoulders and began to spread the soap mixture around. It lathered and bubbled on her soft skin. He moved his hands lower, running them down her spine and lower back. He cupped the mounds of her full ass and squeezed.

She made a small squeaking sound and went up on her toes. "What are you doing?"

"Washing you." He went down on one knee and continued down the backs of her legs. They were strong and supple from all the walking she did in the city. She jerked and laughed when his fingers grazed the backs of her knees. A ticklish spot. He'd have to remember that. When he reached her ankles, he started back up her calves again, and worked his way to her shoulders.

She had both arms out in front of her, using the tiles to support her. Her head was bowed, and the water showered over her. Her breathing was ragged.

He needed to see her face.

He turned her around. Her eyes were closed, and her lips were parted as she dragged air into her lungs. The water washed the soapy bubbles from her body. It swirled around the tiles on the floor before being sucked down the drain. She opened her eyes and blinked several times.

"I'm just getting started," he told her.

"I may not survive." He knew she meant it as a joke, but neither of them was laughing.

"You will." He'd make sure of it. He leaned her against the wall so she was out of the direct spray. The steam from the warm water and the scent from the body wash created a tropical oasis. He didn't have to worry about her getting chilled.

He was hot enough to burst into flames.

Valeriya reached out to wrap her hand around his dick, but he caught her wrist and shook his head. "Not this time." She made him hotter than a teenage boy with his first woman. If she touched him, he'd be inside her in a heartbeat, and he wasn't done playing yet.

He caught both her hands in one of his and raised them over her head. She licked her lips, and the small gesture shot straight to his groin, leaving him panting. "What are you planning to do?" she asked.

Tarrant growled and lowered his head until their lips were almost touching. "I plan to taste every inch of you."

She trembled against him, and he caught the sweet scent of her arousal. He licked water droplets from her collarbone and followed them down to her cleavage. A drop of water was poised to fall from the tip of one nipple. He caught it on his tongue before it could plummet from its precarious perch.

Valeriya moaned and pushed her breast closer to his mouth. He lapped at the tip with his tongue before taking it between his lips. She was so damn sweet and giving. She never held anything back, didn't know how to play sexual games.

She was everything he'd stopped wanting thousands of years ago. He'd never allowed himself to believe he'd ever find her—the one woman who both man and beast desired with equal fervor.

She was dangerous to him. Made him weak. She also completed him and made him invincible. With her by his side, there wasn't anything he couldn't do.

He used his mouth, lips, and tongue to tease her breast and then gave the other one equal attention.

Her breath was coming in big gasps when he finally knelt before her. "Tarrant." She gasped his name, but he wasn't stopping. Not now.

He traced a path down her wet torso with his tongue, dipping into her navel. She tasted sweet. His hands followed the curve of her waist and hips. He loved her figure, full and feminine.

"Part your legs." He wanted to see and taste her.

She lowered her arms from over her head and touched his hair. He looked up. Her pupils were dilated, and her lips swollen and moist from his earlier kiss. Her hair hung like a dark curtain around her shoulders.

She slowly parted her thighs, sliding one foot over the tiles. Satisfaction filled him. She was his, now and forever.

He leaned forward and inhaled deeply, drawing the perfume of her arousal into his lungs. It calmed and excited him at the same time. It was intoxicating.

She gripped his short hair as he leaned inward and flicked his tongue over her clit. She gasped, and he smelled a fresh rush of arousal.

She was hot and wet and his. He slipped two thick fingers into her core. Valeriya went up onto her toes to evade him, but he simply followed.

• • •

Valeriya wanted to come, but she didn't want to come. Not yet. There was something different about Tarrant this time. His sense of urgency was missing. He'd certainly taken his time washing her back. There wasn't a single inch of her skin he hadn't touched or caressed.

And the man had outstanding hands. Big and strong, yet gentle as he'd soaped and stroked and aroused her.

Now he was on his knees in front of her, touching her in the most intimate way a man could touch a woman. He was giving her something she'd never had before. He was putting her first.

He'd let his friends know she was his. He'd saved her life, given her his blood. He wanted her forever. Or so he said.

She was still almost too afraid to believe it. That kind of love was for fairytales, not reality. Tarrant was a creature ripped from the very pages of myth and legend, except he wasn't the villain to be defeated, but the hero.

He started to slip his fingers from her core. She didn't want that, so she followed, coming down off her tip toes. It had been too much when he'd suddenly thrust them into her. Now it wasn't enough.

He wrapped his lips around her swollen clit and growled.

"Oh my God," she gasped. It was like having a vibrator attached to the sensitive bud. He thrust his fingers back into her sheath, and she came, melting around him in the most delicious way.

Her thighs quivered and her knees went weak. She was

grateful for the support of the wall behind her. She wanted to close her eyes but couldn't take them off Tarrant as he brought her the ultimate pleasure.

When he was done, he raised his head. He didn't smile, didn't look smugly satisfied, as he had every right to be. No, there was a warm tenderness in his gaze that made her heart stutter and then race.

He stood, caught her around the waist, and lifted her all in one motion. Then he bent his legs and slid his cock into her still-pulsing depths. They both shuddered and groaned as he pushed his thick shaft inward.

Her inner walls stretched to accommodate him. Already sensitive after just having an orgasm, they rippled around his hard length.

He held her easily with one arm and slapped his other hand against the tile. "You feel so fucking good."

She wanted to tell him how amazing she felt but couldn't manage to speak. They were intimately joined, and it was primal and beautiful.

He caught her chin in his hand and grazed his lips over his. It was such a contrast to the pounding rhythm of their hearts and the heavy pulsing of his cock.

"Tell me you love me," he demanded.

She froze and shook her head. Not because she didn't love him, but because she didn't want to be the only one to make herself vulnerable.

He began moving, pumping his hips up and down, moving his shaft and stimulating every nerve ending in her sheath. "Tell me." He was relentless. There was no give in him. He would have what he wanted.

His lips were still gentle as they caressed her cheeks and chin before returning to her mouth. The heat grew between her legs as he pumped in and out, going deeper with each thrust. His hips moved faster and more frantically.

Caught up in the wild ride, she knew she was close to coming yet again.

"Valeriya." Beyond the command, she sensed a deep need. And loving him as she did, there was only one thing for her to do.

"I love you." She whispered the words. A normal man might not have heard them over the rush of the water, the pounding of their hearts, and the gasping of their breath. But Tarrant was anything but ordinary.

He stilled and then began to pound into her with increasing ferocity. She held onto him as he drove them both over the edge. He called her name as he came. His shaft rippled inside her and pushed her into another orgasm.

Heat and pleasure swamped her even as she buried her hurt at his not returning the words to her. Maybe he couldn't. Actions, she reminded herself, spoke louder than words.

Then why did he need the words from her? Why wouldn't he return them?

There was no time to think. Tarrant raised his head, and this time there was satisfaction stamped on his handsome face. He nuzzled her neck as he liked to do and then carefully withdrew. He was still full and thick, so it wasn't easy.

He grimaced and she gasped. "I'm sorry." He kissed her cheek. He moved her back under the water and began to wash her. There was no lingering this time, only quick, efficient movements. When he was done, he quickly washed himself. She tried to leave the shower, but he simply wrapped his arm around her waist and pulled her back beside him.

She was yawning by the time he turned off the water. She stepped out of the shower and grabbed a towel. "I was going to do that," he told her.

"I've got it." She needed some distance after such a mind-blowing, heart-melting encounter. She'd given him everything. And Tarrant…he'd given her everything but the words.

She ran the towel over her body and then over her hair. Her stomach growled. It had been hours since they'd eaten steak and eggs. She had no idea how long. Tarrant's lair really was the land that time forgot. With no sunlight or darkness to mark the passing of time, and no clocks visible anywhere, she had no inkling of what time of the day or night it was.

Tarrant frowned as he dragged a towel over his broad chest and rippling abs. The muscles in his biceps flexed and moved as he worked. He really was gorgeous.

"You're hungry." It came out as almost an accusation.

"That happens when you don't eat for a while."

His scowl deepened, and he caught her by the arm and practically dragged her into the bedroom. She dug in her heels. "I'm not done in here." It was time to start laying down some ground rules if she was going to be staying with him. While she didn't mind him carrying her from time to time, she wasn't a rag doll.

She told him as much, then she shooed him on. "You can go if you're finished. I want to comb my hair." Since they weren't in her room, she couldn't moisturize her skin. Mostly, she needed a few minutes alone. Tarrant had an overwhelming personality. It would be easy to get lost and subjugated by it if she wasn't careful. He wouldn't mean to do it, but it would happen.

"I'll change the sheets on the bed," he announced. "And then make something for us to eat."

She grabbed a dry towel and used it to blot the water in her hair. "Good idea to change the sheets." She had no trouble with him doing that. "As for food. I want a sandwich. Something with cheese." She didn't want a meal with a lot of red meat and eggs. That was more protein than she needed.

"You need to eat well to regain your strength." He tossed the towel over the rod to dry. Valeriya almost swallowed her tongue as he ambled toward her. It was like watching a tiger stalk toward prey. He didn't walk so much as flow.

And he was naked. How could she not be distracted by that? And he was still aroused.

What had she been saying? Oh, yeah. "I can't eat like you, Tarrant. I want vegetables, fresh fruit, cheese, yogurt, and maybe crackers. But for now, I'd like a sandwich."

"You didn't like the steak?" His voice was neutral, but she caught the thread of hurt.

She put her hand on his chest. "I loved the steak. I enjoy red meat on occasion, but I eat more chicken and fish, and then only a couple times a week."

Tarrant frowned. "Is that enough?"

He honestly had no idea, but he was trying to understand and learn. That meant everything to her. "Yes, it is. Our metabolisms are much different. It's understandable you'd need more food and more red meat in your diet."

He nodded abruptly. "Come to the kitchen when you're done."

She was left looking at the open door. Tarrant detoured by the closet long enough to grab a pair of jeans and haul them on. Then he stripped the bed and got clean sheets from the closet.

Valeriya couldn't stop staring at him, so she closed the door and leaned against it. She got lightheaded and allowed herself to slide down and sit on the floor. What was she going to do?

She was going to love her drakon. They obviously had a lot to learn about one another. Unlike most new relationships, they didn't have the luxury of space or time. They'd been thrown together in a life-and-death situation.

He was trying. And her love seemed to mean something to him. It was enough. It was more than she'd ever had. The words would be nice, but she no longer needed them. He'd saved her life, given her his precious drakon tears, and claimed her in front of his friends.

For a man like Tarrant, that was everything.

Her drakon might not say he loved her, but he did. He might not even realize it.

That understanding propelled her to her feet. She pushed upright and leaned against the door until the room stopped spinning. Her body had been through a lot. She needed a good meal. She also needed to find out what time it was so she could get her body back on some kind of schedule.

Then it was time to start making a normal life with Tarrant. Or as normal a life as it could get between a human and a drakon with a secret society hunting them.

Chapter Twenty-Four

Tarrant didn't want to leave the bedroom, but the bed was made, he was dressed, and Valeriya was still in the bathroom. He could hear her moving around, so he knew she was okay. He wished he knew what she was thinking.

His phone was still tucked into the pocket of the jeans that were lying on the bathroom floor. He knocked and waited.

"Yes?"

He almost growled when she didn't open the door right away. He placed his hands on the wall next to the door to keep from opening it. "I need my jeans. My phone is in there."

And it was a measure of how much he trusted her that he'd forgotten about his phone. He never left his phone where someone else could access it. Never. It didn't matter it was password protected and she didn't have the code. His phone was never more than a few feet away.

The panel opened and she stuck her hand out, his jeans dangling from her fingers. He took his pants and she started to close the door. He wasn't having it. He caught her hand, raised it to his mouth, and sucked her index finger.

She moaned, and he heard a thump as though she'd hit the wall with her free hand. "Tarrant, what are you doing?"

He scraped his teeth over her finger and then nipped the pad of skin at the base. "Making sure you don't forget me."

She gave a quivering laugh. "Believe me, that will never happen."

He wanted to see her face, to kiss her, but he also knew when to back off. Still, he'd left her with something to think about. "I'll be in the kitchen when you're done. Help yourself to whatever you need from my closet."

He released her hand. If he didn't leave now, he was going to drag her out of the bathroom and into bed. He retrieved his phone and tossed his dirty jeans onto the pile of laundry he'd made on the floor. Even in the fight against evil, laundry had to be done. He'd collect the rest later and do a couple of loads.

The door to the bathroom didn't close right away. That gave him some satisfaction. He was feeling good, but his cock was still rigid. He could go for hours, but Valeriya wasn't used to making love so often. He didn't want to make her uncomfortable or sore.

He punched in his password and dialed his brother. Darius answered on the first ring. "What's wrong?"

"Nothing." He shifted his phone to his other ear and opened the refrigerator door. Valeriya wanted a sandwich. "Let me talk to Sarah."

He heard the rustle of covers and knew his brother and Sarah had been engaged in the same activity as he and Valeriya, only they'd done it in a bed instead of a shower.

"Why do you want to talk to Sarah?" Darius demanded.

Tarrant dragged a block of Swiss cheese out of the fridge and set it on the countertop. He had a tomato but no lettuce. Who needed leafy green stuff when there was red meat? Apparently, women did.

He heard Sarah and Darius whispering in the background.

They might as well have been yelling. He could hear every word. He grinned. Right now, his brother was getting a lecture from his woman.

He'd added mayonnaise and mustard to the bounty on the counter by the time Sarah came on the line. "Tarrant? What can I do for you?"

"Tell me about girl food." He had sliced ham. Maybe that would do.

"What?" Sarah asked.

Tarrant shut the refrigerator door and leaned against it. "Girl food?" he repeated. "Valeriya doesn't want meat and eggs again. She wants a sandwich, fresh fruit, and yogurt." There was no understanding women.

Sarah laughed. He might have taken offense, but he desperately needed her help. "I've had the same problem with Darius," she told him. Tarrant heard his brother muttering in the background. It made him feel better about his situation. "We're human. We can't eat as much as you. We also like to eat lighter. Just ask her what she wants. I'm sure she'll let you know."

"I'm asking you." Information was power, and Tarrant was all about information. He should have just gone online and done some research, but Sarah was a good source.

"She's mentioned vegetables, fruit, and yogurt. Ask her what kinds she likes. There are a lot of varieties. I'm assuming she'll like the usual things that go in salads like lettuce, spinach, tomatoes, carrots, radishes, mushrooms, sweet peppers, and such. As for fruit, I like bananas and apples, but she might like melon or grapes, too, or all of it." Her voice softened. "Just ask her to make a list. I'm sure it will be fine."

He was making too much of this. He knew he was, but it was his nature to gather information in any situation in which he felt uncertain. "Okay. Thanks." He hung up the phone and tucked it away just in time. Valeriya walked into the kitchen.

She was wearing one of his flannel shirts that hit just below mid-thigh and pair of socks.

"Everything okay?" She'd halted a few steps from him.

He was standing there like an idiot, staring at her. "Fine. Everything is fine. You need to make a list," he told her.

She cocked her head. "Of what? I've already started my list about the Knights. It's down in your computer lab."

He shook his head and went to her. He wrapped his arms around her waist and dragged her against him. She smelled fresh and clean, with just a hint of arousal and a whiff of him. He liked that she carried his scent.

"Food that you like. If you want all that girly food, I need to know what it is."

Her smile was so bright it almost blinded him. He'd obviously done the right thing. He relaxed, and the boulder of unease sitting on his shoulder dislodged and tumbled away.

"I can do that," she promised. "After we eat. I'm starving." Her stomach growled again, and he turned her so she was facing the counter.

"You're welcome to raid the fridge, but I've got cheese, a tomato, some ham, and other stuff." He wanted to provide for her, to give her what she needed.

"It's perfect. Just what I want."

His sense of pride was far out of proportion to the situation, but he didn't care. His woman needed something, and he'd provided it. His dragon rumbled inside him, content as well.

"We'll go shopping when things die down." It was going to take some ingenuity to get the fresh fruit and vegetables that Valeriya needed, but he was up to the challenge. He could always stock up on canned and frozen, but fresh was best.

"I'd like that." She smiled and went to the counter. "Do you have any bread?"

How had he forgotten bread? Feeling like an idiot, he

opened the refrigerator and then checked the cupboard. There was none there. The freezer was next. He pulled out a loaf of whole-grain bread. "Got it."

Valeriya took the frozen chunk of bread and laughed. "I guess I'll have a toasted sandwich."

He shook his head. "No need." He took back the bread, opened the bag and set the frozen chunk on the counter. "Watch this." He knew he was showing off and didn't much care.

Tarrant allowed himself to feel the burn of the dragon's fire deep within. He concentrated on the heat and blew gently on the bread—not quite fire, but superheated air. The ice crystals melted. He kept at it until he knew not only was all the ice gone, but the bread was warm, too.

"There you go." He stepped back from the counter.

Valeriya was staring at him with a look of wonder in her eyes. "That is so cool." She poked at a slice of the bread. "It's perfect."

He stood a little taller, and she laughed. This time, she poked him in the stomach. "You're all that and a bag of chips," she told him.

He frowned, not understanding the reference. He knew he'd seen it online, but he hadn't paid much attention.

Her fingers curled against his skin, more of a caress. "It means you're special and you know it."

"We should eat." He wasn't blushing, not exactly, but he wasn't comfortable, either. Someone else's approval had never meant so much to him, and he wasn't sure he liked it. Although, it did feel good when she praised him.

They made sandwiches. She made one and he used the rest of the bread to make a stack of his own. He let her have the tomato and piled meat and cheese on his.

She eyed the platter he set next to his seat at the counter. "You can really eat all that?"

"Yes." He didn't tell her he'd probably still be hungry when he was done. He went to the fridge and took out two bottles of water before taking his seat.

"That makes my point." She took a bite and chewed. He liked seeing her eat and knowing he'd provided for her. "I can't eat the way you do."

"I get it." And he did. It had been a long time since he'd lived alongside humans. Plus, both parts of him—the human and the dragon—wanted to take care of her. On a fundamental level, that meant protection, housing, and food.

• • •

Valeriya enjoyed her meal. The ham was tasty and the tomato relatively fresh. But it was Tarrant's effort that made it special. He was trying so hard, and that meant everything to her.

"What will happen?" She hated to bring up the Knights and her sister, but they were never far from her thoughts.

He set down the sandwich he was eating. "What do you mean?"

She shrugged and took a mouthful of water. "Will we live here? How will we avoid them?" She shivered and rubbed her hands up and down her arms. That was the part that worried her. "We can't let them find you." It was her biggest worry, even more so than her possible death.

Tarrant reached out and touched her hair before sliding his hand down to her cheek. "That won't happen."

"You seem so sure," she whispered. She wished she could be as confident. "They've had other drakons." She knew that for a fact. There had always been talk when she was growing up. She'd been a quiet child, and the adults had often forgotten she was in the room with them. Plus, she'd been known to eavesdrop more purposefully on occasion.

His expression turned bleak. "I know. Believe me."

"I'm sorry." She covered his hand. "Were they friends?"

He shook his head. "Drakons are solitary creatures." He frowned. "That's part of the problem. They have no one to call on in times of need."

She nodded and they both went back to eating. She managed another bite, but the conversation had ruined her appetite. "I get how that was the case in days gone by. There'd be no way for you to know what was happening to a drakon halfway around the world. But things are different now. Communications have changed."

Tarrant finished devouring the last sandwich on his plate and nodded. "Communications may have changed, but drakons haven't. Believe me, I've reached out."

Valeriya was smart enough to know if anyone could find reclusive drakons, it was Tarrant. "You've found them."

He nodded. "Not all, but some."

"Will they help if it comes to a war?" Her stomach roiled at the thought, but there was no denying reality.

He shook his head and pushed away from the counter. "Doubtful. They live in their own secure lives they've made and won't risk it. And I wouldn't ask them to."

She understood that. She didn't like it, but she understood. "What about your brothers?" He'd mentioned he had them, but she was reluctant to bring them up. "You didn't say how many you have, but I gather there's more than one."

He removed her empty plate and laid it in the sink. The dishwasher was still filled with clean dishes, as neither of them had emptied it. It was hard to think about household chores with everything else going on.

"My brothers and I stay in touch. We don't live near one another, for safety reasons."

"That's sad. I have a sister I lived with for years, but we were never close. You have brothers you're close with, but they don't live nearby."

"It is what it is." Tarrant put the kettle on to boil and then started a fresh pot of coffee.

"You don't have any chocolate, do you?" It was a weakness, but if a situation ever called for chocolate, it was this one.

He turned away from the coffeepot and tilted his head. "Chocolate."

She leaned her elbows on the counter and rested her chin on her hands. "Yes. I need chocolate."

"Is that another one of those girly foods you need?" he teased. She knew he was trying to take her mind off the direness of their situation. While she appreciated the effort, it really wasn't helping.

"You don't get between a woman and her chocolate. How can you not know that?" He'd lived a long, long time. She couldn't really comprehend the length of time he'd been around. Surely he'd had at least a few long-term relationships. Not that she really wanted to think about them, but still, they must have existed. No one could live alone for that long.

He shrugged and turned away. "I don't bring women to my real home."

She slowly straightened and lowered her hand to the counter. "But I'm here," she pointed out. He'd brought her here. "Or is this not your real home?" Come to think of it, there wasn't really much in the way of personal stuff here.

He dug around in a cupboard and withdrew something, but kept his hands behind his back when he faced her. "Of course this is my real home."

"Of course," she repeated. "But you just told me you don't bring women to your real home." Even as she told herself not to read anything into it, she couldn't help but get excited.

"You're not women. You're Valeriya." He prowled toward her, every inch the dangerous beast he truly was. "My Valeriya."

He came around the counter and scowled down at her. She couldn't stop smiling. Tarrant might not tell her he loved her, but she thought that maybe he did. Every action he took certainly seemed to prove it.

Now that she believed he returned her feelings, she felt as though they could get through anything. They'd face it all together.

"Why are you smiling?" His frown deepened. He really was quite fearsome.

"Because I'm happy." She placed her hands on his rock-solid chest. "You make me happy."

His scowl lessened. Now he looked suspicious. She barely kept herself from laughing again. "I'm about to make you delirious," he informed her. He brought his hand out from behind his back.

"Chocolate? You have a chocolate bar?" She reached out and grabbed the treat. "Dark chocolate, too."

"Anything else is too sickly sweet. This is the best money can buy."

"It certainly is." She ripped open the paper and peeled back the foil. She brought the bar to her nose and inhaled deeply. She ignored the amusement twinkling in his eyes.

"I take it you like it?"

She cracked off a small piece, popped it in her mouth, and let it melt on her tongue. "Umm," she agreed. She broke off another square and held it out to him.

Tarrant took it. He held the treat in his hand and looked it at for a long moment before eating it. She wished she knew what he was thinking.

"It's really good," she told him when the chocolate finally melted in her mouth. Tarrant broke off another piece and fed it to her. His fingers grazed her lips. She was suddenly very aware that he was only wearing a pair of jeans and she was dressed only in one of his shirts and a pair of socks.

"Tarrant." He took the bar of chocolate out of her hand and set it on the counter. The rich, deep flavor of the treat coated her tongue, but it was the brief taste she'd had of Tarrant that was making her crave more.

"You're not just any woman," he assured her. "You're mine." His gaze was direct and his words deliberate.

She finally understood that when he said she was his, he was claiming her in the only way he knew. It was his version of the words she'd given him.

"I love you, too." His eyes widened at her declaration and then grew darker. He growled and captured her mouth.

God, she loved kissing him. He held her head steady in his large palms as he slipped his tongue past her lips. He tasted like chocolate and Tarrant, the most addictive combination on the face of the planet, at least for her.

She wrapped her hands around his thick wrists, or at least tried to. Her fingers wouldn't meet. His wrists were wide and strong, just like the rest of him. He'd make other men appear small. He was a giant of a man with the build to match.

To her, he was simply Tarrant. And he was hers.

Their tongues tangled, the sweetness of the treat mingling with the sweetness of the moment. She still had no idea how they were going to live any kind of a normal life, not with the Knights searching for her. But she trusted Tarrant. With his knowledge and her determination, they'd figure something out.

Together.

Such a simple word, but it meant everything to her. She'd felt alone her entire life. Those days were over. She had a feeling Tarrant wouldn't let her stray too far from his side, and she was totally okay with that. She was a homebody at heart. She liked to draw and write her stories, she liked to read and watch movies. She didn't need cities and stores to be happy.

He drew his lips away. Both of them were breathing

heavily. "Valeriya…" He trailed off and shook his head.

"What?" she asked.

"You must be exhausted. Probably sore, too."

She smiled. Her drakon wanted her again. That was something she knew she'd never get tired of. She ran her fingers up his naked chest, following the swirls of his tattoo. "I'm not too tired."

He growled and covered her hand with his, flattening her palm against his skin. "You're sore?" he reminded her.

She shook her head. "Not too sore." She'd soak in a tub when they were done. Right now she needed Tarrant more. She loved him and he loved her. They were going to face the future together.

Her life had changed so much in such a short time, but for the better. Tarrant had stormed into her life, kidnapped her, and carried her to his lair. She'd gone from fear to love in no time. How could she not? Even when she'd thought him her captor, he'd been kind and considerate. Yes, she'd been afraid and intimidated, but it hadn't lasted. There was something between them that wouldn't be denied.

"You're killing me," he told her. "I'm trying to be all noble and shit."

Only Tarrant could make her laugh at a time like this. She was aching and, quite frankly, horny. She wanted her man, and she wanted him now.

"Be noble later." She pulled her hand away from his and started to slide it down his taut abs.

Before she could reach her destination—the impressive bulge in his pants—an alarm sounded.

Tarrant pulled away, all business as he stalked across the room.

"What is it?" She jumped off the stool and hurried after him. She didn't have a good feeling about this. All of a sudden her instincts were telling her they needed to run.

"Someone is here." He pushed a button on the security system and the noise stopped. Tarrant pulled an electronic tablet from a drawer and went to work, bringing up one picture after another in quick succession before stopping on a particularly chilling scene.

A half-dozen men all dressed in black were moving steadily toward the cabin. "Knights." She gripped the waistband of Tarrant's jeans as she peered at the screen. "Why are they here?"

There was no way they could know she and Tarrant were below, was there?

"Let's find out." He tapped the screen. They couldn't hear any voices, but there was no mistaking the faint sound of movement.

"I don't like this," Tarrant muttered.

Neither did she. She felt totally exposed. "Do you think they know we're here?" She whispered even though she knew they couldn't hear her. Her intuition was screaming they needed to get away. Now.

"There's no way. They're up to something else." He pointed at two of the men. "They're wearing cameras."

They walked all around the cabin and the surrounding grounds before cautiously stepping inside the structure. When the group split up, Tarrant put several images on the screen so he could keep an eye on all of them.

"They're looking for something."

"Most likely *someone*," Tarrant corrected.

"Riggs." Her stomach tightened. Of course her sister would send a team to search for Riggs and his men.

"Yes."

"They won't find anything, will they?" She'd been injured and out of it, so Tarrant had been left to deal with the aftermath all on his own.

He kept his eyes on the screen but reached around and

pulled her in front of him so his arms were wrapped around her. "No. There's nothing."

She shivered and moved closer to absorb the heat from his body. Tarrant had made sure there was nothing to indicate the other group had ever been here. She didn't want to think about what he'd had to do—what they'd forced him to do.

"You okay?" Tarrant kissed the top of her head and then nuzzled her hair.

The last thing she wanted to do was distract him. "I'm fine." There was no reason to be afraid. The Knights had no idea there was a bunker below the cabin, and she was with Tarrant.

Everything would be fine.

"They're leaving." The relief she felt was tremendous. Then Tarrant tensed. "What?" Horror filled her as she watched two of the men setting what looked to be explosives around the cabin.

Tarrant tossed the table aside, scooped her into his arms, and sprinted toward the big metal door at the end of the hallway.

They weren't going to make it.

Chapter Twenty-Five

Tarrant raced to the door guarding his lab, desperate to get Valeriya to safety. He'd be fine, but she was all too human. Fragile. She was calm in his arms, even though she had to know the world above them was about to explode.

He wanted her as far from the blast zone as possible. He hoped they had a lengthy timer on the explosives, but was doubtful, given the way the men had hustled out of there.

He felt the vibration before he heard the explosion. Acting on instinct, he shifted. His jeans ripped away as his body grew. There was no time to get Valeriya deeper underground and into his computer lab, which was the most secure place he had.

His body shifted as his dragon burst forth, eager to protect his treasure. He faced the titanium door and curled his large body and tail around Valeriya. She peered up at him, and he caught the fear on her face just as the blast echoed around them.

Something crashed and smashed on the floor. The entire place shook as the aftershocks rocked them. He used his head to pushed Valeriya closer to his body. Covered in armor-like scales, he was impervious to anything short of a nuclear bomb, and maybe even that. He'd never tested it to find out.

He heard a whoosh and smelled smoke. It was coming through the ventilation system. He swore.

"What is it?" Her voice trembled, making him angry. She should never have to be afraid. Not anymore.

"Smoke." His voice was deeper and more guttural in this form.

Then he felt the heat. Whatever they'd used in their bombs was fast burning and incredibly hot. They wanted the cabin destroyed quickly and completely. They were probably outside watching and filming the destruction.

Valeriya coughed and turned her face into his chest.

He was an air drakon. He could put that fire out in a heartbeat, but if he did, the men outside would know something was wrong. They'd know someone or something was here and wouldn't stop until they found them.

She coughed again.

If he did nothing, she'd die.

"I'm going to douse the flames and clear the smoke."

Valeriya jerked back, her expression fierce. "No. They can't know about you." She beat on his chest. He barely felt it. "I won't let them have you."

Once again, his woman was willing to die to protect him.

He wanted to roar with the injustice of it all. She was the kindest, the bravest woman he'd ever known.

The heat was making her sweat. Perspiration rolled down her forehead. He had to do something.

He was an air drakon. The element was his to manipulate.

He inhaled and pulled all the clean air toward him and created a bubble. It was still hot, but not fatally so. The air was also breathable.

Tarrant focused like he never had before. He put

everything he had into maintaining the bubble of protection around himself and Valeriya. Without his security system, he was working blind. He couldn't see if the men were still out there. And with the fire crackling and burning above them, there was no way he could possibly hear them, either.

His phone was most likely destroyed. If his shifting hadn't done the job, the blast and heat had. And even if it was working, he couldn't use it in his dragon form. All he could do was maintain the perimeter of safety around them and pray.

Valeriya's breathing became labored. The air around them was clean but very warm, bordering on hot. He was fine, but she was struggling.

"Control your breathing," he ordered. He knew he sounded gruff, but he was scared to death. He couldn't lose Valeriya. He'd just found her. After thousands of years alone, he wasn't about to let that happen.

He moved one of his claws and dragged it across his opposite arm. It wasn't easy to pierce his thick hide, not even with a drakon talon. "Drink," he ordered her. Maybe his blood could help save her.

She stared up at him, her green eyes glazed. He wasn't sure she understood him. He tried to ease her forward but ended up pushing her against his arm. She whimpered and he cursed. "Drink." He said it louder, put more of a command behind it.

She turned her head and touched her lips to his skin. He couldn't tell if she was drinking or not. There was no time to check. His shield was starting to collapse, and he was forced to direct all his attention toward maintaining it. If it failed, she was dead for sure. Her human body couldn't withstand the intense heat and lack of oxygen.

His muscles trembled and his own lungs began to strain, but he held on. He'd die before he'd release the shield protecting Valeriya.

It seemed like years instead of minutes until the heat began to recede. It wasn't much, but it was enough to tell him the worst of it was over. He couldn't even risk a glance at Valeriya, fearing he'd lose his concentration if he did.

There was nothing he could do for her until he could clear the air. Until then, he was doing the only thing possible.

The air inside the bubble grew stale as the oxygen diminished and carbon dioxide built up. It was time. Tarrant only hoped that the team the Knights had sent was either gone, or that the lowering of the flames would be seen as natural.

He had to act quickly so Valeriya didn't suffocate on the smoke-filled air filling his home.

Tarrant took a deep breath, dropped the protective shield, and exhaled. He wanted to send the dirty air billowing from the hidden ventilation shafts but didn't dare. It took skill and patience to direct it slowly out the ducts. He counted to ten and then inhaled, pulling fresher air back inside. It wasn't totally clean, but there was enough to make the space livable for Valeriya.

He shifted back to his human form and staggered to his feet. Valeriya lay on the floor, unmoving. He spread his arms wide and hit the security plates. They turned green, and he input the code into the keypad on the door. The elevator doors opened, releasing hot air.

Tarrant scooped her into his arms and stepped into the box. "Down," he ordered. When it reached the bottom, he used the retinal scanner and the door opened into his lab. The air was cleaner here as the ventilation duct was farther from the cabin.

He staggered into the room and lowered them both to the floor. Valeriya wasn't moving.

Blood stained her lips, but he had no way of knowing how much of it she'd ingested. "Valeriya?" He lightly shook her.

Fear filled him when her head simply lolled to one side.

He placed his head against her chest but couldn't hear a heartbeat.

"No. You can't die." He ripped the shirt she was wearing open and listened again. Nothing.

He grabbed her head and tilted it back so her mouth was open. It was difficult to force himself to go slow and be gentle. If he exhaled too deeply, he'd overinflate her lungs and possibly kill her.

He placed his mouth over hers and gave a soft puff of breath. He watched her chest rise and fall. Then he did it again.

"Don't you fucking die," he ordered. Frantic now, he placed one hand on her chest and pressed gently. He was so strong he might accidently crush her chest if he wasn't careful.

His arm had healed, but he manifested a claw and sliced it open again. He placed the cut over her lips. "Drink." Droplets slipped down her chin, but some of it dribbled into her mouth.

"You can't leave me alone with those damn Knights. You can't." He sat behind her and propped her against his chest. With his arm still pressed against her mouth, he implored her. "Drink. For me. Please, Valeriya."

Desperate, he gave her his heart. "I love you. Don't leave me."

• • •

Valeriya heard a voice as though from a great distance. It was unbearably hot. Her throat was parched and her lips were dry. Her inner organs felt as though they'd been roasted, and her lungs ached like she'd been running full-out for miles in the thick heat of midday at the height of summer.

Something wet brushed against her mouth, and she instinctively parted her lips. Some of it trickled down her throat, easing the burn. It tasted delicious, better than the coolest spring water.

She swallowed, letting it soothe her terrible thirst as she drifted in a cocoon of safety, content just to be. As she grew stronger, reality intruded. The armed men. The explosion. The fire. Tarrant.

She gasped and jerked forward. It hurt to draw a breath, but she didn't care. Where was Tarrant? She tried to say his name, but all she could do was cough.

"I've got you." His deep voice settled some of her panic. He was okay. He was here with her. Of course he was. Her drakon wouldn't leave her.

Memory came flooding back. He'd protected her, using his body and his abilities to create a protective bubble of some kind around them.

She tried to sit up and turn around so she could see him, but was too damn weak. "You okay?" she managed to get out.

He lifted her as though she weighed nothing at all and turned her so she was lying across his legs with one of his arms supporting her shoulders. His hair was damp and his torso gleamed with sweat. A cut on his arm healed before her very eyes.

She ran her hands over his chest and shoulders. "You're okay."

He nodded. His eyes were glassy and his expression bleak. "You're the one who almost died." He jerked her tighter against his chest. "Don't ever do that again."

It was an irrational demand. "I won't," she promised.

He nodded and kissed her forehead and her cheeks. "I thought I'd lost you. Again." His hand shook as he pushed a damp lock of hair away from her forehead. She stank of smoke and sweat, and so did he, but they were both alive and safe. Nothing else mattered.

"You saved me." She touched his cheek. "I knew you

would." It was important he understood she trusted him completely and without reservation.

"Valeriya." He buried his face against her hair. Something solid fell across her face. She caught a glitter of green before it fell to her lap. She picked it up and held it in her hand. A drakon tear. Now she knew the gems were the physical manifestation of his tears, she didn't want any more of them. She'd cherish the ones she had, but she never wanted him to hurt this badly again.

She'd cry, too, but her tear ducts were completely dried out from the heat.

A fever began to build inside her. "Tarrant."

"What is it?" His eyes were a little bloodshot but they were steady.

"Heat. Burning me from the inside." It was familiar, and not like the burn from the fire.

"That's my blood healing you." He kissed her cheeks. "I'm sorry it has to hurt you to heal you."

She sucked in a breath and swallowed a moan. The last thing she wanted was for Tarrant to worry any more than he already was. "I'll be fine," she managed to get out between bursts of pain. "Doesn't hurt a bit."

"Liar." There was such love in that one word. He pressed his lips gently to hers and held her as the spasms rocked her. She closed her eyes and hung on until the burning finally eased and left a delicious cooling in its wake. She knew what to expect this time, and that made it easier to endure.

When she finally opened her eyes, Tarrant was leaning against the wall with her in his lap. "You saved my life again. It's becoming a habit." She ran her fingers over his hard jaw. "Thank you."

He scowled. Amazing how that expression, which had once scared her senseless, she now found endearing. "Let's not do it again."

"I'm all for that. It's no picnic." She knew her drakon didn't want to talk about it. That was fine by her. Almost dying wasn't something she particularly wanted to relive.

"You're naked." She'd really been out of it not to notice that until now.

He gave a small chuckle. "There wasn't exactly time to change out of my jeans before I shifted."

She supposed not. It had all happened so quickly.

"You're not much better."

She glanced down to find the shirt she was wearing holding only by the last button on the bottom. The rest were gone. She tugged the shirt closed and changed the subject. "What's happening outside?" It was easy to forget there was an entire world outside Tarrant's home.

"I don't know." He leaned his head back against the wall. For the first time since she'd met him, he looked tired. It must have taken a tremendous amount of energy to protect her like he had.

"You need to rest." She wanted to take care of her man. She had a feeling he tended to push himself until he dropped.

He dropped a quick, hard kiss on her mouth. "Later." He gathered his strength and stood, never relinquishing his hold on her. He carried her to the chair he favored and sat. She knew it was useless to try to get away from him, and since she didn't particularly want to, she leaned against him and watched as he pulled up the outside footage from the security cameras.

"Oh my God." There was absolutely nothing left of the cabin but a pile of smoldering rubble. Thankfully the flames hadn't spread to the nearby trees and set the entire forest ablaze.

"Whatever they used had burned hot and fast. That was smart. The last thing they'd want would be to cause a forest fire. That would bring a huge investigation. As it is, no one may ever know the cabin burned down. There's no one around for miles, and the smoke it already starting to dissipate. Thankfully, they didn't wait around. If they had, they might have noticed one wall didn't burn like the others."

"The secret staircase." She'd forgotten all about that.

"Yup, but don't worry. I'll seal off that entrance and make another," he promised.

Tarrant's fingers flew over the keyboard and he started the footage from where the men left the cabin. Valeriya rested her head on Tarrant's shoulder and watched the men race away from the area.

She jumped when the building exploded. "Wow." The whole thing seemed to implode. Then the fire started. She swallowed hard. "I'm sorry they burned down your cabin."

He shrugged. "I'm not. Hopefully they'll leave this site alone now."

There was that. She hadn't thought about it that way. "From their perspective, they destroyed Darius Varkas's safe house."

"And your sister is sending you a message."

Yeah, she hadn't wanted to think about that. She and Karina might not have been close, but she never thought they'd ever reach a point where her sister would try to kill her.

Tarrant moved his arm so her head tilted back. His eyes were an icy blue but she could see the warmth smoldering behind them. "You know that, don't you?"

She nodded. "Yes. She's letting me know there's nowhere for me to hide. She doesn't know if I'm still in the area, but she's making it so I have no shelter to run back to."

He nodded. "My family is yours now. Karina was never truly your sister. She belongs to the Knights of the Dragon."

"I know." It still hurt, even though she'd known that all her life.

He skimmed a finger down her cheek. "Don't be sad. You

have three brothers now."

She pushed upright and grabbed his shoulders. "You have three brothers." That was unbelievable. She'd never known that drakons actually formed those kinds of familial bonds. "Real brothers, not just close friends?" Living thousands of years could create close ties between people.

Tarrant smiled. In spite of the sweat, dried blood, and smoke, he was still sexy as all get out. "Real brothers. Same dragon sire but different mothers."

A lightbulb suddenly went off. "Darius Varkas." There had been something familiar about him when she'd seen him, but she hadn't been able to put her finger on it. Now it made sense. He reminded her of Tarrant, just a rougher version with different coloring.

"Yes, Darius is my older brother."

"Wow." That was a lot to wrap her head around. "And the other two?"

He ran his finger down her nose and then tapped the end of it. "Ezra and Nicodemus."

"Ezra and Nicodemus." She repeated the names. Tarrant really had a family. Then she frowned. "I thought Darius was an earth drakon?"

"He is." Tarrant pulled open a drawer and pulled out another phone. "I need to let Darius and the others know. The fire hasn't made the news, and most likely won't, but I'd rather they hear about it from me first, just in case."

"Of course." They might not live together, but they seemed close. She had no experience with that kind of relationship with a sibling. They were technically only half-brothers since they had different mothers, but that didn't seem to matter to Tarrant.

He dialed a number and then put it on speaker so she could hear. She smiled her thanks. "What?" The deep voice wasn't one she recognized. This wasn't Darius Varkas.

"Ezra. Figured you'd be out for a swim."

"Why are you calling?" It wasn't annoyance Valeriya heard in his voice but concern. She already liked the man, even though they'd never met.

"Ah, there's been a small explosion." Valeriya rolled her eyes. Tarrant was the king of the understatement.

"Are you okay?" Ezra demanded. "Darius, get your butt down here," he yelled before turning his attention back to the conversation. "Well?"

"I'm fine. Valeriya is fine, too, but the cabin is toast."

"Shit. What happened?"

Before Tarrant could answer, another male voice demanded. "What the hell is going on?" This one she recognized as Darius Varkas.

Tarrant winked at her. "The Knights paid us a little visit and burned down the cabin."

"You're okay?"

In spite of their gruff, direct manner, it was obvious to her the men all cared deeply for one another.

"It was a little dicey for a while, but we're fine."

"Valeriya?" Darius asked. His concern took her aback.

"I'm fine," she answered.

"Good."

Ezra broke back into the conversation. "What are we going to do about the Knights?"

"Right now, they don't know about me or you. Only big brother." Tarrant began to absently rub his hand up and down her arm. "They have no idea the bunker was below the cabin. That means we should be safe here as long as I move the exterior entrance before someone comes back to investigate. Let me keep doing research on the Knights and see what I come up with."

"Sarah and I are moving soon."

"Where will you go?" Tarrant asked.

"Undecided, but I don't want to put Ezra in danger by staying here much longer."

"You and Sarah are welcome to stay as long as you need."

She could tell that Ezra meant it. They had big hearts, at least where family was concerned.

"I know, but it's safer for all of us if we're not together. Not until we know what's happening with the Knights."

"I agree with Darius." Tarrant dragged in a deep breath. "Listen, I need to go and inspect the damage to my home. Valeriya needs to rest. She almost died in the heat and smoke."

"Tarrant needs to rest, too," she added. "He expended a huge amount of energy creating a protective bubble so I'd survive. Then he gave me more of his blood."

He frowned, but she winked at him. He simply shook his head. "I gotta go."

"You take care of yourself," Darius told him.

"Will do."

"Call later," Ezra demanded.

"I'll be in touch. One of you call Nic and fill him in on everything that's happened." Tarrant ended the call and then tucked the phone in the pocket of the shirt she was wearing. It was the only place to put it, since he was naked.

He pushed out of the chair and headed toward the elevator. "Let's go see what's left of the place."

Chapter Twenty-Six

Tarrant wouldn't admit it to anyone, but he was tired. Talking with his brothers, connecting to them, had helped settle him. He was still jittery about almost losing Valeriya. It was closer than he ever wanted to come again.

They rode the elevator in silence and stepped out into the smoky hallway. "Turn your face toward me." She didn't hesitate, but buried her face against his neck. He took a deep breath and blew.

Wind whipped up around them. He used his skill as an air drakon to direct the smoke toward the vents. He breathed in and out again and again until every lungful he drew in was nothing but fresh air. He'd never thought of the placement of his air vents as being a security risk, because it hadn't been to him. Now that he had Valeriya, he'd have to make some changes.

"Is it okay?" she asked.

He kissed the top of her head. "Yes. All the bad air is gone." The walls still smelled smoky. They'd have to be washed and repainted. The furniture that couldn't be fumigated would have to be replaced. It was an irritation, but doable.

She patted his arm. "Put me down."

He shook his head. "No. You're only wearing socks, and I'm not sure how much broken glass or debris might be lying around." He headed for the kitchen and living room areas. Those rooms were directly under the cabin and were the hardest hit.

"Oh my God," Valeriya whispered.

The place was a mess. The fountain that used to trickle down the far wall was dry. Dust and ash covered the sofas and entertainment center. Glass had exploded in the kitchen and plastic had melted. The huge stone countertop was cracked in several spaces.

"I'm so sorry." Valeriya wrapped her arms around his neck and hugged him tight. "They destroyed your beautiful home."

He sent a cool blast of air over one of the stools to make sure the metal was no longer hot before he deposited her onto it. It didn't matter if it made her dirty as they were both already filthy. "I need to get some pants." It was easy to forget he was still walking around naked.

The distress in her face was momentarily replaced by a flash of desire as she skimmed her gaze over him. "Ah, yeah, probably a good idea."

He liked that he could distract her, even with all the destruction around them. "Stay there," he told her. "I'll get your shoes." He didn't look back, but he felt her eyes on him as he walked away.

The broken glass and debris didn't bother him as he crunched his way to his bedroom. The minor cuts healed almost as soon as they happened. He went to the closet and snagged a pair of track pants. Once he had them on, he pulled on a T-shirt and jammed his feet into a pair of boots. This room didn't smell as bad as the outer ones, but there was no mistaking the odor of burning wood.

Tarrant hurried across the hallway and found Valeriya's sneakers. What little clothing she had reeked of smoke. They needed to get cleaned up and do some laundry, assuming his water pump was still operational. "One thing at a time," he muttered.

He strode back to the kitchen, happy to see that she'd obeyed him. The last thing he wanted was for her to be hurt again. She'd been through so much—had almost died twice since she'd been here.

The Knights of the Dragon had much to pay for.

He went straight to her and went down on a knee. He slid one of her shoes onto her foot and quickly laced it. Then he retrieved the second and did the same. "There. Now your feet should be protected."

Her hands touched his face, and he glanced up. There were tears in her eyes. "What is it?" he demanded. "What's wrong?"

She shook her head. "Nothing. Well, other than your home being destroyed and my almost dying." She gave a shaky laugh. "That's not why I'm crying." She waved her hand in front of her face and swiped at a single tear as it escaped. "Thank you for taking such good care of me."

He couldn't believe his ears. "They almost killed you," he pointed out.

"Yes, and they would have if you hadn't protected me, hadn't saved me. You're an incredible man, Tarrant."

His heart swelled in his chest. "I'll protect you," he promised. "Always."

She leaned down and rubbed her nose against his, the gesture playful and touching at the same time. "And I'll always protect you."

"You're stuck with me," he warned.

She slid off her chair and he rose to stand in front of her.

Valeriya wrapped her arms around him and settled her body against his. Such a simple gesture, but something inside him seemed to snap into place.

This was his woman, his life. Drakon that he was, he'd protect her with everything in him. The Knights had made a huge mistake. When they'd come after his brother, he'd been hot with anger, ready to blast them.

Now they'd attacked his woman, and he was coldly furious. He wouldn't rest until every last one of them had paid for what they'd done. If they wouldn't leave the drakons alone, he'd destroy everything they'd ever built, and then he'd destroy them.

He didn't think he was being overly harsh. Drakons had left the humans alone for thousands of years, wanting only to live in peace, but the Knights wouldn't stop. Would never stop. He understood that now. Their greed for money, power, and the hope of immortality would never allow them to.

They had to be eliminated.

"What are you thinking?" Valeriya peered up at him, concern etched on her pretty face. "Whatever it is, it's not good."

She already knew his moods almost as well as his brothers did. He stroked a smudge of soot from her brow. "This is war." He wouldn't sugarcoat things. Valeriya needed to understand who and what he was.

She looked stricken but nodded. "I know." She glanced at the refrigerator. "Do you think the bottled water might have survived?"

She was changing the subject, but he understood. Her sister was going to be a casualty of the war between the Knights and the drakons, and there was nothing she could do to prevent it.

"I'll check." He didn't want to leave her, not when she was upset, but he forced himself to take the half-dozen steps to the fridge. He opened the door. The power was still on, thanks to his underground generator, and everything inside seemed untouched by the blast and heat. He grabbed a couple bottles of water and shut the door.

He handed her one of the bottles. "Let me taste it first to make sure." He unscrewed the top and took a long swallow. The water flowed down his parched throat. "It's good."

She followed suit, taking smaller sips.

"I'm sorry," he blurted. He hated feeling like this. Uncertainty was not a state of mind he was familiar with. He always had a plan, always knew what he was going to do next. He wasn't used to having to factor in someone else's views or opinions.

"I know." She set the bottle on the cracked counter. "You've left them alone for years."

"We've basically hidden for centuries, not wanting to start a war." That had galled many of the drakons. "We figured, out of sight, out of mind."

"It didn't work."

He shook his head and downed the last of the water in the bottle. "No, it didn't."

• • •

Tarrant's throat rippled as he drank. He looked grim when he set the bottle down next to hers.

"The Knights kept looking for you." She knew enough about the history of the Knights, and about human nature, to know they'd never leave the drakons in peace.

"You got that right. They trekked to the highest mountains. They didn't climb Everest simply because it was there, but because a drakon lives there."

"Really?" Now that was fascinating.

"Yeah, he mostly sleeps, but every now and then he rolls

over and reminds them he's there. They'll never get to him."

She could already imagine writing a child's story about a dragon living in a mountain. Or maybe not. Better not to give the Knights more ideas.

"We never wanted to hurt anyone." There was resignation in Tarrant's voice. She noticed the fatigue in his eyes and the slight slump of his shoulders, so unlike her drakon.

Even though there was nothing she could do to change things, she reached out and placed her hands on his chest, offering comfort. "I know."

His eyes began to glow, and she caught a brief glimpse of the creature dwelling inside him. "I do now," he continued. "I want to eliminate every threat to you and to my brothers. That means they have to die. All of them."

For a woman who'd done her best to walk away from the dark, violent history of her family, it was ironic she was right in the thick of things, and on the opposing side. "I know," she repeated. It made her sick to think about how many people would die in this war, but the Knights had made their choices, had known what they were doing.

She shivered and slipped her arms around his waist. "I'm scared. For you, for them. It's worse now that they have computers and satellites, maybe even the help of the military. I'm not sure there will be any winners in this war."

"I'm not worried about their satellites or the military. I have more control over them than they could ever imagine."

That was both a scary and reassuring thought.

He wrapped his arms around her, offering her his strength. "I won't hurt any innocents. We're not like the Knights." He kissed her temple.

That hurt, but she knew it was also true. Her sister and the others had no trouble harming those who wanted nothing to do with their pursuit of drakons. Just look at what had happened to her. Her own sister had sent a man to hunt her down.

"It's all crazy."

"I know." He gripped her shoulders and eased her away from him. "I can't promise neither of us will be hurt again, but I'll do my best to prevent it."

She licked her parched lips and stared into the face of the man she loved. She'd never fully appreciated what military spouses dealt with, knowing their loved ones were heading into a war against overwhelming forces. At least her man was a drakon. Just being what he was protected him against much of what their enemies would throw against him, and she was still terrified for him.

"I'm a weakness, a chink in your armor."

He scowled. "I don't wear armor. Knights do."

She found his hatred of all knights endearing. "I stand corrected. I'm a chink in your scales."

The corners of his mouth tipped up. It wasn't quite a smile, but it was close enough to make her heart flutter. "You're my strength, not a weakness."

She couldn't quite believe that. "I make you vulnerable," she pointed out. "I'm human." She would never be a drakon, could be hurt more easily, and would age unless she continued to drink his blood.

He rubbed the pad of his thumb over her cheek. "You'll keep me working smarter and sharper because I have to protect you."

There was no point in arguing about it. Her drakon was stubborn. Nothing she could say would change his mind. "What do we do first?" Better to take one step at a time rather than try to process everything at once.

He sighed and glanced around. "We see what we can do about this place first. You tackle laundry. All the sheets, towels, and clothes need to be washed. I'll work on securing the outside entrance and then clean up inside. I'll have to leave most of the cabin rubble as is. I expect other members of the Knights to come snooping around to find out for themselves what happened."

It was weird to be thinking about such mundane tasks when their world had literally exploded such a short time ago. Her sister and the Knights wanted her dead, and they'd want to capture Tarrant if they knew about him. A war was coming, but she needed clean underwear.

"Where's your laundry room?"

He took her hand and led her to the first door on the left, past the kitchen. "In here." The room was small but contained everything necessary. There was a fairly new washer and dryer. There was also a sink and counter.

"I can handle this." She didn't mean the laundry, but the upcoming conflict with the Knights and her sister.

He tilted her chin up and brushed a kiss across her lips. "I know you can." She knew he understood, and his confidence bolstered her resolve.

"I'll get started on the laundry." She wanted to stay with him, but they both needed time to think. There was also way too much work to be done.

• • •

Luther Henderson walked into Herman Temple's outer office. He knew he was pushing his luck, having put the man off for so long, but he'd needed sleep. He'd also wanted time to weigh his options and plan his next move.

It had taken him time to ditch his tail and head to the second apartment he kept under an alias. That was where he truly lived, not the tiny apartment in Manhattan listed on his employment records. Then he'd had to sneak back into his official residence so his tail could pick him up once again.

He'd spent hours reading the valuable book he'd

retrieved from Gervais Rames's bookstore. For something so simple—nothing more than paper and ink—it was incredibly dangerous.

As always, Victoria Marshall was seated at her desk. He wondered about the exact nature of her relationship with Temple, but didn't delve too deep. Still, it angered him to think of a woman as smart and beautiful as her in bed—possibly both literally and figuratively—with someone like Temple. Maybe she was nothing more than his receptionist, but she had to know that more went on than just regular business. That made her as bad as Temple.

Not your business, he reminded himself. "Is Temple in?"

Most people reacted to his size. He was a big man and drew attention, all of it unwanted. It was the reason he always wore suits. People seemed less afraid of him when he was dressed that way. He looked at it as camouflage. Even though he'd been wearing them for years, had his suits tailored specifically for him, he never felt entirely comfortable.

He was a jeans and T-shirt guy at heart.

But Victoria had never shown any reaction to him one way or the other. She treated him as she did everyone else—in a cool and competent manner—and it irked him.

In spite of his many talks with himself about what a bad idea it was, he was attracted to Victoria. He was a man used to looking below the surface, and his instincts screamed there was much more to her than the facade she presented to the world. Or maybe he was just seeing what he wanted to see.

"He's been expecting you." There was neither annoyance nor approval in her tone. She was as businesslike as always. "I'll tell him you're here."

He waited while she picked up the phone to the intercom system and spoke to Temple. Luther half expected his boss to fire him, and that simply wouldn't do. It didn't fit with his plans.

"He'll see you now." Victoria's gaze met his, and he nodded, not showing just how jolting it was to peer into her clear-blue eyes.

He turned his attention to the matter at hand and opened the door. Temple was seated behind his desk, as though that gave him authority. It was all Luther could do to keep from smiling at the pompous ass.

He shut the door behind him, reached into his jacket pocket, and drew out the second book he'd taken from Rames's bookshop. "Don't think it's of much use, but it was the only thing I found of value." A lie, but Temple didn't know that.

Temple raised an eyebrow and tapped his steepled fingers together. Without a word, he leaned forward, took the book, and leafed through it. Luther saw the covetous look in the man's eyes, even though he was trying to hide it.

It occurred to him that Victoria was much more adept at hiding her true feelings than Temple was. Before he could follow that train of thought, Temple dumped the book back on the desk.

"That's it?"

Luther nodded. "There are a lot of books there, first editions, and some that appear valuable, but that was all I found that might be of interest to you."

Temple sat back in his chair again. Luther could only assume he was trying to appear in charge of the situation. "Just where have you been all this time?"

Luther knew he was skating on thin ice and decided to give up some of the truth. "It took a long time to search the shop. There were a lot of books." He was curious to see if Temple would admit to having him followed.

"My men said you weren't there past dawn."

He crossed his arms over his broad chest. "Your men are fools. I ducked out for a bite to eat, evaded them, and went back."

Temple didn't look convinced.

"There was a secret room in the shop. I was in there all day. I couldn't risk leaving in case someone looked in the window and saw me."

"A secret room?" Temple sat forward again. "Tell me about it," he demanded.

Luther shrugged, knowing it would make Temple crazy. "Looked as though someone else had already been there. Either that or Rames moved some things before he died. I went through what was left but found nothing else of interest." He had no plans to tell Temple about the book he'd taken and hidden away.

"You will take me there and show me." After issuing his edict, Temple stood and walked to the antique coat rack to retrieve his coat. "And next time, you'll call in and update me. You don't leave me waiting."

Luther didn't bother responding one way or the other. Arrogant as Temple was, Luther knew he'd take that as compliance with his orders. Luther would do what he always did—whatever he felt was best.

Victoria glanced up from her laptop as they exited the office. "Will you be back again today, sir?" she asked Temple.

"No." The man didn't even glance her way as he left.

Luther couldn't help himself. He caught her eye, and winked. He kept his smile to himself as he followed Temple out of the building and into the waiting limo.

Chapter Twenty-Seven

Valeriya fell into bed totally exhausted. The linen was clean and so was she. The faintest smell of smoke still lingered. All the walls and ceilings would have to be washed and painted, the floors scrubbed, and some of the furniture replaced, but they'd made a good start.

Tarrant had obliterated any sign of the old entrance through the cabin, sealing it tight and burying it. He had a second one through the cave system in his basement. It was a long tunnel that opened up in the middle of the woods, but at least it was safe and very well hidden. They'd use that one for the time being.

Valeriya tried to stay awake until Tarrant joined her. She could hear the shower running as he cleaned up. The sound was soothing, and she closed her eyes. She had no idea how much time had passed when she became aware of Tarrant's large body wrapped around her. Cocooned in his warmth, she drifted back to sleep.

Several times, she woke to go to the bathroom, always tumbling back into his welcoming arms. When she opened her eyes again, she felt rested. Hungry, too.

In spite of the uncertain future before them, she was happy. She inhaled, drawing in the fragrance of his soap and Tarrant's unique scent. Her entire body quivered.

He drew his big hand down her spine and then up again. "Go back to sleep."

She shook her head, rubbing her hair against his chest. "I'm done sleeping. I don't think I've ever slept this much or this hard in my life."

"You needed it." His voice rumbled, deep and low, the vibration of it flowing through her.

"I've lost all track of time. I don't know if it's day or night, or even what day of the week it is." It was strange not to be aware of something she'd always taken for granted, but it was becoming the new normal.

"Does it matter?" His calmness floated through her. "Neither of us has to leave home to go to work."

That made her laugh, and she rubbed her hand over his taut abs. "No, I guess not." It felt strange to not have a schedule. It made her realize just how much she'd depended on hers. Most people did.

She made little circles just above his belly button. "So, what do we do?"

He rolled suddenly and she found herself flat on her back with Tarrant looming above her. His legs were between hers, and there was no mistaking his arousal, not with his thick shaft pressed against her inner thigh.

"Whatever we want," he replied.

She linked her hands behind his head, grateful the light was on in the bathroom. The door was almost closed, but it gave enough of a glow for her to see him. She didn't have his preternatural vision.

"And do you have any ideas?" Before he could suggest anything, she decided to tease him. "I know. We could get up and start washing the walls and ceilings."

He growled, sounding more animal than man. He nipped at her chin and then kissed a path to her ear. She shivered and gave him a mock frown.

"Don't like that idea? There's still more laundry to be done." She'd only gotten through about half of it. "Or we could survey more of the damage outside."

When he sighed, a whoosh of warm air fanned over her ear and neck, sending goose bumps running down her arms. "If that's what you want." He pressed his hands against the mattress and started to lever himself up.

She clung to his neck and twined her legs around his thighs. "Beast."

He grinned and lowered himself back down, supporting most of his weight on his hands. "Don't you forget it." He grazed his lips over hers. "I always get what I want."

Breathless from his kiss and wanting more, she used her grip on his neck to pull herself slightly off the pillow so she was closer. "And what is it you want?" She liked this playful side to their relationship.

His eyes turned molten blue and began to glow. "You." Her heart clenched, and a deep warmth spread outward all the way to the tips of her fingers and toes.

"I'm yours." She was fully committed to him, to their relationship.

"Valeriya." The worshipful way he said her name brought tears to her eyes. There was no more teasing, no more play. He captured her lips and kissed her like he needed her more than food or air. And maybe he did. Her need for him went that deep.

Mine.

She caught the echo of thought and knew it wasn't her own. Tarrant's? Not quite. It was more primitive. The dragon side of his nature?

Then his tongue plunged into her mouth and she didn't care about anything but returning the caress stroke for stroke.

He supported his weight on one strong forearm and cupped her breast with his free hand. She moaned and pushed upward, wanting more of his touch. Her nipple was a tight nub, and he flicked his thumb over the tip.

She ran her hands over his wide chest and down to his narrow flanks. Ignoring his growled warning, she wrapped her hands around his shaft and stroked.

"Fuck. Valeriya. Feels so good." His words were forced out between gasps. He buried his face against her neck and ran his teeth over the sensitive skin.

She sucked air into her lungs. Every nerve ending in her body was alive with sensation. Emptiness pulsed between her thighs. The need to celebrate the fact they were both still alive and together was overwhelming.

"Tarrant." She had to have him now.

He understood what she needed and reached between them to position his cock at her opening. There was no more foreplay. He flexed his hips and pushed inward, sliding past her body's initial resistance and right into her wet warmth.

She clung to his biceps. His tattoos seemed to glow in the darkness, becoming almost alive. It was fascinating and beautiful. She traced the edge of one swirl.

Tarrant groaned and kept up the inward pressure until he was buried to the hilt. He dropped his head forward, panting like he'd run for miles.

It was always like this between them—urgent but tender. She didn't know how else to explain it. "Tarrant." She whispered his name as he began to rock against her. There were no hard thrusts, but this somehow felt more out of control.

Maybe it was the love. It welled up inside her as he moved in and out of her body. His thick shaft stimulated every nerve in her slick channel, pushing her closer to the edge each time he slowly slid back in.

• • •

Tarrant had made love to many women over the course of his long life. He'd even made love to Valeriya before. But not like this. Nothing had ever felt like this.

The two of them were one. He could feel her inside him. She invaded his mind, his body, and his soul until the two of them became one entity. He was feeling an extra buzz, as though his dragon was close to the surface. His tattoos tingled, something they'd never done before.

He felt alive like never before. His intellect was unrivaled, his determination and will made of titanium, but this small woman made him forget his own name.

And he wouldn't have it any other way.

She was his and he was hers.

She moved with him, traced the curves of his tattoos, dug her nails into his skin. Her touch was at times soft and gentle, at others demanding. He wanted to give her whatever she needed.

"I love you." Her breathy declaration was worth more than all his treasure combined.

He felt her tremble, sensed the desperate grip of her muscles around his cock, heard the way her breath caught in her throat before she released a deep moan.

His own release welled up from deep inside him. He caught her face in his hands as he came. "Look at me," he demanded. Her green eyes were glassy with passion, like shimmering emeralds.

Something deep and primitive welled up inside him. His body shook with the power of the creature living inside him, the part he'd inherited from his sire. He willed it back, unwilling to do anything that might hurt his Valeriya.

The dragon part of his nature responded to his worry and eased back. It had all happened in a split second, and then he was shaking from the power of his release.

His big body shuddered as she milked him dry. Her sheath gripped him so hard he swore he saw stars. Her lips were moist and parted, so he captured them for another kiss. She gave him everything she was and then some. And he took it.

He managed to roll onto his side while staying inside her. She burrowed closer and sighed. They lay there a long time. Eventually, she stirred. "I guess we should get up."

As much as he loved lying there with her, Tarrant was starting to get jittery. He hadn't been out of contact with the world for this long in years. "We should." He kissed the top of her head, disengaged their bodies, and rolled out of bed.

"I didn't mean it had to happen quite that quickly," she groused.

He laughed and playfully swatted her bare butt.

"Ouch." She frowned and pointed at him. "I'll get you for that."

"Promises," he teased. He strode into the bathroom and stepped into the shower. He made mental lists as he quickly washed and dried. By the time he was finished, Valeriya was standing in the doorway.

"That was fast." She yawned and headed toward the shower he'd just exited. He loved watching the way she moved. She was a delight of feminine curves, from her full breasts to her firm ass.

"Work to do."

She sighed as the water cascaded over her. "More cleaning?"

He leaned against the vanity and enjoyed the view. His cock stirred to life, but he managed to ignore it. He needed to give Valeriya time to recover. "Business. I still have an empire to run."

She didn't bother with her hair and quickly finished. He snagged a towel and handed it to her, watching as she ran the cotton over her arms and legs before wrapping it around her body. He'd never been jealous of a piece of cloth before.

Tarrant raked his fingers through his damp hair. "I need to see to regular business, and we also need to keep looking into the Knights. The clean up around the place will take days. I need to order furniture, paint, food, and more." There was so much they needed.

She padded across the tiled floor and stood in front of him. He dropped his hands to her hips and pulled her in close enough that she could feel his erection. Her eyes widened and then half closed.

"Just how do you get supplies?"

Not what he'd expected her to ask, but then she was always surprising him. "I have a system," he told her. "I'll show you. You need to order clothes."

She laughed and hugged him. It was quick, but it warmed his soul. Not to mention what it did to his dick.

"That's an understatement. I need to borrow another one of your shirts." She left the bathroom, and he was right behind her. "I have clean underwear and jeans, but my shirts haven't fared so well."

"Take whatever you want." He quickly pulled on a pair of faded jeans and a T-shirt. When he turned around to find her watching him, he cocked an eyebrow. "Like what you see?"

She flashed him a quick grin. "Very much." He started for her, but she backed away. "Work," she reminded him. "We've been down for hours."

He hated that she was right, but that didn't stop him from kissing her senseless. When he finally backed away from her, she was breathless. Satisfied, he headed toward the door.

"I'll make us something to eat. We can take it down to the computer room." He wanted to make sure no one else had been lurking around while they'd been sleeping. No alarms had gone off, but he wasn't taking chances.

The place looked clean, but the faint scent of smoke still lingered. He'd have to clear away the charred remains of the cabin at some point. Having that above them wasn't helping. But he needed to leave it for at least a couple of weeks. By then any interested parties should have come and gone.

By the time he'd made a stack of grilled cheese sandwiches, Valeriya had started another load of laundry and joined him. "I want juice." She poked in the refrigerator. "Do you have any?"

"Check the freezer for frozen. There might be a can." He didn't drink it often, but he did sometimes get in the mood.

While he gathered napkins and a tray to put everything on, Valeriya found a jug and mixed up the orange juice. "Just bring the whole thing," he told her. "There are mugs in the computer room we can use. There's also a coffeepot and a kettle. Bring the teabags."

Less than a minute later, they were in the computer room. Everything was humming, and Tarrant immediately set the platter on an empty spot and sat in his chair.

He was aware of Valeriya puttering around, but he was soon lost in the cascade of information flowing around him. There was so much, from world affairs to the economy, and his searches on the Knights.

His stomach growled and he reached out and snagged a sandwich, then another and another. When he got thirsty, he discovered a large mug of juice next to his hand. He just drained it and kept scrolling.

When he reached out to the platter and found it empty, he looked up. He had a sense that a lot of time had passed but had no idea just how much. Valeriya was curled in what he now thought of as her chair with her sketchpad open.

When she sensed her gaze on her, she glanced up and smiled. "Everything well in the world?"

She didn't seem upset even though he'd brought her down here and then ignored her for hours. "You tell me."

She laughed and set her sketchbook aside. "Tarrant, I know who you are. You need information like most people need air. I get that. I also know things won't always be this intense. I suspect you need less sleep than me and will play catch-up while I'm in bed."

Damn, the woman knew him well. He grunted and nodded. "What have you been doing?" Her cheeks flushed a pale pink. Intrigued, he rolled his chair toward her. "Now I really have to know."

She slowly picked up the sketchpad and opened the cover. There he was, sitting at the desk, fingers on the keyboard. He took the pad and studied the likeness. "It's amazing." He flipped the page and found another drawing. This one was of him in his dragon form. Then another of the little dragon from her children's book, and still more of the fairies. "You've been busy."

She shrugged. "I know my career as a children's writer is probably over, but that doesn't stop the stories from coming."

He carefully closed the pad and set it aside. "We'll find a way to make it work. You won't be able to visit your agent or publisher in person, not for a while anyway, but there are ways." He held up his hands and wiggled his fingers. "King of the internet," he reminded her.

She laughed, reached out, and took his hand. "As long as you don't do anything to endanger yourself or your brothers."

And speaking of his brothers. "I think we should go visit Ezra before Darius and Sarah take off. I want you to meet them." It felt right.

"You do?" Her excitement was palpable.

"I do."

"Isn't that dangerous?" Valeriya pointed out. "For all of you to be together in the same place?"

He nodded. "It is, but we won't stay long, and we'll be careful." He needed to connect with his family, but more than that, he needed them to meet Valeriya. "Maybe we can even get Nicodemus to tear himself away from Vegas long enough to join us."

"You don't seem to be as close to him as you are to the others."

"Nic is different. He actually likes people." Tarrant shuddered, and Valeriya laughed at his obvious discomfort.

"That does make him very different."

"There are four of us," Tarrant continued. "And as I mentioned before, we all had the same sire but different mothers." He lifted her out of her chair and onto his lap. "We're all different kinds of drakons, too. That's not decided by what the sire is. It develops in each individual drakon."

"Really? I had no idea. That's so cool. So your sire wasn't an air dragon?"

He smoothed her hair back from her face. "No. He was a fire dragon. Nic is the only one who took after him in that regard. Darius is an earth drakon and Ezra a water drakon."

"That's incredible. And we're really going to see them?"

He wanted his family to know Valeriya and for her to know them. "Yes."

She began to chew on her bottom lip, a sign she was worried. "What is it?" he asked.

"I need clothes," she blurted. When he started to laugh, she smacked his arm. "It's not funny. I'm not meeting your family looking like a reject from a thrift store. I can't keep wearing your clothes, and most of mine are worse for wear after the past week."

With her in his lap, he wheeled her back to his main

console and brought up a popular online store. "So shop."

"I can't use my credit cards," she pointed out. "Maybe you can access my bank account for me."

He scowled. "I'm buying you clothes."

She shook her head. "That's not right."

"Woman, I'm loaded." He softened his tone and brushed a kiss over her lips. "Let me do this for you." He didn't just want to provide for her, he needed to. For him, it was another way to show her how much he loved her.

Epilogue

"How do I look?" It had taken them about two weeks to get everything planned, but she and Tarrant were finally standing on a shoreline in Maine. It was November and the wind was buffeting them. Thankfully, she was wearing boots and dark jeans, as well as a shirt and a sweater beneath a thick jacket.

Tarrant looked handsome, as always, in faded jeans, hiking boots, and a soft cashmere sweater. He also looked toasty warm. She tried not to resent him for that.

"You look perfect." He tugged on the end of her ponytail. "And warm," he teased. He knew how much she detested being cold.

"I need gloves." She started to stuff her hands into her pockets, but Tarrant caught them.

He frowned when he felt just how chilled her skin was. "You really are cold." He cupped her hands in his much larger ones, bent over them, and blew. Warm air circulated around her fingers, driving out the cold and slowly warming them.

"Thank you."

He brought her hands to his lips and kissed them. "You're

welcome."

The sound of a boat getting nearer caught her attention. It was being piloted by a tall, lean man with extremely broad shoulders and shoulder-length brown hair that caught in the breeze. He had on even less clothing than Tarrant, was actually wearing a tank top. Swirling blue tattoos outlined in turquoise ran up and down his left arm and the part of his chest that was visible above the neckline of his top. Valeriya shivered.

The man pulled the sleek speedboat up to the dock and nodded. She shivered again, but this time it wasn't from the cold. This man had a forbidding nature that made her glad Tarrant was with her.

"Ezra this is Valeriya. Valeriya, this is my brother Ezra." He scowled at his brother. "As always, I love your warm welcome."

Ezra sighed. "Get in the damn boat. I don't like being this exposed."

Tarrant hoisted their bags over one shoulder and guided her into the boat. There was no talking as Ezra backed the craft up, turned it around, and headed toward the small island.

She still had a hard time wrapping her head around the idea the man owned an island. It was beautiful in a wild and untamed way. She glanced at Ezra. It suited him.

Tarrant wrapped himself around her and blocked the worst of the wind, but it was still cold. The boat was open, with nowhere to hide from the chill. She guessed it didn't really bother Ezra.

Thankfully, the trip was a short one. She was more than ready to get inside when they finally docked. The house Ezra led them toward was constructed of stone and thick logs. It looked as natural in the surroundings as its owner did.

The front door opened and a man stepped outside. She recognized him from their video chat, but the small screen hadn't done him justice. Darius Varkas was even more imposing in person. Big and broad, with shoulder-length black hair, there was something solid and enduring about him.

A woman stepped around him and smiled in welcome. Valeriya had never been so relieved to see another person in her life. Sarah was human, like her. At least she wouldn't be alone with four drakons.

Not that she thought they'd hurt her. Tarrant would never allow it. That didn't stop her from being uncomfortable around so much barely contained power, not to mention the testosterone.

"Tarrant." Darius stepped forward and enveloped Tarrant in quick bear hug. Tarrant slapped his brother on the back. It would have felled a lesser man. Darius didn't budge.

"This is Valeriya." The pride in Tarrant's voice boosted her courage.

She stuck out her hand. "Nice to meet you." Darius's huge hand smothered hers. His grip was firm, his handshake brief.

"I'm Sarah." The woman pushed around Darius and gave Valeriya a hug. "Nice to meet you."

"It's so good to meet you, too." The heartfelt relief in her voice made Sarah laugh and the men frown.

"You get used to them," Sarah assured her.

"I'll take your word for that." She wasn't sure she'd ever get used to being surrounded by this much animal magnetism. They were all tall and made her feel incredibly tiny even though she was five-seven.

Sarah laughed again. "I've made lunch. Chicken soup and sandwiches, since we weren't exactly sure when you'd arrive."

"That sounds perfect."

"Where's Nic?" Tarrant asked. He put his hand on the small of her back as they went into Ezra's home. He'd already slipped inside. Valeriya wasn't taking it personally, since neither Darius nor Sarah seemed surprised by his actions. She had a feeling Ezra preferred to be alone, which made it even more amazing he'd opened his home to all of them.

"He'll be along later tonight," Darius told them. "You know him. He got a line on some artifact he simply 'has to have,' to quote our brother. Once he buys it, he'll join us."

Tarrant set the bags down in the entryway and bent down to whisper in her ear. "Nic collects antiquities and paintings and all kinds of interesting things."

She knew that, because he'd already told her about Nic, she but appreciated the reminder. Ezra was leaning against the counter in the kitchen holding a mug of what smelled like coffee.

"And you, Ezra?" she asked. "What do you collect?" Tarrant had never told her.

He slowly set his mug down on the counter. "Treasure."

Tarrant wrapped his arms around her from behind, making her brave enough to ask another question. "What kind of treasure?"

One corner of Ezra's mouth tipped upward. She wouldn't call it a smile by any means, but it did make him appear a fraction less forbidding. "Sunken treasure."

That made sense since he was a water drakon.

"Let me take your coat." Tarrant slid the garment down her arms after she unbuttoned it. Ezra's gaze went straight to the necklace she wore. Tarrant had taken the emeralds, the drakon tears he'd shed for her, and had them made into the beautiful piece of jewelry. He must have paid a huge sum to have it made so quickly.

The setting was silver, since she wasn't fond of gold. The emerald teardrops were set at intervals around the double length chain. She loved it.

Sarah put her hand to her mouth and gasped. Then she reached inside her blouse and drew out a gold chain studded in diamonds the same shape as the emeralds. Valeriya knew they had to be drakon tears, and they'd come from Darius.

Ezra swore and pushed away from the counter. He stalked over to her, pulled her roughly into his arms, and kissed the top of her head. "Welcome to the family."

Apparently, those drakon tears meant more than she'd even suspected. "Thank you." Her voice was muffled against Ezra's chest.

Tarrant growled and dragged her away from his brother. "Get your own woman."

Ezra flashed a grin. It was so fast she almost missed it, but it made him seem so much younger. Handsome, too. "Not many of them floating around the ocean."

The rest of them laughed, but Valeriya caught an undertone of longing beneath the humor.

"Let's eat." Sarah bustled over to the stove and took the lids off two large pots. The yummy smells of chicken and spices filled the air.

"What can I do to help?" she asked.

"You can take the plastic wrap off the sandwiches and set the platters on the table."

As the women worked, the three brothers stood together by the big window in front of the table. In spite of their different coloring, it was easy to see the resemblance when they were all so close.

They were big men, but it was more than just their size. It was in the way they canted their heads when they listened, the way they stood, and the intensity that surrounded them.

Tarrant must have felt her studying him, because he left his brothers and came over to her. "Everything okay?"

She knew the rest of them could hear her, but that was fine with her. "Everything is perfect." She went up on her toes and kissed him.

He lifted her right off her feet. She heard Darius chuckle and Sarah laugh. She was warm from her head to her toes by the time Tarrant released her.

"Perfect," she repeated. Then she handed him one of the platters and they joined the others at the table.

This small group was the family she'd always wanted. And it had taken a drakon to give it to her. No matter what they faced in the future, they'd do it together.

Valeriya knew the war with the Knights of the Dragon was just getting started. As though sensing her unease, Tarrant reached out and squeezed her hand. "You sure you're okay?" he asked.

She nodded. "I am." Because no matter what happened, she was with the man she loved. Together, they could get through anything.

Acknowledgments

Thank you to Heidi Moore. I love working with you!

Thank you to Liz, Bridget, Crystal, Heather, and everyone at Entangled. Your hard work, support, and dedication does not go unnoticed or unappreciated. You guys rock!

About the Author

N.J. Walters is a *New York Times* and *USA Today* bestselling author who has always been a voracious reader, and now she spends her days writing novels of her own. Vampires, werewolves, dragons, time-travelers, seductive handymen, and next-door neighbors with smoldering good looks—all vie for her attention. It's a tough life, but someone's got to live it.

www.njwalters.com

Discover the **Blood of the Drakon** *series…*

DRAKON'S PROMISE

Discover more Entangled Select Otherworld titles...

Once Bitten

a *Wolves of Hemlock Hollow* novel by Heather McCorkle

One night was all it took to change everything. But the biggest danger? Ty: history professor, super sexy Viking werewolf, and the man who's been assigned by the Council to teach me how to survive becoming a werewolf.

The Black Lily

a novel by Juliette Cross

As the leader of the underground resistance against the vampire monarchy, Arabelle concocts the perfect idea to gain the attention of the Glass Tower. Her plan? Attend the vampire prince's birthday ball and kill him. But her assassination goes awry, and Arabelle flees, leaving behind only her dagger. Marius is desperate to find the woman whose kiss turned into attempted murder, hunting for the mysterious assassin he can't push out of his mind. But what he uncovers could change the course of his life forever...

Shifter Planet

a novel by D.B. Reynolds

Determined to remain on Harp to learn its secrets and call it home, Earthling Amanda Sumner sets out to become part of the planet's elite Guild. While he wants the Earthlings gone, Shifter Rhodry de Mendoza is reluctantly drawn to the fierce and lovely woman who's determined to prove herself. The pair is thrown together in what becomes a fight for their lives. And they might just lose everything–including each other–in their battle for the right to live in peace.

The Queen's Wings

an *Emerging Queens* novel by Jaime Schmidt

FBI dragon Reed's disdain for humans can't mask the magnetic attraction he has for Carolyn, but when she tells him she's going to shift into a dragon he thinks she's crazy. A female hasn't been hatched, or shape shifted, in over a thousand years. He's proven wrong after Carolyn shifts and is named the new Queen on the block. When the Cult of Humanity kidnaps Carolyn to sacrifice her, Reed must face his fears—and feelings, racing to save the woman he realizes he can't live without.